FREEPORT PUBLIC LIBRARY
100 E. Douglas
Freeport, IL 61032
OCT 2 2 2018

W9-AAR-056

THE PATRIOT BRIDE

This Large Print Book carries the
Seal of Approval of N.A.V.H.

THE PATRIOT BRIDE

KIMBERLEY WOODHOUSE

THORNDIKE PRESS

A part of Gale, a Cengage Company

Farmington Hills, Mich • San Francisco • New York • Waterville, Maine
Meridian, Conn • Mason, Ohio • Chicago

Copyright © 2018 by Kimberley Woodhouse.
All scripture quotations are taken from the King James Version of the Bible.
Thorndike Press, a part of Gale, a Cengage Company.

ALL RIGHTS RESERVED
This book is a work of fiction. Names, characters, places, and incidents are either products of the author's imagination or are used fictitiously. Any similarity to actual people, organizations, and/or events is purely coincidental.
Thorndike Press® Large Print Christian Romance.
The text of this Large Print edition is unabridged.
Other aspects of the book may vary from the original edition.
Set in 16 pt. Plantin.

LIBRARY OF CONGRESS CIP DATA ON FILE.
CATALOGUING IN PUBLICATION FOR THIS BOOK
IS AVAILABLE FROM THE LIBRARY OF CONGRESS

ISBN-13: 978-1-4328-5656-4 (hardcover)

Published in 2018 by arrangement with Barbour Publishing, Inc.

Printed in Mexico
1 2 3 4 5 6 7 22 21 20 19 18

This book is lovingly dedicated to my outrageously incredible-one-and-only-son: Josh. Who somehow along the way earned the nickname of George. You've been a delight to me since before you were born (even though you broke one of my ribs). And I've loved you more and more each day. As a baby you were cuddly, smiley, and really quite chunky. (I'm sure you're loving me for writing that in this dedication. I *should* include a picture. . . .) You never met a stranger and could cheer up and encourage everyone you encountered. You entertained us and made us laugh and gave the very best hugs. Your creative genius still amazes me and it *almost* makes up for all the Legos I stepped on in your room over the years. It's hard to believe that you are grown and married (gasp! How did I get that old? And how did you survive with a mom who homeschooled you and tortured you with math drills and diagramming sentences? And let's not forget all the book tours? Especially once you were old enough to handle all the hookups on the RV . . . I won't go into details, I promise) — but I've treasured watching you grow and mature into the amazing man that you are today. I'm sure I've embarrassed you plenty over the years, but it was all worth it, right? You are incredible, and I couldn't be prouder. You amaze me every day. I could never tell you how much you mean to me and what a thrill it is to be your mom. Oh, and one more thing . . . just remember that I love you more.

Dear Reader,

How exciting to be back with the Daughters of the Mayflower series. I hope you have enjoyed *The Mayflower Bride, The Pirate Bride,* and *The Captured Bride.* As the fourth book in this series, *The Patriot Bride* follows the descendants of the Lyttons and brings us to a fascinating part of our history: the Revolutionary War. Make sure you watch for *The Liberty Bride* and *The Cumberland Bride* also being published this year.

In documenting the great events of our country's history in this series, it is important for me to remind you that this is a work of fiction. While I strive to be as historically accurate as possible, in many places I had to take artistic license.

For instance, George Washington; Benjamin Franklin; and his son, William, are integral pieces of American history and are also key characters in *The Patriot Bride.* But please note that even though I did extensive research, there's only so much I could ascertain about personalities and other details. So good ol' George and Ben are depicted in the way my imagination created them for this story. I created their dialogue and traits, although I based my interpretations on information gleaned from numer-

7

ous biographies. The part they play in Matthew's life in this story is not based on any fact; it is purely fictitious. The part that George plays in Faith's life is also a creation of my mind. As is Benjamin Franklin's role in the story. It is not my wish to take anything away from these brilliant men who were founding fathers of our country. Any mistakes are also purely my own. Please see the Note from the Author at the back of the book about other details and a timeline discrepancy with Benjamin Franklin as well.

Might I suggest some wonderful nonfiction books to read if you wish to truly know these great men? *His Excellency George Washington* by Joseph J. Ellis is an excellent biography of our first president. *Washington: A Life* by Ron Chernow is also a brilliant read (even though the tome is tiny print and more than eight hundred pages long). *George Washington: A Collection* compiled and edited by W. B. Allen is a fabulous compilation of the writings of this amazing man. *The Autobiography of Benjamin Franklin* is also an incredible read and one of my preferred choices. It is definitely a classic. One of my favorite parts is seeing how he scheduled his day. Lots to learn from both of these fascinating and honorable men.

Charles Thomson was the secretary of the

Continental Congress and also one of the Sons of Liberty, along with Paul Revere, Alexander Hamilton, Samuel Adams, John Hancock, and even Benedict Arnold, along with many others. Their depiction in this story corresponds with events that actually occurred in history, but all the details are created for the purpose of this story.

For your ease of reading, I've written the majority of the manuscript in modern English with just a few hints here and there of colonial expressions to help create a sense of the time period. This was to aid the flow of the story and make it understandable for the modern reader.

For more details on the actual events of the American Revolution and the people who truly lived during this time, I've given sources, websites, and links in the Note from the Author at the back of the book.

Enjoy the journey,
Kimberley

Daughters of the Mayflower

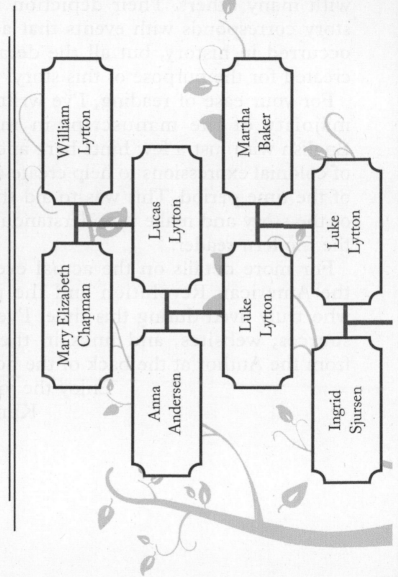

William Lytton

Mary Elizabeth Chapman

Lucas Lytton

Anna Andersen

Martha Baker

Luke Lytton

Luke Lytton

Ingrid Sjursen

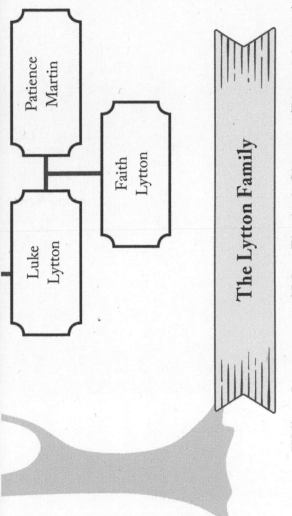

The Lytton Family

William Lytton married Mary Elizabeth Chapman (Plymouth 1621)

Parents of 13 children, one who was Lucas

Lucas Lytton (born 1625) married Anna Andersen (Massachusetts 1649)

Luke Lytton (born 1652) married Martha Baker (Massachusetts 1675)

Luke Lytton (born 1677) married Ingrid Sjursen (Massachusetts 1699)

Luke Lytton (born 1700) married Patience Martin (Virginia 1730)

Only child was Faith Lytton

PROLOGUE

Monday, May 11, 1752
Across the Rappahannock River from
  Fredericksburg, Virginia

Ten-year-old Faith Lytton placed her hands on her hips — like Mama did when she was exasperated — and looked at the sad little group of puny troops allotted to her. Why must the bigger and mostly older boys always insist that their teams be so mismatched? A huff left her lips.

"What're we gonna do, Faith?" Tommy kicked the dirt. "They win every time."

Several of the other boys whined their discontent. It wasn't that she didn't like her team. In fact, come rain or come shine, they had been the same team for almost forever. It's just they were all . . . well . . . *small.*

Taunts echoed across the field from their opponents, the League of Victorious Virginians — a ridiculous name for ridiculous boys. Obsessed with playing war and pre-

13

tending to be soldiers, the league wanted nothing more than to *win,* so much so they fought their skirmishes against younger, smaller opponents.

Faith narrowed her eyes. The only girl under sixteen years of age within ten miles amidst uncountable boys, she had learned to hold her own with the lads a long time ago. Now, she found herself a leader. Even if it was of the scrawny crowd.

How could she teach the other team a lesson? They weren't *all* older, nor were they smarter. Just because they were bigger and stronger shouldn't mean that they should get their way every time. It was almost like they just wanted to tromp all over the smaller, skinnier, and more studious kids.

Of which she found herself a part.

Another huff, but this time bigger. If only the other team could feel her aggravation all the way across the field. She was tired of getting tromped. Plain ol' tired of it. She wanted to win.

"Faith?" Charlie poked her in the shoulder. "Come on, we gotta come up with something."

"I'm thinking." She glared at the boy she outweighed by probably twenty pounds, even though he was five months older and she was thin as a rail, as Mama would say.

14

Scrawny indeed.

"Well, don't take all day. My ma won't let me eat supper if I show up late again."

Faith glanced around at the other nine members of her team. Skinny, short, a bunch of boys who'd rather stay at home and work their sums than play war every day. Then she took a long look at the others. Taller and stronger. There really wasn't a contest. But . . . She tapped a finger against her chin. They weren't that bright. In fact, there wasn't a truly intelligent one in the bunch. Mama would scold her for such thoughts, but Mr. Brickham — her tutor — would laugh because it was true and he loved what he called "Faith's inquisitive intelligence." The thought made her smile.

Her team had been going about this the wrong way for too long.

The only way to win would be to outsmart them. And while the bigger boys might have the brawn, her team definitely had the brains.

She turned toward the pond. An idea struck her in an instant which caused her smile to grow. Trying not to giggle with glee — because soldiers didn't giggle — she gathered the rest of her group into a tight circle and whispered her plan.

Several of her team looked to the pond

15

and shrugged, while the others appeared concerned . . . or was it confused? It really wasn't that difficult.

Tommy crossed his arms over his chest. "I don't know, Faith. That sounds awfully risky." He crinkled up his nose.

"It'll work. Trust me." The grin that split her face couldn't be contained. Wait until she wrote George about it. He'd be impressed with her plan, she just knew it. The letter she'd received from him yesterday was sitting on her dresser waiting to be answered, and boy, wouldn't it be grand to write her friend about a victory?

As her team walked to the center of the field, she thought about what she would write. George Washington was more than just a friend — he was her best friend. Add to that, he was her family's closest neighbor. Since Faith was an only child, she'd followed George around all her growing-up years. Wherever he went around their two farms, she'd traipse along behind him. She looked up to the boy as an older brother. And when he'd left to go learn more about surveying for Lord Fairfax, she'd cried. That day had broken Faith's heart, because George was her pal. But he'd promised to write her letters and visit as often as he could.

While penmanship had been her least favorite to study, she'd put great effort into learning how to correspond with him. From the time she was five years old until this day, she'd been determined to pen her own letters to George. Much to her mother's consternation.

Not because Mama didn't want her writing letters or learning penmanship, but because she had given Mama fits over what she wanted to learn and *when* she wanted to learn it. On more than one occasion, Mama — whose Christian name was Patience — had proclaimed that the good Lord above had a sense of humor since she had to practice the virtue from sun up to sun down with Faith. That was probably half the reason Papa hired Mr. Brickham so early for her. Oh, he might have told her it was because she was so smart and they wanted her to have the very best education they could provide, but she knew better.

Because she wanted to impress George — and didn't want to exasperate Mama — she worked harder and soon wrote flowing letters to her pal. They were quite grown-up too. George often said so.

She'd always wanted to be grown-up like him — he was ten years her elder — but George told her there was no rush to take

17

on the responsibilities of an adult. And he should know, having lost his father when he was only eleven.

He constantly reminded her there were plenty of children her own age.

Plenty of children, yes, but there was one problem. They were all *boys.* So George taught her to use her smarts and keep up with them.

Well, wouldn't George be proud now?

The two teams came together in the center of the field. Robert — the leader of the league — gave her a smirk and shook his head as he looked down at her. "Which side of the pond do you want? Since there's no chance of ya winning, we'll let you choose this time."

Faith put on her best frown and crossed her arms over her middle. War was serious business. Even if it was just a game. Time for them to take her seriously. "We'll take the west side."

Several moans came from the boys behind her. Never mind them. She knew her plan would work.

Robert laughed. "Sure, Faith. You can have whatever you want." He gestured to two of his team. "Post the flags." He turned back to her. "Same rules as always. No one can leave their side until the horn blows. If

18

you are captured by another team member, you're out. Whichever team captures the other's flag first, wins. Agreed?" He stuck out his hand.

Faith grabbed it and shook.

"You've got thirty minutes to get to your flag, plan your attack, and then John will blow the horn for the battle to begin." Robert snickered then turned back to his team.

With a wave of her hand, Faith motioned for her team to follow, and she ran for the reeds on the west side of the pond. The pond was always the chosen battleground because to capture the opponent's flag, you had to venture through woods and dense undergrowth while trying to avoid the enemy. The league was good at hiding people along the route so that she normally lost a good portion of her team before they even reached the halfway point. The time would be different. The other team wouldn't expect them to do anything out of the ordinary.

As her little band crouched in the reeds in front of their flag, she kept looking to the woods. "Ya know, they're going to set up just like they always do because they *always* win with that strategy. They will hide enough of their team to try and capture us along the way in the woods, but we won't be

19

there. Let them think we don't have any other plan. So just stay here. We'll pretend we are coming up with a plan — which we already have — while they think it will be like every other time, and then when we start, they will get into position. The two they'll send to advance on our flag will wait to scare us, but since we're not going to take that route, we should have about twenty minutes to make it to the other side."

Charlie chuckled. "I can't wait to see their faces when we surround their flag." He lowered his brow. "Hey, why didn't ya come up with this plan sooner?"

"Do I have to do all the thinking around here?" Faith pushed his shoulder.

"No. But I just wish you woulda — 'cause we're gonna win!"

The rest of the group caught on to the excitement, and Faith enjoyed listening to the boys chatter about what they wanted to chant for their victory. While the entire team was educated at home and quite studious, Faith's private tutor taught her more than just arithmetic and reading. Mr. Brickham had a passion for history, and since Faith had a leaning toward tomboyish ways, she often coerced him into teaching her about famous battles. Mr. Brickham told her it was fine with her parents unless she began to get behind in other studies.

While the strategy she'd devised was only for a game, she knew her teacher would be proud.

A shuffle in the reeds next to them made her hush the group. The horn hadn't sounded yet, so which one of the other team was trying to sneak in and cheat?

She held her breath while her teammates appeared to do the same. Eyes glued to the shifting reeds on the right.

A familiar face split the stalks. "George!" Faith's relief made her put a hand to her chest. "What are you doing here?"

Several of the boys moved closer. George was quite a fascination for them, being named the surveyor of Culpepper County at a mere seventeen years of age. All the boys wanted to be like him.

"I came home to visit Mother and wanted to stop in and see how you were first." Her lifelong friend sat in the reeds, glanced around, and dipped his head low, which was quite a feat. He was really tall. "And it seems you are doing very well. Is this one of the battles you have told me about in your letters?"

"Yes." She couldn't help but smile up at him as she thrilled in her team's admiration for her friend. Lifting her shoulders back, she hoped George saw her as a leader and not just a child, but her emotions won over and she threw her arms around his neck. He was here! And he would be able to watch her team finally win. Joy bubbled up inside her.

But it was time to be serious. She had a battle to win.

Faith pulled back and stuck a finger in his face, trying to stand as tall as she could and look as authoritative as possible. Even standing she barely topped a couple inches above his seated frame. "But I need you to stay hidden. We haven't begun, and I have a plan to beat the league once and for all." Nodding, Faith wiped her hands on her dress. This was more important than ever — George was here to witness it.

"What?" He put a hand to his chest. "I came to offer my assistance, Captain Lytton." He gave her a wink. "You do not want my help?"

"Oh, couldn't he?" Tommy pleaded. "We could win for sure!"

Charlie shook his head at the same moment Faith did. "Any other time, we'd love for you to be on our team, but you're too big."

"And" — Faith piped up — "we need to win on our own. They'd never admit to us winning if we allow you to help."

George looked a bit amused. He crossed his arms and sat hunkered in the reeds.

Faith placed a hand over his. "I can do this."

He cocked an eyebrow. "I have no doubt. So when does it begin?"

The horn sounded across the pond.

"Now." Faith left George and crawled to the edge of the pond, waving for the others to follow. Not even looking back to see if everyone was with her, she climbed into the small skiff. Each *thunk* behind her told her another teammate had climbed in as she kept an eye on the sides. So far so good. They didn't seem to weigh it down too much. Give another point to the scrawny team. Taking one more glance to the rear, she looked at Charlie. He nodded from the back. They were all in and crouched down. Faith and Charlie each had a paddle and started rowing as quietly as they could toward a small island covered with trees in the middle of the pond. The scent of algae and grass filled her nose. Her nose twitched. Holding in a sneeze to keep from giving away her team's position, Faith scrunched up her nose and shook her head.

A few minutes later, her face cracked into a smile as they reached the island. All was quiet. So far, the other team hadn't noticed the new strategy. The league had no idea what they were doing. Faith held a finger over her lips as her team snuck out of the boat. They kept quiet as they picked up the skiff and carried it through the trees.

At the breach in the trees on the other side, Faith hurried them forward. "We are almost there." She kept her voice as low as possible. "From this point on, it's run across the beach and then row as fast as we can."

Anticipation glowed on the boys' faces. The win was within their grasp, and they all knew it. It took more than a half hour to run around the pond, and that was without hindrances of watching for the enemy. It had been maybe ten minutes, and they were over halfway there — and their opponents were still unaware of their strategy.

Running for all she was worth, Faith dragged the band of small boys along with the boat to the shore. Once they were back in the water, her energy surged, and she paddled with every ounce of strength she had.

A yell echoed across the water. "Where did they go?"

A few more yells answered back. No one from the league knew where her team was. Not even risking a glance behind, Faith paddled the last few strokes. They reached the opposite shore and tumbled out on top of each other. She grinned. The other team's flag stood in front of them not more than twenty feet. Could George see them? Wouldn't he be proud?

"Come on!" Faith ran toward the flag and didn't care if anyone heard her. "Let's capture it together! All of us!"

Robert ran from the north side of the woods and his jaw dropped. He waved his arms, screaming at his team to come out from hiding.

When her team reached the flag, Faith yelled for all she was worth. "We won! We captured the league's flag!"

Robert kicked at the dirt then started throwing rocks which splashed in great *kerplunks* in the pond. Apparently he was the one who should have been guarding their flag.

It wasn't hard to determine that he wasn't happy about losing. After several moments of his fit, several other boys raced to his side and the calamity only grew. Until they spotted George across the pond, walking toward the field.

Faith knew the exact moment they spotted him because they all straightened up and stopped acting like two-year-olds.

25

Robert pulled the horn from inside his shirt and blew three short bursts calling everyone back.

Faith grabbed the flag and marched to the field area where the two teams had met before they began. Her team chanted about their victory while she carried the flag, and her chest swelled with pride. She'd done it. Well, *they'd* done it. But it had been *her* idea, and it worked.

It took a long time for everyone to reach the field. Several of the league boys were covered in mud and leaves — obviously from the places they'd been hiding to ambush Faith's team — and none looked too happy.

George strode toward the group and immediately the bigger boys from the league approached him with their cries of cheating. He shook his head and smiled. "They did not cheat. I watched the whole thing. It was a brilliant and well-executed plan."

Robert began to argue again. But George held up a hand and stopped him. "Every time you play — win or lose — you learn a little more. Faith's strategy was a good one, and it will challenge all of you to come up with different strategies next time." He laid a hand on Robert's shoulder and winked. "It helps to have a sneaky girl and smaller

26

teammates sometimes — everyone can have value on a team. Not just the strong ones."

Faith beamed under George's praise. Not only had her team beat the undefeated League of Victorious Virginians — a name she would demand they change considering today's loss — but her dear friend had helped to teach those big boys a lesson. And they *always* listened to George.

Maybe next time they would suggest dividing the teams up evenly. But as Faith gazed around at her group, she wasn't sure she'd want a different troop of soldiers. Her team — scrawny as they were — lifted her up on their shoulders, and she waved the opponent's flag. Smiling at George, she yelled quite dramatically, "Victory or death!"

Her older friend laughed. "Let us hope it never comes to that, young Faith . . . er, excuse me, Captain Lytton." He bowed low.

Movement behind George's bent frame caused Faith to jump down from the boys' shoulders. Morton — her father's valet — ran toward them looking quite grim.

Morton never ran.

Her heart drummed and sank. Dread drowned out her joy of victory. Then she saw it. Smoke.

Rising in the distance above her home

27

George stood by the fireplace in his mother's parlor and listened to Morton and the Lyttons' solicitor. A man George knew all too well because Mr. Crenshaw had also been his father's solicitor. Over the years, the gentleman had steered George in understanding his own inheritance. Small as it was, if not for Lawrence — his older brother — and Crenshaw, George would have been lost. His father's death at such a young age had dealt a huge blow to him. How would Faith deal with double the loss? How could he help her?

But he had to. He stood straighter under the new weight he carried.

She was now his ward.

At age twenty, George began to feel the full scope of what lay before him. Faith had always been like a puppy following him around. She was like another little sister to him. She adored him. And he had always enjoyed the little sprite's company.

But now he was responsible for her wellbeing. For managing her estate until she was old enough to inherit.

He turned his attention back to Crenshaw. Luke and Patience Lytton had been killed in a blaze that took out half the manor in minutes. The Lyttons had property, slaves, servants, and a vast amount of wealth. Faith was their only child.

Before he died, George's father — Augustine, otherwise known as Gus — had been best friends with Luke. Apparently, Luke had asked Gus to take care of his family in case anything happened to him. And in case of the loss of both Mr. and Mrs. Lytton, Gus Washington would become Faith's guardian until she turned twenty-one and inherited her family's fortune.

The mantle had passed to George when his father died. Lawrence was too far away at Mount Vernon to handle anything here. Luke Lytton had never wanted his will changed, telling Crenshaw that if anyone would look out for Faith and her best interests, it would be George.

But Luke couldn't have thought he'd leave this life so soon. Faith was but the tender age of ten. George a mere twenty.

He looked out the window. Not only would the Lytton manor need to be restored, but the staff would all need taking care of, the estate would need to thrive so it would provide stable income for Faith's future. And then there was the question of where she would live. The life of a surveyor was not a decent life for a young girl, and it would hardly be appropriate for him to drag her along on his journeys. She certainly couldn't stay with his mother. Mary Ball Washington would neither understand nor abide Faith's precocious nature — one of his favorite things about his young friend. He'd hate to see it squashed.

His heart ached to think of her dealing with the loss of both parents. Faith was strong, but their family had been very close. Much closer than George had ever felt with his.

A knock at the door brought his attention back to the room. Mary — Mrs. Lytton's maid — came toward George. "I am sorry to bother you, sir" — she bowed — "but young Faith wants no one but you. She has done nothing but cry, and we cannot convince her to eat or sleep."

George straightened and nodded. "Let me accompany you back to the house and see what I can do." He turned to the solicitor. "Is there anything else that needs my attention at the moment?"

"No." He gathered his things. "I will bring the papers to you in the morning."

"Thank you." George bowed and then kissed his mother's cheek before heading out the door. As he walked the short distance between the two farms, a new idea formed. Maybe a change of scenery would be good for Faith. The Martins in Boston didn't have any children and George trusted them with his life. Would they take Faith in for the rest of her upbringing? If they'd be willing, she could have the finest of schooling and tutors and would be surrounded by the best society had to offer. He'd have to get a letter off immediately.

But if he moved Faith to Boston, it would be difficult for him to visit as often. Unless he chose a different line of work. An option that held some appeal.

Stepping into the Lyttons' parlor, his eyes watered. Smoke still hung in the air. Faith couldn't stay here. Neither should the servants. On the settee, Faith was curled up into a ball, her dress still covered in dirt from her jaunty game of war, and her arms wrapped around her mother's shawl. With swollen green eyes, she looked up at him. Tears streamed down her face in silent rivers of pain.

George understood the heartache etched into her features all too well. He reached for her hand. "Let us go for a walk, shall we?"

She nodded and took his hand but kept the shawl tucked under her other arm.

31

They headed toward the apple orchard. One of her favorite places.

Silence stretched between them for a good while as he led her to a little hill and settled down on the grass. The air was sweet and fresh. Faith sat beside him and rested her head on his arm.

Unsure of where to begin or how to reach her broken heart, George thought it best to be honest. "I lost my father when I was about your age."

She nodded against his arm.

"It devastated me, and I felt lost for a long time. But the good Lord above saw me through."

Faith began to sob.

"It is not within my power to bring them back or take away the pain, dear girl. But I can promise that I will do my best to take care of you and make certain that all is well for your future."

"I do not want to stay here right now. It scares me. Can I go with you?"

Exactly the question he'd expected from her. He sighed. "I don't think so, but I have an idea. It may take me a bit to arrange everything. But I will make sure you are happy and well."

"You will send me away?" She sounded resigned. Her tone so matter of fact, even though he noticed the quiver of her lower lip.

"It will not be like that, little Faith. I have trusted friends in Boston. If they are in agreement with my plan, I think it will be the perfect place for you to be for a while."

She nodded. "I do not like the thought of being so far away, but I do not want to be here right now. Maybe not ever." A small sigh made her shudder. "Will you come visit?"

"Yes."

"And write letters? Like before?"

"Yes. I will even write more often."

She tucked her hand back into his. "It hurts really bad, George."

"I know." He squeezed her hand. "But the ache will ease a bit over time. And you will always have your wonderful memories. Your parents were the finest people I've ever known."

Sniffing, she sat up. "I want them back." Her voice cracked.

It was hard to imagine that mere hours ago, he'd watched Faith be carried on her team's shoulders in victory. Independent and strong-willed, the young girl had cried, "Victory or death!"

The contrast now was chilling. She seemed smaller and fragile, as if she could

33

shatter into a million pieces at any moment.

Loss could do that. But could that fiery, fearless leader come back from such a blow? He hated to see her defeated and worn. He'd have to do everything he could to help Faith survive and become vibrant once again.

Maybe they both needed to leave Virginia for a while.

Boston sounded better the more he thought about it.

"George?"

"Yes?"

"I'm an orphan now, aren't I."

His heart felt like it stopped for a breath as he looked into Faith's sad eyes. What could he possibly say to her to help ease the pain? "No." The sigh that left his lips felt heavy. "You are a child of our heavenly Father, so you are never truly an orphan. And don't forget . . . you have me." He tapped her nose like he used to when she was just a toddler following him around. "You will always have me while I'm here on this earth."

"I completely trust *you,* George." She took in a shaky breath and wiped tears from her cheeks. "But I do not like that God took my parents from me."

The hurt and anger in her voice surprised

34

him, but he knew it would stay with her for a while. It was part of grieving someone you loved. But George sat up a little straighter. Part of being Faith's guardian meant steering her in the truth. "I do not believe that God *took* your parents from you, Faith. And He's far more trustworthy than I am. But I will do my best to be His representative here — to show you how good He is."

"I feel very alone."

He wrapped an arm around her shoulders. "You are never alone, my friend."

"But what about when you leave?"

"God will be with you. I promise."

CHAPTER 1

Thursday, September 22, 1774
Philadelphia

Matthew Weber sat hidden in the corner of Charles Thomson's study and waited for word from him. Charles was not only a good friend but the secretary of the Continental Congress as well. His appointment as secretary had been fortuitous for them all. The plan had been to meet after the Congress so they could discuss what needed to be done next. A tap sounded on the door, and Matthew ducked deeper into the dark shadows. His heart pounded.

It wasn't the planned signal.

Who would be coming to the secretary's home tonight?

Matthew couldn't let anyone loyal to the King know he was here. And no one knew for sure when they might run into a Loyalist. It made things exceedingly difficult as the weeks passed.

A familiar face entered. A broad grin stretched across his face, Benjamin Franklin shut the door. "Matthew, I presume that is *you* hidden over there?"

Relief rushed through his veins. Shaking his head and letting his breath out in a great *whoosh,* Matthew laughed and stepped into the light. "Yes, 'tis me, Ben. But you did not use the appropriate signal, and by the way, wouldn't that have been a tad risky — mentioning my name — when you were not sure 'twas me?"

"If I had not been *sure,* yes." The older man shook a finger at him. His gray eyes twinkling. "But Simpson acknowledged you were already here. And frankly, I wanted to see how you would handle the situation. Good show, had I not known you were here, I wouldn't have seen you."

"Ah, I see." Matthew moved forward to shake Franklin's hand still working to get his heart back to normal. "These days, we can be none too careful." The definite need to practice at hiding and controlling his anxiousness pressed into his mind. The job before him grew more stressful by the day.

"I agree." The older gentleman nodded several times and placed his hands behind his back as he paced the room. " 'Tis hard to believe how things have changed over the years."

"Yes, indeed."

"How's Deborah?" Matthew hadn't seen Ben's wife in a while.

Ben smiled. "As lovely as ever."

"Please give her my regards. Have you spoken to William?" Matthew kept his tone low.

"No." The instant frown and gravity of the single word gave Matthew more than enough to understand the man's disappointment. William and Benjamin Franklin had been on different sides of the political spectrum for some time.

Matthew turned back to look at the bookshelves. "I am sorry to hear that."

"I appreciate your sincerity, but you know William. This is, I fear, what comes from a thirst for power." Franklin took a deep breath and then let it out in a long sigh. "Back to business, how are you, dear boy?"

A slight smile lifted his lips. Only Benjamin Franklin could think of him — a thirty-six-year-old man — as a dear boy. "I am faring quite well."

"Ah . . . an answer that is vague." Light laughter came out of his friend's mouth as he shook his head.

"You taught me well." Matthew grinned back.

"We will get to the crux of it in a moment. . . . Have you tried an air bath yet?"

"No." Matthew tried to keep a straight face. "I cannot say that I have. Nor have I had the privacy."

" 'Tis quite invigorating. Stimulating to the system."

"I am sure." Goodness, the subject needed to change. Sitting in front of an open window in nary a piece of clothing wasn't his idea of *healthy*.

"Still no word from Thomson?" Franklin tapped his fingers on the back of the chair in front of him.

"Not yet."

"Well, things are escalating quickly, and we must act." Franklin rubbed his hands together. "With the British troops occupying Boston, I believe they have drawn a line."

"What do you mean?"

"A line that will only lead to war."

Relations with Britain had been declining for a long time. The Tea Act giving the East India Trading Company a monopoly on tea trade made men in Boston so angry they dressed up as Indians and tossed over three hundred crates of tea into the harbor. In retaliation, Parliament passed the Intolerable Acts — laws denying constitutional rights, natural rights, and colonial charters to Massachusetts. Fear this denial of basic rights would spread through all the Colonies had pushed many in America to the point of revolution.

Loyalists still faithful to the Crown of England were in direct conflict with the Patriots and their quest for independence and relief from taxation.

Matthew pondered the quandary. What did the King seek to gain?

The taxations were getting out of hand and many of the colonists were tired of being ruled by a monarchy across the ocean and paying the debts of England through their taxes. Something wasn't right. And people knew it.

Now the British were keeping trade from other countries from coming to the Colonies, so of course, the Patriots were discussing boycotting all trade from Britain. All appeals to the Crown had no effect, so they were once again at an impasse. The Continental Congress was meeting to determine a way to appeal to the King. Again.

Matthew shook his head.

"What is ruminating in that fine mind of yours?" Ben cocked an eyebrow.

"Just thinking on how we arrived at this place in time. You are correct to say that we must act. Tumultuous times are upon us."

"But they are also exciting times, don't you agree? Our thirteen governments with their people cover a great deal more land than that of England. We have got fifty-six men from twelve of the Colonies coming together for the first time at this Continental Congress. We are going through growing pangs, are we not? Imagine what could be accomplished if we can persuade the Loyalists that we'd be better off independent of England?"

Matthew held up a hand and gave a slight laugh. "I admire your enthusiasm, my friend. And I do agree, but it has been almost ten years already, and we have a long way to go before we are free of British rule. Besides, the Loyalists are too afraid of the British military." He couldn't help the sigh that escaped his lips. Exhaustion pounded behind his eyes. It was a legitimate fear. England's army and navy were the mightiest in the world.

"I hear the weariness in your voice, my boy. This has taken its toll on you, has it not?"

Could he tell his mentor the truth? That any thoughts of a bright future seemed blotted out by the prospect of war? Matthew could manage a simple nod but couldn't allow his emotions to climb their way to the surface. "We'll do anything for our cause, will we not?"

"Yes, we have all made sacrifices, but this is *me* you're speaking to. You may not be my flesh and blood, but I can see what's lurking behind your eyes and I understand, even though you are working so hard to keep it hidden." Ben came forward and put a hand on Matthew's shoulder. "The future is hard to look forward to now, yes, but remember that all we are seeking to accomplish is for a better future for our children and grandchildren."

But what if he never had a family to give a brighter future to? Those children and grandchildren that Ben spoke of. He was already sacrificing his life and reputation for the cause of the Patriots — which was a truly great endeavor — but the thought of having not one soul to pass along that bright future to made a deep sorrow wash over him. At age thirty-six, settling down and starting a family in the middle of this turmoil were hard to imagine. In fact, they were quite unthinkable. And very selfish of him. Time to get his mind back on the tasks at hand.

Three taps on the door — the signal they were *supposed* to use — brought Matthew out of his thoughts and back to the present. He gave Ben a look and smirk. "See? That is how it works."

Benjamin just winked at him.

The master of the house entered the room with a smile on his face. "Good evening, gentlemen."

As Charles walked over to his desk, he motioned for them to sit. "A boycott will be in place the first of December."

"Of all British goods? That should shake things up quite a bit." Benjamin tapped his knee.

"It should, yes." Charles pulled out papers. Most likely his notes from the meeting. He perused them for a moment. "Each of the Colonies has been encouraged to develop and train their own militia."

Another hearty nod from Benjamin. "Good, good."

Matthew took a deep breath. Just what he'd suspected. At some point soon, war would be upon them. A reminder that it was a good thing he *didn't* have a family. This was no way to live — with no foreseeable, positive outlook for the future. Would this revolution ever end?

Another three taps on the door.

44

"Come in." Charles looked to the door.

George Washington opened the door and walked in with a nod. Matthew stood to greet his childhood friend. As a delegate to Congress, George would also have good insight into the meeting. "Good to see you, Matthew. I hope I have not missed too much." He smiled as he gave a firm handshake.

"Not at all." Matthew shook his head. "Charles had just begun to tell us of the boycott and preparations for militia."

George took a deep breath and then sighed heavily. "I believe the time has come." He ran fingers through his powdered hair leaving streaks of auburn in their wake. "We have much to discuss."

The group gathered chairs closer to the fire as George launched into his recall of the Continental Congress.

As the youngest in the group, Matthew sat back and listened to the insight from the men around him. While George was only a few years his senior, his longtime friend had much more experience in practically everything. The smartest and strongest man he'd ever known, George was steadfast and noble, and Matthew couldn't think of a man he respected more. Thomson was a few years older than George and had the distinguished appointment of secretary for the Congress. Then there was Benjamin Franklin. The eldest in the group was one of the most amazing men Matthew had ever met. Author, inventor, and statesman — and everything in between — Benjamin was his mentor and friend. Providence had blessed Matthew to be among these ranks.

Ben looked to him. "Matthew, I know you have been preparing for this for a good while, but the risks are high. Are you sure you are fully ready for what lies ahead?"

Knowing what his mentor spoke of, Matthew took a deep breath and nodded. "I am a Patriot and will do whatever it takes." He might have just laid his whole life and future on the line. But he couldn't be selfish. Not at a time like this. At least he could help provide a brighter future for those who would come behind him.

Several hours later, the group disbanded. While everyone else could go out the front door, Matthew had to wait and exit through a tunnel from the main house that came up into the barn. It had been dug for just this purpose, and now was the time to put it to use. Even though Philadelphia wasn't as tricky as Boston, there were still eyes and ears everywhere. He'd worked too long for the cause and built relationships to aid in it for him to be caught this early in the game.

As he pulled the black cloak around his shoulders, he made his way through the tunnel. Once in the barn, he tugged his cocked, felt hat lower over his brow. The sweet smell of the hay mixed with the strong aroma of manure. As he left the protection of the building, a crisp wind hit his face and gave him an even better excuse for concealment.

Lifting the stock around his neck closer to his chin, he moved forward. With a flick of his hand, he pulled his cloak's collar high up around his ears. Even though it was dark, he couldn't take the risk of being seen. From here on out Matthew must play the part of the Loyalist. He needed to entrench himself among the enemy. Abandon his friends and everyone else he knew, so that he could become the man he'd been creating for such a time as this. The only way to win independence would be to win the trust of those loyal to the Crown and gather every bit of information that he could.

It hadn't been easy forging friendships the past couple of years. Especially with his ties to George. Many had been hesitant to allow a childhood friend of a staunch Patriot into their midst. But since William Franklin — the Royal Governor of New Jersey — had vouched for Matthew, and William was

known to be at odds with his own father —
a Patriot — Matthew had finally found
some footing among the men who had influ-
ence.

His secret advantage was Ben. The older
man had incredible ties and relationships to
England. In fact, he'd spent a lot of his time
traveling back and forth and speaking on
behalf of the Colonies. But the open lines
of communication were failing. While deep
down, Matthew knew that the elder Franklin was heartbroken the revolution was
dividing him from his son, it still amazed
Matthew how Ben didn't hesitate to share
what he could about how to work his way
into William's good graces. For the good of
the cause.

And it had worked. Matthew found himself in the inner circle with the Royal
Governor. But as tensions mounted, he
would have to be on guard continually.

The depth of the situation hit him. No
one could know he wasn't just another af-
fluent Loyalist seeking to better his country.

No one could know the real Matthew
Weber. Not anymore.

His life was now on the altar of the Patriot's cause. And he'd give everything — even
his last breath — for freedom.

He was a spy.

■ ■ ■ ■

Faith Lytton Jackson stood and smiled as
her butler announced Mrs. White. "Thank
you, Clayton." She nodded and rushed
across the parlor to greet her friend. "Lavonia, what a pleasure to see you." The lavender silk on her friend was lovely. "Your dress
is enchanting. Is it new?"

"The pleasure is all mine, my dear. Although I wish the circumstances were different." The white-haired woman smiled
back and gave Faith a brief hug. "And yes,
this just arrived from Paris, but I wasn't sure
if the color suited me. I must say, that yellow silk taffeta on *you* is simply gorgeous. I
knew it would be."

"You do have a talent for choosing the
best fabrics, Lavonia."

"I might have an eye for the fabric, but
you, my dear, you make them exquisite."

Clayton announced several other guests
and kept Faith from responding although
she shot Lavonia a smile. Even in the direst
of circumstances, her friend always found
something to compliment.

Warmth filled the room as women she

adored and trusted entered. A crackling fire in the massive stone fireplace added to the cozy feeling as everyone spoke of the contrasting chill in the air outside.

Faith greeted each one and invited them to sit. "Clayton, would you ask Sylvia to serve the tea, please?"

"Yes, ma'am." Her stoic butler had been with her for more than a decade. He would do anything for her, she had no doubt. But she often wondered about his friends. Did he have any close confidants? Did anyone other than her staff care for the man? And was he always so stiff and reserved? The thoughts made her chuckle to herself. Why on earth was she all of a sudden so concerned with Clayton? He'd always puzzled her, but he was loyal and trustworthy.

She gazed around the room and shot a prayer heavenward. *Lord, I need Your focus and divine wisdom. We need Your guidance now more than ever. Help us to do what we can.*

Strengthened by her prayer and resolve, Faith quieted the women and stood before them. "We shall begin our meeting today by continuing through the reading of the Psalms." She picked up her Bible. "I believe we are beginning the 119th?"

Several murmurs of affirmation filled the room.

Faith began reading:

"Blessed are the undefiled in the way, who walk in the law of the Lord. Blessed are they that keep his testimonies, and that seek him with the whole heart. They also do no iniquity: they walk in his ways. Thou hast commanded us to keep thy precepts diligently. O that my ways were directed to keep thy statutes! Then shall I not be ashamed, when I have respect unto all thy commandments. I will praise thee with uprightness of heart, when I shall have learned thy righteous judgments. I will keep thy statutes: O forsake me not utterly. Wherewithal shall a young man cleanse his way? by taking heed thereto according to thy word. With my whole heart have I sought thee: O let me not wander from thy commandments. Thy word have I hid in mine heart, that I might not sin against thee."

The ladies looked to her when she was done reading. Where to begin?

"Ladies, as you know, the revolution is intensifying. It has not been easy thus far, and I dare say it will only get worse. Espe-

51

cially with the British troops here. We have committed to do what we can to help, and it is vital that we do our part." Faith took a deep breath before diving into the next discussion. "But we also need to tread more carefully than ever."

"What is it that you are unwilling to say, Faith?" Lavonia raised one eyebrow with her question. Always to the point, she was smart and steadfast. "No need to guard your words with us. We can shoulder the responsibilities."

Murmurs and nods filled the room.

With a sigh Faith allowed her shoulders to relax a bit. "The leaders of the Patriots have asked for our help again and they have also asked us to be exceedingly vigilant in whom we speak to and trust. The dangers have increased along with the number of infiltrators."

Several of the women's faces turned ashen.

Claudia leaned forward. "So I take it they are worried about spies? Even among the women?" Voicing the words that must have been on the ladies' minds, her friend shook her head and *tsked*.

The room erupted in chatter.

Faith held up a hand and waited for the women to quiet. "Yes. Ladies, it is imperative that we keep everything we speak of here *only* amongst ourselves. We will not be able to invite any new ladies to join us again for a while."

Lavonia stood and joined arms with Faith. "I think we all understand the depth of importance to which we hold this secrecy, right, ladies?"

Affirmation filled the room.

Lavonia continued, "I suggest we make a pact. Right here and now."

The other ladies stood and made a circle. No hesitation. No questions. Lavonia stuck her hand in the middle and swore herself to secrecy on behalf of the Patriot cause. Fifteen other women joined their voices with Mrs. White's and stacked their hands in the middle of the circle.

Lavonia grinned. " 'Thy word have I hid in mine heart, that I might not sin against thee.' I have another suggestion. I think we should start memorizing more scripture, ladies. To help us through the tough times ahead and to keep our minds trained."

"Oh, yes!" Margaret echoed. " 'Tis also another good reason for meetings. We must be vigilant in how we plan and what we say. Everything must have a purpose and a reason in case we are questioned."

Lavonia pointed at Margaret. "Excellent point."

Faith beamed. This group of friends amazed her. Already thinking ahead. No one could ever say the Patriot women weren't intelligent and thoughtful.

The other ladies nodded and took their seats again. All looked to Faith.

As she looked around the room and met each woman's gaze, a powerful emotion flowed through her. Pride. In who they were. In what they were trying to accomplish. They might not be able to serve in the government or fight in any battles — God forbid it get to that point — but they could serve their cause valiantly nonetheless.

When her gaze met that of Mary Wallace, she realized this young woman was the newest member of their group and probably didn't understand all they had already accomplished. "Mary, I apologize. I just realized you are quite new to us. Do you have any questions?"

The young woman shook her head. "I will listen in and ask my questions at the end, if that's all right with you."

"Of course. I just want to make sure you are comfortable."

"Quite. Thank you."

Faith looked back to the rest. Mary was

married to a man whom George knew well, so Faith had complete confidence that the woman could be trusted. But since she hadn't been part of the group for as long as the rest of them, it might be a bit daunting to take it all in. "Well, ladies. Back in '69, we produced with our other sisters in arms over forty-thousand skeins of yarn and wove 20,522 yards of cloth. But now we need to do more than just weave and make yarn. We may be asked to do a great many things to help the men."

"We are willing," Lavonia piped up.

Nods were all around. Shoulders straightened. Chins lifted.

Sylvia arrived with the tea at that moment, and Faith smiled. God was good to anoint them with such spirit. "Let us bless the tea and then we will discuss the details."

After giving thanks, Faith took a seat as Sylvia served the tea.

Mary came and sat next to her. "Might I ask you a few questions now, Mrs. Jackson?"

"Of course, and please . . . call me Faith." She nibbled on a piece of shortbread — her favorite since childhood — and let the buttery goodness melt on her tongue. Maybe she could get to know more about this young wife of George's friend.

"You are a widow?"

"Yes." The word no longer pained her since she'd been a widow for twelve years.

"May I ask about your husband and what happened to him?" Mary took a sip of her tea.

Faith smiled. "Well, you know George. I was a child when my parents died, and he became my guardian. Over the years, he wrote hundreds of letters and visited as often as he could. And most of the time, he brought someone along with him. Normally one of his soldiers. Joseph — my husband — was one of those visitors. He told George one day that he loved my spunky personality and George, of course, told me all about it. It wasn't long before Joseph and I were married. Sadly, he was killed in battle only a week after our wedding."

Mary laid a hand over one of Faith's. "I am deeply sorry. You never remarried?"

Faith shook her head and took a long sip of tea. The mint leaf Sylvia had placed in her cup with the tea refreshed her senses. Something she needed a lot of lately. "No. While I did not know Joseph extremely well, I did love him. I entered our union with my inheritance from my family, and he was quite wealthy. So there was that . . . I wouldn't be destitute if I didn't marry again.

"But it was devastating to lose him so

soon after we married. My young heart and mind had already faced so much loss. I felt numb. After mourning for a year, I thought I would be ready to consider suitors, but it wasn't to be. My heart was not ready. Even if society dictated that it should. Then, when I finally decided I *was* ready . . . Well, I found that men were interested in my fortune but not necessarily in *me.*" She chuckled. "It didn't help that the suitors seemed to lose interest as soon as they found out I had my own opinions and wasn't willing to give up my independence. So now I find 'tis best to just keep to myself and work with the women for our cause."

A smile lifted Mary's lips. "I imagine that George is quite a formidable man to cross as well. What does he have to say in all this?"

"Oh, he'd love for me to remarry so he can be 'Uncle George' to my children, but I'm afraid it is probably too late for me."

Twinkling eyes met hers as Mary laid a hand on top of Faith's. "It is never too late, and you are a beautiful woman."

Even though she longed for children of her own, Faith wasn't sure about remarrying. God would have to bring the right man directly to her if she were to consider it. And she'd have to know — without a doubt — that she could trust him with her life.

Her father and George had set high standards for her to compare any man to. "I appreciate the compliment, Mary, but we will have to leave it in the Lord's hands. For now, we have much work to keep our hands busy."

Mary nodded. "You are correct. I promise not to play matchmaker."

"Good. Because George does enough of that already."

They laughed together and then Mary's face sobered. "Back to the reason for this meeting. My husband has sent me with a private message for you. Instructions for our group."

Faith took the paper offered and opened the message. She couldn't help but gasp at some of the instructions. Her eyes widened as she glanced at Mary.

Her friend covered her hand again and nodded. "Now . . . what can I do to help?"

CHAPTER 2

Saturday, November 5, 1774
The candle on Anthony Jameson's desk cast an irritating, shadowy glow on the paper he read. Not at all the news he wanted to hear.

Not at all.

Apparently, the King was denying his request. Again.

After all the promises he had made to Anthony, this was unacceptable.

Blasted King George was the only reason he was in the Colonies. And after all Anthony had done for the monarch, this was how he was to be repaid? Why, he'd practically given the man every piece of information that was needed for his . . . conquest. He'd curried favor and fawned and eavesdropped his way into the royal's graces for ten long years. All he'd asked for in return was a measly title. Nothing fancy. Just something adequate enough for him and his future bride.

Something deserving of his name.

Anthony took a moment to look at himself in the mirror beside his desk and slicked back a rogue hair on the side.

The land and position offered to him decades ago in the Colonies was not holding the worth and prestige that Anthony had hoped. He'd come to the Americas to gain the status that he couldn't gain in Britain — that of a noble. Even after all he'd done for the King, it wasn't enough to gain the good graces and earn what he'd worked so hard for all this time. What a waste. It was like a slap in the face.

He lifted his chin. This wouldn't do. Not for one moment longer.

The revolution had been an inconvenience up to this point, but maybe it was time to use it for his benefit. Not that he cared one whit which side won. As long as it benefited him. He'd called himself a Patriot to those who had the means to profit him as such. At one time, he would have stayed loyal to the Crown, but if this was how he was to be treated, then good ol' King George could forget about enlisting Anthony's help.

The rumors of all-out war had been whispered for many years. As tensions rose, maybe he could count on just that — war. And quite possibly it could help him achieve a status in the new country that would equal a British royal. The thought made him puff out his chest. Yes, that would work.

Once America's colonies were out of Britain's clutches, the opportunities would be endless. He just needed a little investment to do what needed to be done. And he knew just the handsome young widow who had it. She would surely be pleased with his attentions.

He tilted the paper toward the candle and burned the missive in his hand. A slight chuckle lifted his lips.

If the King wouldn't give him what he wanted, then he would just get it another way.

Saturday, December 17, 1774
Faith breathed in the crisp air. Snow sifted down in a soft curtain of white. It made everything feel fresh and clean even though the world around her was in turmoil. The walk back to her home had given her far too much time to contemplate the fact that the mutterings of war could become real at any time, and it drained her of energy. Why didn't she just take the carriage? Sometimes her independent nature clouded her judgment.

Clayton opened the door for her almost

as if he had anticipated the very moment she set foot outside the threshold. That man's senses were uncanny. Shaking her head, Faith suppressed a smile. Her butler might be odd, but he was the best of the best.

Inside her home, the fireplace roared with a great fire, but it couldn't cut the chill that had seeped in through her layers. A shiver raced up her spine as she stood in front of the fireplace. Even with three petticoats, she longed to wrap herself up in a blanket.

Surveying the room as she turned to warm her other side, she pondered her lavish surroundings. The parlor was furnished in lush reds and golds. The deep mahogany wood her husband loved was featured throughout the house, and she found that it comforted her. Some of the women thought the dark wood was too masculine, but the gold silk on the couches seemed to brighten up the room. Even though it was all beautiful, it seemed a waste when it was just her. Lavonia had tried to convince her to redecorate last year, but why spend the money now when they were in the midst of such turmoil?

With a glance to the clock, she realized the ladies would be here in a just a few minutes for their next meeting. They had worked on many intense projects for the Patriots, but the most difficult had been their latest. Learning to write coded messages. They'd been given the training and then had to practice. Lots and lots of practice. The codes were hidden in messages from the women so that if anyone tried to trace it back it just appeared to be a lady friend sending a secret note rather than anything political. Faith wasn't sure the plan would work, but all the women had worked very hard on the project. While it made a few of the women blush to even think about writing a letter that could be called scandalous, they all knew it was for the cause of freedom. And for that, they'd do whatever they could.

When her hands finally felt a bit warmer, she looked down at her dress. Maybe she should change before the ladies arrived. "Clayton?"

"Yes, ma'am?" The man was always close when she needed him.

"I've decided I need a few moments before the meeting. Would you please welcome my friends and offer them some hot beverages in case I'm not back before they arrive? I believe hot apple cider and tea sound very appealing right now."

"Yes, of course." He bowed and headed

toward the door.

Faith slipped up the stairs to her massive bedchamber. The scent of leather and beeswax drifted over her like a welcoming blanket. The deep mahogany furniture graced this room as well — it had been her husband's choice, but she'd loved it for many years and the staff rubbed the beeswax into the wood every week. Now the familiar smells and gleaming wood greeted her in a way that begged her to stay — she longed to just slip under the covers of her bed and sleep away the cold. The busyness of the past weeks was beginning to catch up with her. And she doubted it would slow down any time soon.

As her maid entered the room, the thought of going to all the trouble of changing her gown seemed wasteful. Faith shook her head. "I've decided I'll just return to the meeting, but thank you."

Marie nodded. "Yes, ma'am. The ladies have begun to arrive."

"Thank you." As she watched her maid leave, Faith let out a long sigh. Back to work she must go. A good night's sleep would help to aid her weary mind. But that would have to wait.

She took the stairs at a slow pace and the chatter below made her smile. Some time with the ladies should refresh her.

As she entered the parlor, the women turned toward her. "Please, everyone, have a seat." Faith made her way to her chair. "It seems we have much to discuss again this evening. But first, we should continue with our scripture reading. Who memorized the verse Lavonia gave us?"

Everyone's hand raised. What a wonderful group of women.

"We are in Psalm 120 today." She paused and gave them all a moment to turn to the passage before she began reading:

"In my distress I cried unto the Lord, and he heard me. Deliver my soul, O Lord, from lying lips, and from a deceitful tongue. What shall be given unto thee? or what shall be done unto thee, thou false tongue? Sharp arrows of the mighty, with coals of juniper.

"Woe is me, that I sojourn in Mesech, that I dwell in the tents of Kedar! My soul hath long dwelt with him that hateth peace. I am for peace: but when I speak, they are for war."

A hush fell over the ladies. *War* was a word used far too often of late.

The bell outside rang. Faith looked about. Everyone was already present; they weren't expecting anyone else. Curious.

A moment later, Clayton entered. "A Mr. Lewis is here to speak to your group, ma'am." With a bow, her butler exited.

Mr. Lewis took a moment to look around the room and then bowed. "Good evening, ladies."

Silence permeated the parlor like a heavy, wet blanket. Several women narrowed their eyes at their guest. Faith would have found it humorous had she not been curious and hesitant about the man as well. "Good evening, Mr. Lewis. How may I help you?"

He strode forward and offered her a missive sealed with a red wax. "Mr. Washington has sent me." He held the note out to her with another bow and nodded.

Faith took it and broke the seal. Opening it, she recognized George's script immediately:

Lewis is a good friend and trustworthy. At great risk, we've sent him with an important request. Please aid him on his return journey as I know you will. But do not under any circumstances alert anyone else to his presence.

66

She closed the note and looked around the room. "Ladies, it is of utmost importance that we keep our guest's visit a secret. Are we all in accord?"

Quick affirmations filled the air. Faith nodded back to Mr. Lewis. "Please tell us how we can help."

The man licked his lips and took a deep breath. "I will attempt to be brief. The request is for one of you ladies to become a messenger. It would be an ongoing mission of sorts because it's vital that the messenger's familiarity in the area become regular in case she is seen in the vicinity. The meetings need to be out of sight as much as possible, but people need to see the messenger as a regular patron in the area. To maintain the facade of normal, everyday outings."

No one spoke.

Faith tilted her head. "A messenger to whom?"

"One of our men." Lewis straightened his shoulders.

What was he not saying? Faith glanced at Lavonia and could see the same questions burning behind her gaze. "Is this dangerous?"

"Quite so." The man lifted his chin and then looked down to his shoes before continuing. "But we need your help, and none of our men can attempt it without getting caught. The Patriots believe that one of the ladies — one of you — can aid us in this case."

"Who will the messages be delivered to exactly? You have only told us 'tis one of your men."

"He's a spy. Well placed within the Loyalists."

Gasps were heard throughout the room. The women began to whisper to one another.

"Just to ensure that we are understanding what you are requesting . . ." Faith took a deep breath. "You need one of us to get messages — on a frequent basis — to a man posing as a Loyalist?"

"Yes."

"Will that put our reputation at risk?"

Lewis shifted his weight from one foot to the other. "There is that possibility if you are seen together. And there is a good probability of that. Thus the need for the rest of the plan."

Several of the women looked to her with brows raised and eyes wide. A few of the others whispered to each other.

"This would not be requested unless it was of greatest importance. The leaders are convinced this is the only way and will provide us with the highest advantage. Both in time and in confusion. They will not be looking for women to be spies."

The room erupted as the women voiced their shock.

Faith held up a hand like she usually did when she needed their attention. "Friends . . . please." She closed her eyes for a brief moment and shot a quick prayer heavenward. "There is no need to go into hysterics."

Lavonia nodded. "Indeed. There is nothing wrong with Mr. Lewis giving us the details in an honest manner."

Normally timid Lydia spoke up. "But I do not think my husband would allow for his wife to be a . . . a . . . spy."

Several of the other women nodded and voiced their concerns.

Faith listened and watched Mr. Lewis's shoulders droop an inch. How could they allow fear to keep them from helping out the Patriot cause? It couldn't be borne.

"Ladies!" She stood and stomped her foot. "What of freedom? What of independence? What of honoring what the good Lord above has given us by using our minds and our hands to accomplish what is right?" Faith took a deep breath. "I, for one, will not let this chance go by — knowing that we could help. Let it never be said that the Patriots failed because they did not have the aid that we can provide."

Every lady — except Lydia — stood and nodded. Lydia glanced around and closed her eyes. When she came to her feet, all the women applauded.

"Now . . . the question is, who will be the brave one to take on this task?" Lavonia put her hands on her hips.

The room quieted again. Everyone looked around.

Five hands raised. Some with a bit of hesitance, but they were still raised.

As Faith's gaze roamed from woman to woman, a startling thought plunged into her chest. She was the only one without a husband or children to tend to. How could she even think to allow any one of them to take on a possibly dangerous mission? Shaking her head, she raised her hand high. "As proud as I am of all of you, I cannot allow any of you to do this task. You all have husbands and children that will be put at risk if you do this, and I do not —"

"Will that not make it even more dangerous for you? Being alone? A widow?" Lydia shook her head vehemently. "We cannot abide it if anything were to happen to you."

70

Murmurs filled the room.

Lavonia moved forward and took Faith's hands in hers. Her eyes pierced to Faith's very soul. "Are you sure about this?" she whispered low.

"Quite."

Her friend nodded. "Then so be it." She kept hold of Faith's right hand and turned to face the others. "It seems we have a volunteer, Mr. Lewis. And you will not find a braver woman in all of Boston, or even New England I dare say."

Mr. Lewis came forward and bowed before he took Faith's hand. "I will get the message to the leaders right away and will be in touch forthwith." With a nod, he retreated out of the parlor.

Lavonia shook her head and smiled. "You always had the spunk that none of us had, my dear. We will do whatever we can to assist you and your valiant undertaking."

"Here, here!" The women clapped again and surrounded Faith.

She had to admit, a little thrill of excitement ran through her at the thought of being so useful to the cause. But as soon as it washed over her, a new feeling crashed in behind it.

Was she ready for this? To be . . . a spy?

■ ■ ■

Saturday, December 24, 1774
Mount Vernon

George Washington sat behind his desk and scanned the ledgers in front of him. Everything looked as it should. Thankfully. He didn't want to spend extra time managing the estate right before Faith arrived. He worked hard to keep everything in order and had good men working for him. Knowing that he'd checked before her arrival would give him a clear mind to spend with his dear friend and guest.

It had been several months since she'd journeyed to the plantation to see them, but it was their tradition to try and spend the Christmas holiday together. Martha always insisted that Faith feel like part of the family.

He shook his head and smiled. Martha had loved Faith since the day she found out about his young ward.

Leaning back in his chair, George looked out the southwest window toward the Potomac River. He loved this home. The latest expansion would take years to finish in detail work, but Mount Vernon had a hold on him that the farm of his youth on the

Rappahannock River could not. The years had been hard on him but good in the long term. Providence had taught him to learn from any and all circumstances because they weren't by chance.

Reflecting on the past, George was amazed that Faith survived those early years. After he served as county surveyor, he'd been commissioned for England and served as a major and then lieutenant colonel in the French and Indian conflict back in the early '50s. Later resigning his post, he then served as an aide to General Braddock and eventually was given command over all the troops in Virginia. By age twenty-six the conflict was over, he resigned another commission, and returned home. God had been good to him. Especially to take care of Faith during those days when his world revolved around being a soldier. The Martins had been a gift from God above to take her in.

Then Martha had entered the picture, and life changed for the better. No longer in the army, he married and went home to Mount Vernon and worked to build the family estate. It had been almost sixteen years of his dream life. He served in the Virginia House of Burgesses and enjoyed being a gentleman and a farmer.

As snow fell from the sky outside his

home, George wished it could wash away all thought of war. Just like the blanket of white made things look clean. But a new conflict had been brewing for far too long. His meetings with the Patriot leaders were more frequent and he was certain that he would be called in to assist at any time. He'd shared as much with Martha, but she advised him not to borrow trouble. When the moment came, it came. They would enjoy their time together until then.

A light rap sounded on the door in front of him. "May I come in?"

The oh-so-familiar voice pulled his gaze from the window, and he jumped out of his chair. "Faith! You are here!"

Her effervescent laughter washed over him, and he went to hug her.

" 'Tis been far too long." He tried not to sound too fatherly, but she brought it out in him.

"Yes, it has. Which reminds me, you promised to visit me in Boston." She gave him a sideways look and placed her hands on her hips.

Feeling a bit sheepish, he cleared his throat. "Well, you see . . ." There really was no explanation.

She placed her hands on his shoulders and tugged him down. A tradition she'd followed since she was young. Standing on tiptoe, she kissed his cheek and then made her way to one of the chairs by his desk. "Do not even try to make an excuse. I know how much you love it here and hate to leave. Although I know you have made the trip to Philadelphia for the Congress." She pointed a finger at him and then positioned herself in the chair and gave him a large smile. " 'Tis all right, George. I completely understand. But I do love to get the letters from you and Martha."

"Does she know you are here?" He headed for the doorway. "If I don't let her know, I will get quite the scolding."

"Stop your teasing. Yes, she knows. I went to see her first so that you and I would have time to chat before dinner."

George chuckled and went back to his chair. Only those he invited were allowed into his study, but Faith was welcome without exception. There would always be a special place in his heart for his young friend. Framed by irrepressible dark blond curls, her face held its usual spirit, but something seemed to weigh on her mind. Of course, she would never again be the little sprite who followed him around; she was a grown woman. But he'd always think of her as needing protection.

Memories washed over him. Faith was an independent little thing. Even after her parents died, it was only a matter of days before her spunk and spirit returned. Yes, he'd always been her protector, but not because she couldn't take care of herself — that was for certain.

"George?"

"I am sorry. I was remembering you when you were just a little, precocious girl." He shook his head. "What's on your mind, Faith? I can see that something is troubling you."

She tilted her head to the side, squinted her eyes, and pursed her lips. A sight that always made her more endearing. She was smart and quite opinionated. " 'Tis not necessarily that anything is troubling me. I am quite determined in my decision."

Oh boy. What had she gotten herself into now?

"But 'tis hard to stop my thoughts from processing it all. I want to do the very best job that I can."

It was his turn to make a face. He lowered his brows and frowned. "Why is it I get the feeling that you have volunteered for something dangerous?"

"You're the one who sent Lewis to us, George. You even wrote me the note saying

76

he could be trusted. I cannot believe for one moment that you didn't have any inclination that I would take the job."

He closed his eyes and sighed. So *she* was the new messenger. He should have known. "Did no one else volunteer?"

She huffed. "Of course there were other volunteers. Every woman in there would give her life to see her children have the opportunity of a free country. But that's just the thing . . . It had to be me. I'm the only one without a husband or children to sacrifice."

And she was the bravest and probably most stubborn of them as well. George could easily envision how it had played out. "I cannot say that I'm pleased with your decision, Faith. It could be very dangerous." The words sounded like a rebuke, and he couldn't help it. They were out, and he couldn't take them back.

She stood to her feet and leaned over his desk, her cheeks matching the red of her dress. "I am shocked at you. Why . . . were you not the one who taught me to follow my instincts and not let anyone think less of me because I was a woman? When I inherited everything and then lost Joseph too, were you not the one who stood by my side and encouraged me to find my strength in the Lord? Told me all things were possible with God? And were you not the man who encouraged me to put my ladies group together so that we could help the Patriot cause? Goodness, George. I am thirty-two years old. I believe I can handle this job whether you approve or not." Hands on her hips again — a sign that she was not to be argued with — she lifted her chin, gave him another little huff, and sat back in her chair.

He took a deep breath and tried not to smile at her outburst. This was his Faith. He shouldn't expect anything less. In the back of his mind, yes, he'd always thought she could be the one to volunteer. He'd just conveniently blocked those thoughts from surfacing. "I'm sorry, Faith. 'Tis not that I doubt your abilities. But as your guardian for all those years, it is difficult for me to let go sometimes. You forget that I know the ugliness of war. I do not wish that for anyone." He and Martha would probably pray uncountable hours for their "girl" and worry for her safety every moment . . . but he couldn't stand in her way. They all had to sacrifice. He wiped a hand down his face.

She softened and reached out to lay her hand atop his. "I'm sorry for my outburst, George. And the last thing I want to do is add to your worry." She sighed and lifted her eyes to the ceiling. "Heaven knows that Martha will give me a stern talking to as well. But you know this is something I *must* do."

All he could manage was a nod. They would need a lot of strength for the days ahead, and Faith definitely had plenty of that. "Weber better keep you safe." He stood as well and leaned toward her, tapping her nose with his finger.

"That's God's job, George. You taught me that."

He came around his desk and offered her his arm. "Right, you are, my dear. Now why don't you accompany me to dinner. I have a feeling it will take a lot of convincing to keep Martha from accompanying you back to Boston to watch over you."

Faith's laughter filled the room as the aromas of a sumptuous feast pervaded his senses. It was Christmas after all. Time to celebrate the birth of Christ and put all the rumblings of war aside.

After they told Martha.

Thursday, January 12, 1775
Hingham, Massachusetts
Matthew crouched behind the stone foundation of Old Ship Meetinghouse and waited as the sun went down. The sky was

79

streaked with pinks and purples, and on any other night, he'd take the time to enjoy the beauty. But tonight was the first time he was to meet his messenger. His nerves felt frayed. The thought of a woman being sent as a messenger to a spy was the equivalent of leading her into the lion's den. But that's what the Patriots had asked her to do! How could they do such a thing?

He closed his eyes and took a deep breath. Calm was what he needed at this moment. This was their first test meeting. They needed to know who the other was, they needed to feel familiar with several different rendezvous points. It would take them a few weeks of practice, and then prayerfully, it would all be ready to go before things got out of hand. The fear within the Patriots was of a British attack. And no one knew how soon that could happen. It had taken years to get to this point, but everyone felt the tension in the air.

Sending a prayer heavenward, he praised the Lord for the beauty in the sunset and for another day to worship Him. If Matthew could just keep his focus there — worshipping God — all the time, he'd probably have a much better go of it.

Opening his eyes, he determined to do just that. The only way they'd gain freedom was if they followed Him. Thankfully, the leaders of the Patriot movement were God-fearing men.

The night sky darkened around him and the only sound was that of his own breath. Time was of the essence. Prayerfully his new messenger wasn't lost.

The crunch of snow underfoot sounded from the north side of the church. Was that her?

Waiting at the appointed meeting spot, Matthew kept close watch on everything else around him. The trees were covered in ice and snow and the wind was utterly still. No movement of any kind broke the quiet, except for the continued footsteps.

Light and quick, the weight sounded to be from a woman. A man's steps were farther apart and more plodding.

Turning to his right, he held his breath and kept his chin tucked so that his face wouldn't be visible in the dim light. Just in case it wasn't his expected guest, he couldn't be too cautious.

The footsteps slowed and then stopped. But whoever it was hadn't rounded the corner of the building yet. Was she in trouble? Or possibly second-guessing herself?

Matthew moved a few steps closer and

waited. The scent of roses wafted over him.

Nothing happened.

The seconds dragged by as if he were holding his breath and simply relishing the scent. Had she changed her mind?

A little huff sounded and then a step.

Matthew exhaled.

Five more steps and then a voluminous gown that seemed gold in color in the waning twilight appeared around the corner. The small woman in the fine dress stepped all the way toward him.

As she came closer, Matthew couldn't breathe for a moment. She was the loveliest woman he'd ever seen. When George told him that his friend would be helping them and she was a widow, Matthew had fully expected to meet an older — in fact he'd envisioned a *much* older — lady.

"Are you . . ." She licked her lips. "Are you Mr. Weber?" Her voice was so soft, he almost couldn't discern the words so it gave him an excuse to step closer.

She didn't hesitate and stepped toward him too.

The bottom of her skirt swished against his boots. Whoever she was, she had great wealth. And no lack of confidence. Her eyes shone with it.

"Mr. Weber?"

He nodded and tried to convince his brain to engage in the conversation.

"I'm pleased to meet you." She held out a hand. "My name is Faith Jackson."

"Mrs. Jackson." His manners kicked in and he bowed but almost knocked her in the head with his own, they were so close. "My apologies." He felt the heat rise to his cheeks, but he didn't step back. Thankfully, it was almost fully dark.

"George told me that you were a trusted friend of his from his surveying years." No censure, no hesitation. She kept a close eye on her surroundings, and it made her appear quite smart. "I remember him writing about you. He always thought his stories would be boring to me, but I could imagine a great adventure occurred almost everywhere George went."

It all hit him in that moment. As he gave a slow nod, a rush of memories flooded him. So she was *that* Faith. The inquisitive, precocious, and spunky young girl he'd heard so much about.

She tilted her head and narrowed her eyes. "Did I remember incorrectly?"

"No." He shook his head. "It just occurred to me that you were the Faith that George told me about . . . the one he had written to all those years." The beauty before him had been George's ward. It all made sense now. All the stories his friend had shared over the years of the neighbor girl who had the bravery of ten men. She'd lost her parents as a child, and if he remembered correctly, she'd lost her husband only a week after their wedding. His eyes widened. Newfound respect flooded his chest. "When George told me about my appointed messenger, he forgot to tell me that it was you."

Mrs. Jackson laughed and then covered her mouth. "My apologies," she whispered and looked around her as if the sound would have drawn spectators. "He did not tell me anything about you either, other than that he trusted you and had worked with you for Lord Fairfax."

"I heard stories of you all those years, so I am quite familiar with Faith Lytton — um . . . Faith Jackson." He couldn't help the smile. He'd always wanted to meet the little "sprite" George described. But these were not the circumstances he'd been expecting.

"Well, I am sure we will get acquainted the next few months." She smiled up at him. "I am thankful that this first meeting went well. I don't believe anyone has seen us." She causally checked the surroundings.

"No, I don't believe they have."

"I look forward to meeting you again, Mr. Weber." Her broad smile flashed white teeth at him.

"Please, call me Matthew."

"Then you must call me Faith. At least when we are alone like this." Her brow furrowed. "Which I guess will be every time we meet, since we are not supposed to be seen together."

The clouds moved away from the moon for a moment, and he got a better glimpse of her eyes. They appeared a light brown in the light, but he couldn't determine the color with certainty. She seemed highly intelligent and not at all afraid, in fact her courage astounded him. So what had been the hesitation when she first arrived? Had she been checking to see if anyone had followed or seen her? And what of her tiny huff? These were the things that he wanted to ask but knew he would have to wait until a later time.

"I suppose I should be going." Faith took a step back. " 'Twas a pleasure to meet you . . . Matthew." Her smile was a beautiful sight.

"You as well." He bowed. "I look forward to seeing you next time."

She nodded and turned around. As she walked around the corner, she looked over her shoulder and smiled at him again.

When her footsteps faded into the quiet of the night, Matthew leaned up against the wall of the church. No longer affected by the bitter cold, he pondered what had just happened.

He'd met his messenger. And she wasn't anything like what he expected. George was of course to blame. It all would have been so much easier if he had simply told Matthew that it was Faith.

But then, he'd been completely distracted by her. Not a good thing.

He'd do better next time. He had to. She was only a distraction because he hadn't known what to expect. Now that he knew who she was, he could prepare for their next meeting and be a perfect gentleman. It was all for the Patriot cause and none other.

Providence had shined down on them all. The tasks before him weren't as daunting as they seemed a few hours prior. It must be the confidence Mrs. Jackson exuded. Or the fact that he felt instantly that he could trust her.

Who was he kidding? He couldn't wait until the Patriots had a message to give him. Because he wanted to see Faith Lytton Jackson again.

CHAPTER 3

Tuesday, January 31, 1775

Faith took her basket to the market near Hingham where she was assigned to meet Matthew. It was a much different area than that of her own home in Boston. She'd need to get better acquainted with it. Meandering through the market, she tried to appear like a regular customer. Even in her simplest gown, she stood out a touch. Perhaps Marie could sew her something different to wear.

Mr. Lewis's words ran through her mind. He had returned to visit after her first meeting with Mr. Weber to give her detailed instructions for future contact. Since it went well and no one saw them, they were ready for the next phase. The actual exchange of messages.

But Faith had to acquaint herself with the other locations first.

Last week, George had asked her to meet him in Philadelphia, and he went over everything again. Of course, he plied her with questions. Probably to make sure she was ready. While she'd been adamant about her preparedness to George, there had been a slight niggle of fear in her mind.

The list of things to remember was lengthy. But she was up for the task. She was. George knew it — and it shone in his eyes. She could tell he was proud of her for taking up the cause, but also worried for her well-being. He'd even expressed as much, although he was a quiet man of few words. But George had always been one to worry about her. Even though she could take care of herself — a point which Mr. Washington should know quite well.

Ticking off the main things to remember, she walked to the candle maker's shop.

Be a regular patron in the area.

Make friends with the ladies around — especially those with husbands of the loyalist inclination.

Smile.

Act as if nothing were amiss.

Never take the same route to a meeting, but use regular routes within town.

Don't let anyone see her exchange the letters.

Try never to be seen with Matthew. But if so, they had to make it look like a couple in

88

love meeting in secret.
Keep the drop-offs short.

Not too difficult. At least, she hoped not.

The key would be to spend money at the shops, earn people's trust, and blend into the regular crowds. She needed to be recognizable but not well-known.

As tensions continued to rise, British troops were seen on a much more common basis. It seemed startling to see them in the streets and shops, but George had warned that this was coming. He'd gone back to Mount Vernon, the estate he'd inherited when his older brother died. And for some reason, it made Faith feel a bit more alone.

She longed to return to her parents' home in Virginia. But she'd only been back once a year to ensure everything was still working ever since Joseph died. The pull seemed incredibly strong in her heart. Maybe after her job of messenger was complete, she would be able to return to Virginia and stay. There really wasn't anything holding her in Boston, although she did love her home and her friends.

After loading her basket with the most expensive candles — she'd informed the chandler that she needed them for an important dinner — she made a large order for everyday candles and told him she'd send one of her servants to pick them up at a later time. The man practically bowed all over her feet, he seemed to be so grateful for the business. Most homes had servants who would make all their candles, so only the elite would buy them, and it was always a rank of prosperity when a household purchased their candles.

Were things really this difficult nowadays? She'd heard rumors about times getting tougher because of the taxations and boycotts, but apparently, she hadn't paid enough attention. Perhaps she would need to be more frugal in the days to come.

Thrice she had made appearances in the marketplace and shops. A few people greeted her as if she were familiar, but she wasn't at all sure if the plan they'd put into place was working. She still didn't feel much familiarity. But George had been correct that the best way to get used to her surroundings was to observe it all in the daylight.

She'd just take a walk — the long way around the square — so she could ensure she remembered every part of the area.

A carriage pulled up beside her and impeded her path. "Mrs. Jackson. How lovely to find you here."

The all-too-sweet and sniveling-sounding

voice was familiar and made Faith inwardly cringe. But she pasted on a smile and turned to look up at Anthony Jameson. "Good day to you, Mr. Jameson." While she'd avoided the man in social circles for many years, this past year, he'd seemed to take an interest in seeking her out. For what reason, she couldn't even guess. . . . The man believed everyone to be beneath him. Always talking about his relationship with the King and expecting the world to bow at his feet.

"This is an awfully long journey from your home." The pompous man looked around him. "Might I offer you a ride back to Boston, ma'am?"

"No, thank you. I have got quite a bit to do yet today, and my driver is with me."

"Then perhaps I could interest you in a companion as you walk?" The large man descended from his carriage.

Faith sighed. The man never took no for an answer. "That would be . . ." She bit off the last of what she wanted to say. No use offending the man completely.

Out of the corner of her eye, she could see him start to offer his arm, so she stepped forward at a brisk pace and hoped he could read her hint. Even if she did manage to deftly ignore his gesture, the man needed an education in pursuing women.

When it all boiled down to it, he was not as smart as he tried to convince people he was.

"Mrs. Jackson." He huffed. "I do believe we should slow our pace a bit."

"Whatever for?" She furrowed her brow and tried not to smile. "I enjoy walking. It is so invigorating."

"Humph." He mumbled something she couldn't discern. "But I was hoping for a leisurely stroll. Where we could get to know one another better."

"Oh, that is very kind of you, Mr. Jameson. . . ." Faith picked up her pace and stared straight ahead. She had no desire to know Anthony Jameson at all. "But I do have quite a few things that I need to accomplish yet this afternoon, if you remember. I do like to stay busy."

"But you have a staff and plenty of people to serve you, ma'am. Why not let them earn their keep?"

She narrowed her eyes. Earn their keep? If she didn't know better, she would have thought Anthony Jameson had crawled out from under a rock. How had this man found favor with the King? And with the upper classes? Was he really wealthy enough to just buy his way in and then treat people however he wanted? The thought disgusted her.

His quick footsteps and heavy breathing reminded her that he was still trying to keep up with her. Bother.

"I believe the good Lord above has given us instruction as to how we should live. And I don't believe being idle and waiting to be served is one of those instructions." She tried to be nice. She really did. But sometimes that man could bring out the worst in her, and she feared her tongue would get away with her. If only George were here, maybe he could help get rid of the pest of a man. But George wouldn't be able to tolerate him at all. Why had Anthony Jameson decided to give her attention? She'd never encouraged it. Of that she was certain.

"But you deserve to be pampered and taken care of, my dear."

Not by him, not ever. Faith could only keep walking. And bite her tongue, so she didn't say anything rude. He couldn't be that daft. Surely, he'd get the point and leave her alone.

"I would like the opportunity to show you the life you deserve."

The last words made her stop and turn toward him. "Mr. Jameson —"

"Yes, my dear." Anthony moved closer with the opportunity. His wig sat at an odd

93

angle after their brisk walk. "I am so glad I've gained your attention —"

"No." She held up a hand. No. No. No. Never. She took a deep breath. "I am sorry. But I must put an end to our walk today. I really must go." Faith lifted the edge of her skirt and took off what could almost be called a run — to find her driver. It didn't matter to her that it was unseemly. She didn't care who was watching.

All she knew was that she *must* get as far away from that man as she could.

Wednesday, February 15, 1775
Philadelphia
Matthew stood at the back of the room and listened to the group of Loyalists discuss the turmoil around them. Tobacco smoke hung thick in the air while voices competed to be heard. They'd met in secret but spoke of many other Loyalists and of the many British troops to the north.

"We've sent word to London and to Parliament about the rebellious nature of the Colonies." Lord Williams tilted his chin up. Matthew always took it as a gesture to dare anyone to argue with him.

"But what of their militias they are building?" John Masterson tapped his finger on the table in front of him. "We cannot rush into anything without backing from the King."

"I for one" — a man Matthew didn't recognize stood with his thumbs tucked into his jacket — "am tired of the rumblings. We are British and should remain as such. If they are not loyal to the King, then they should just go elsewhere."

"Here, here." The one known as Robert Sims stuck his quill in the air and then went back to recording the meetings proceedings.

Matthew forced himself to nod so that no one would be suspicious. William Franklin was supposed to meet him here, but he hadn't arrived yet. It was vital that he got William's take on things because he was scheduled to meet Faith in three days' time and he needed to send a message on through her.

Faith. He'd had a hard time getting the lovely widow off his mind. And he'd looked forward to nothing more than to see her again. But circumstances were not conducive for a courtship right now. Matthew lifted a hand to his brow and rubbed it. What was he thinking? He needed to get back to the task at hand. Focusing on the discussion around him, he wondered if everyone in the room truly believed that the best future for their Colonies lay under British rule.

One of the men mentioned the Royal Governor of New Jersey — that was William — and how the man had done commendable things for the British Navy. Even gaining Patriot secrets to share with the commanding officers.

Secrets? What secrets had William gotten a hold of? And from whom?

William's leanings had been increasingly toward the strict Loyalist, and he always seemed in the know on the word from London. The fact that Matthew had been welcomed into this secret group showed the power that William held. So why wasn't he here? And how was he obtaining secrets from the Patriots? Matthew would have to investigate this further.

No matter Franklin's thoughts, it appeared the British wanted to lay down some hard lines for the Colonies and attempt to remain in control. A very difficult and risky proposition with the monarchy across the vast ocean. The leaders in Parliament — and even the King, for that matter — couldn't possibly understand what was happening here in the Americas.

Why couldn't meetings and conversations be held? Why wouldn't the monarchy take the time to listen? Didn't they understand that boycotts and taxes and rules and demands were not the way to run the Colonies? It was as if the ruling class in England believed that everyone in the Colonies were nothing more than . . . slaves.

A deep sense of foreboding hit him in the gut. War seemed more real each day. And even though Matthew longed for the Colonies to be independent, he couldn't justify a war in his mind. What were they to do? The ugliness of every battle he'd seen raced through his memories. There had to be a better way. But what was it?

The conversations continued around the room, and Matthew noticed that any official discussion was over. Still no sign of William. He'd been so lost in thought again that he'd missed the end of the meeting, but did it really matter? It seemed lines were being drawn in the sand. Deep ones, without the option of erasure.

The thought weighed heavy on his heart. If there wasn't a chance of working through the differences of opinion, then war was imminent.

Shaking his head free of the thoughts, he put his hat in place and snuck out of the room. A visit to his mentor would help him sort through it. It would be a risk, but he could slip in through the kitchen door. Pulling his black cloak high up around his neck, he stepped into the shadows.

He took several different turns and rounded two separate blocks three times just in case anyone was watching or tried to follow him. When he was sure no one had seen him, he made his way toward the back of Benjamin Franklin's home.

When he knocked on the kitchen door, he expected Charles — the butler — to answer like usual. But the old man himself answered the door.

"Matthew." Franklin's shocked whisper floated into the night. "Good heavens, son, 'tis late and it is freezing. Come in, come in." Ben's hair was disheveled as if he'd fallen asleep in his chair. It had been barely two months since his wife had died, and it had aged the man.

"Thank you, sir." Matthew walked straight through the kitchen to the fire to warm himself. "I was hoping to see your son tonight and have more information to pass on via messenger, but he wasn't at the meeting."

"I see. There have been a lot of murmurings lately. William has had his hands full as governor." The sigh that left his friend's lips showed a bit of the discouragement the man must feel to be on separate political sides.

"I fear our relationship is at an impasse. I don't believe I will be speaking with William anymore in the future. If ever."

Matthew sucked in a gulp of air. "Truly? Has it come to that?" He couldn't believe that a father and son could be divided so much over politics as to split the relationship. Perhaps Deborah's death had altered his thinking in more ways than one.

"I fear it is so. He's been secretly reporting Patriot activities to his authorities, and I cannot abide his willful abandonment of my thoughts and wishes. He has no regard for them, even with all I have done for him — to gain him his position to say the least. And after the loss of his mother . . ." Ben swiped a hand down his face. "Well, she had raised him. He thought of her as his mother." He released a heavy sigh. "Come, let's sit in the parlor for a while. The fire is just as warm in there, and we can discuss different topics."

With a nod, Matthew understood that the subject of Ben's sweet wife had to be closed. But he couldn't cover his shock. If Ben and William could be so divided, what did that say for the Colonies and Britain?

Ben eased himself into a chair and picked up his glasses. "What's on your mind, son? I can see that something is greatly troubling to you."

How could he tell his friend and mentor that the split in his relationship with his son seemed to be the final nail in the coffin? It truly was here. War. As much as he didn't want to see it, didn't want it to happen, it was here nonetheless.

"Go ahead, Matthew. I can see your mind is in a whirl of motion." Ben leaned forward.

Everything he'd heard that night made sense. It all added up. And the conclusion was the same no matter which way he turned. That meant the message that needed to be passed on through Faith would have to show the truth of the dire situation.

Faith. He'd been thrilled at the thought of seeing her again. And in the back of his mind, he'd hoped that there was a future ahead . . . but could they even think of a future if war was on the horizon?

"Matthew?" Ben's voice broke through his reverie.

"My apologies." He'd only just met Faith. There was no use even contemplating the future at this point. "I was lost in thought."

"So did you need to discuss anything else that you heard or saw this evening?" Ben put his glasses on and rubbed his hands together. "I'm all ears."

"Actually" — Matthew removed his cloak

and sat in one of the large wingback chairs — "I was hoping to discuss a different matter."

Ben raised his eyebrows. "Of course. Anything for you. What can I help you with?"

" 'Tis about a woman."

"You know my history in this area, young man." The older gentleman chuckled and stood.

"Yes, but since I believe we are on the precipice of war, I need some education in this matter. I have always been working, or fighting, or surveying . . . and no one has ever captured my interest."

"Ah, but there is one now."

"Yes. And even though the times we see each other are short — and a bit dangerous — I cannot seem to get her from my mind."

"Well now, that is a dilemma." Ben walked over and patted Matthew on the shoulder. "I am glad you have found someone that's caught your interest, 'tis about time, you know."

Matthew shook his head and laughed. Good ol' Ben. Never mincing words.

"But I think we need a drink to have this discussion." He winked, and Matthew followed him back into the kitchen.

Even on the brink of war, he looked forward to seeing Faith again.

CHAPTER 4

Saturday, February 18, 1775
Boston

The heavy scent of manure made Faith bring her gloved hand up to her nose. And leave it there. Why on earth had they chosen to meet in a barn? The nosegay pinned to her stomacher couldn't even begin to cut the stench.

She spent so little time around animals that the overwhelming sensation to gag on the smell made her eyes water. This was no way to meet Mr. Weber again. She had to show that she was strong and capable of such a job.

When she was younger, she'd spent uncountable hours in the muck and mire, playing with the animals and getting covered in who knew what filth. But that had been long ago. Before her parents had died. Before she'd been taken to Boston to be raised. The Martins had been wonderful people,

103

but they spoiled her. She knew that. That never stopped her curious and precocious nature, but since they had no children of their own, they poured everything into Faith. Which had been a wonderful thing for her. And when they also died, it was almost like losing her parents all over again. Through it all, she'd become even stronger and more independent.

And quite wealthy.

Not only did she have a substantial inheritance from her parents — the Lyttons — but she'd also gained her husband's fortune. Then the Martins' wealth passed on to her a few years later because they had bequeathed everything to her. It was true: she would never want for anything monetarily or materially, but she did long to be loved by someone. Everyone she'd loved had died. All except for George.

And while she knew that George would always be there for her — as long as he was alive — she still longed for someone to call her own.

For years, she'd wanted children. Still did. But she'd had to push the ache aside. The Patriot cause seemed to have been sent by God — something for her to pour her time and efforts into — but she knew there had to be more. Even though she had to tuck those feelings deep inside.

From the moment she'd met Matthew, the spark she'd felt had started a new flame of longing in her heart. Granted, they'd only met a couple of times — barely a few minutes each — but there was some sort of connection. Did he feel it too?

Removing her gloved hand from her nose, she realized her mistake and replaced it. She'd have to get more accustomed to the smell before he arrived. It wouldn't do to stand here with her face covered the whole time they spoke. But then, she'd also arrived quite early. Anxious to see him again, she couldn't help it.

The barn door creaked, which made the geese in the corner stall raise a ruckus. Should she hide until she knew who it was? She'd never been given instructions on this part — Matthew had always been waiting for her at the arranged meeting sights. Maybe she should at least ease her way into the corner. The shadows would hide her for now. Her heart jumped into a faster rhythm.

"Faith?" Matthew's whisper floated over to her.

Releasing a sigh of relief, she moved toward his voice. "I am so glad it is you. I realized how unprepared I am for other visitors."

He moved toward her until she could see his outline in the dim light.

She lowered her hand from her face. "You should probably take the time to instruct me on what I am to do in case I run into someone else."

"I would be happy to." He turned, but she couldn't see what he was doing. "But first, we need a bit more light. Wait here."

Faith couldn't see where he went, but she could hear his rustling footsteps on the hay. She lifted her hand again and planned to keep it up by her nose as long as possible. A small circle of orange light headed back toward her.

"Here. I brought a candle with me, in hopes there would still be some embers burning in the fire."

As he moved closer, she could see the lines of his face, and the deep brown of his eyes. Was it just her imagination, or did they dance with joy when he came near her? The smile that lifted his lips made her hope that he felt something of the same excitement she did.

"That was very smart of you." She returned his smile and clasped her hands at her waist. With him near, the smell didn't seem to affect her.

"I must admit that it was in hopes we'd

have a few moments to get to know one another better." The earnest look in his eyes stirred her heart. "Do you have the time to spare?"

"Why yes, of course." Why did she feel like a young girl all over again? She was thirty-two — closing in on thirty-three — years of age. Goodness, she needed to get a grip on her feelings. They weren't children. Maybe it would be best to conduct their business first. "Any brilliant advice to me on how to behave if there are other visitors?"

His smile made her stomach do a little flip. "Always remember that you are supposed to be there. Wherever it is. So act as such. If it makes you feel better, think ahead of time about what you would say if questioned. Come up with a valid reason, and then your brain will be able to relax."

"That is very good advice, thank you." If she could just keep her heart at a regular rhythm, she was sure she could manage it. But with Matthew so close, that was quite difficult. "I have a message for you." Reaching through the slit in her skirts she found the pockets hanging from her waist. She'd had Marie take extra precaution and pin them in addition to tying them around her waist so there was no risk of losing them.

She pulled out the paper.

Matthew took it and began to read it. "Thank you." His face shadowed for a moment. "It is as I feared."

She cocked her head. "Feared? Are things getting worse?"

His face softened at her worried query. "I'm sure you are well aware of all that has been going on."

"Most of it, yes."

"All this time, I have been hoping to avoid all-out war, but I fear that was just a whim — reality is so much more harsh than we'd like to admit." He reached into his coat and brought out a folded paper. "I need you to deliver this message back."

"Of course." As she took the message, their fingers touched, and she allowed her hand to linger. Looking into Matthew's eyes, she saw the heartache he felt. War wasn't unknown to him — she knew he'd fought battles at the side of George in the French and Indian conflict, she'd received many letters mentioning his bravery and honor — but she wished it could be. Especially now.

As much as everyone behind the Patriot cause wanted their freedom, it would be nice if it could be won without a fight.

"I am sorry for the location of our meeting — the smell is quite overpowering." He released a slight chuckle. "But I was hoping for some quiet and a little bit of warmth so we could visit."

"I appreciate your thoughtfulness." Although she could quite do without the stench. She put her hand back to her nose to inhale the lavender scent on her gloves. She'd have to thank Marie with an extra abundance tonight for always putting the sachets in her dresser.

"Would you like to sit for a moment?" He motioned to two bales of hay sitting in the corner. "Allow me." He took off his cloak and laid it over one of the bales for her. "Now there won't be any chance of mussing your beautiful gown. Please . . . sit."

Faith smiled up at him, admiring his blue coat with elegant, brocade trim. "Thank you." Taking a seat, she felt bad for him sacrificing his outer cloak. It was still quite chilly in the barn.

"I would love to know more about you, Mrs. Jackson — I mean Faith." He appeared to be a bit nervous. "I mean . . . George has told me a lot about you over the years, but I am afraid 'tis mainly from when you were much younger."

She couldn't help but laugh. "I can well imagine the stories you heard. I was an interesting child. Precocious is the word that George used a lot, along with many others that weren't quite so complimentary." She laid her hands in her lap. "Poor George, he had his hands full as my guardian all those years."

"But he loved every bit of it. I'm sure you know that." Matthew leaned in an inch closer and cocked an eyebrow.

A tingle raced up Faith's spine. "I do. I never had any siblings, and George was better than any big brother I could have imagined."

"He's an exemplary man. Someone I look up to."

"I'm sure. I have never met a better man, other than my father, of course."

"I would have loved to have known your father. George looked up to him as well." Matthew leaned closer and put his elbows on his knees. "Would you tell me more about your parents?"

Tears pricked the corners of her eyes. It had been a long time since she'd spoken of them. "Would you mind if I asked you to wait for another time? I find myself quite unprepared for the emotion at the moment." As she peered into his eyes, she saw concern that she'd never seen in a man's eyes before. Other than George's.

"Of course. My apologies for bringing up such a delicate matter."

It was her turn to lay a hand over his. "No need to apologize. One day I'd love to share with you about them. But I probably need to prepare myself for it." She gave him a small smile. "Would you like to tell me about your family?"

"There's not much to tell. My parents died of the small pox when I was surveying with George for Lord Fairfax. I have an older sister who is married and lives in Plymouth. She has two children whom I love to dote on."

"My family is from Plymouth originally. How fascinating." Faith had been longing to take a trip there and see her family's history.

"Ah, yes. My sister — Amelia — told me she knew of some Lyttons. Years ago when I was sharing stories from George. When did your family come to Plymouth?" His genuine eagerness to learn of her family made her heart soar.

"They were passengers on the *Mayflower* and the *Speedwell.*" She hadn't told the story in far too long. Almost giddy with the joy of sharing it with someone, she sat up a little straighter and couldn't help the huge smile.

"You don't say. Fascinating. So they weren't married when they came over?"

She shook her head. "In fact, they'd never met. My father told me it was a story passed down through the generations how my great-great-great-grandfather was one of the Strangers while my great-great-great-grandmother was one of the Saints. They started off on separate vessels, and then when the *Speedwell* could no longer make the journey, they spent the voyage to America together on the *Mayflower.* Mary Elizabeth Chapman started a journal on that trip, and it's been passed down for all these generations."

"So I take it you've read it?" Matthew inched closer again, his eyes alight with curiosity.

"I have. And even better than that, 'tis one of my most prized possessions."

"Am I to assume that they fell in love on the trip? I've heard that was one of the worst voyages in history."

Faith couldn't help but laugh. "I dare say." She shook her head. "From the details in her journal, 'tis amazing to me that any of them survived the trip. But yes, they fell in love during the trip over, and then she stuck by his side when he was accused of being a spy. Mary Elizabeth told everyone that William Lytton was too honorable a man to be a spy." The memory made her so proud of her ancestry. Why hadn't she gone to Plymouth before now?

The smile fell from Matthew's face. He opened his mouth and then shut it. His expression clouded, and he stood to his feet and paced away from her. "I suppose you think that being a spy is not an honorable thing." His voice was soft and sad.

His words struck her heart like someone had hit her in the chest. "Oh, Matthew. That is not at all what I meant." She stood as well and walked over to him. When would she ever learn to think things through before she spoke? "Don't you see? We're *both* spies. But this is a different situation. This is to aid our fellow man. William was accused of being a spy in a way that would hurt the people he loved."

He turned and looked down at her. "I am not sure you understand how difficult it is for me to pretend to be someone I am not. I know this is for the greater good, but it feels like I'm lying all the time."

Faith had struggled with the same feelings when she'd first been asked to carry the messages. "You know, I have had quite a few doubts myself, and I haven't been at this as long as you. Matthew, what you're doing is a very honorable thing. Your goal is to save as many lives as you can, and to keep them from the shedding of innocent blood. We are fighting for freedom."

"I know that. I do." He reached out and took her hands. "I'm sorry." Releasing her hands, he stepped back. "That was inappropriate of me. I just didn't realize how much it meant to me — what you thought. That is . . . what your opinion of me is . . ." He lifted a hand to his forehead. "I'm sorry. I am making a mess of things."

Faith led him back to the hay bales and sat down. "The way I see it, we are like the spies in the Old Testament. Joshua and Caleb in the book of Numbers. They had to spy out the land. And then there was Rahab, the woman who lied on their behalf to save their lives. She knew they were from the Lord. I am not saying that 'tis right to lie, but sometimes what is required of us is more difficult than we could ever imagine and will put us in situations that we never would have guessed."

Matthew nodded. "I haven't doubted for a moment that what I was called to do was the right thing. But hearing your voice there a moment ago . . . I realized how much it *did* matter to me — at least it mattered what you thought of me." He shook his head and laughed. "Let's get back to your family, I'd love to hear the rest of the story."

She understood all too well what Matthew was saying. Even though they'd only known each other a short while, she cared deeply about the opinion he held of her. But it would be much better to stay on safer topics. Her heart was already inclined to think too much of Matthew. "Well, he was a carpenter, and they stayed and helped build Plymouth and had twelve children and forty-two grandchildren. My great-grandfather was one of those grandchildren."

"How fascinating. Do you stay in touch with much of your family?"

A wave of sadness washed over her. "My mother tried to correspond with as many as she could, and sadly, after she died, I was too young to keep up with all of them. A lot of my parents' books were burned in the fire that killed them, and so I don't have addresses or even names."

"We can fix that. My sister knows a few of them — or at least she did — and I am certain with a little effort, we could reconnect you with your family."

"Really? You wouldn't mind asking her?"

"Not at all. It sounds like great fun. An adventure to find your family." Matthew smiled and took her hand. "It will be something joyous in the midst of this madness."

"I would love that." She put a hand to her chest. The thought of reconnecting with her family — even in these tumultuous times — gave her heart a little jolt. And all because this man cared.

She studied him for a minute and just smiled back at him. Here was a man that didn't seem to care one whit about her money or her inheritance, but cared about her. He wanted to know about her. *And* her family. What a nice gentleman. "You have given me something to look forward to, Mr. Weber."

" 'Tis Matthew, remember?" He stood and bowed. "And I think it's you who has given me something to look forward to."

The look in his eyes stirred something deep inside. It was way too early for her to be feeling anything of the sort. Wasn't it? Trying to diffuse the charged air between them, Faith laughed, "I think we've already broken one of the rules."

His brow furrowed and he sat down again. "Whatever do you mean?"

"One of the rules they gave me about delivering messages."

One eyebrow shot up. "Oh, pray tell. What is this rule?"

"Keep the drop-offs short."

Matthew laughed. "Well, yes, I am guessing we have broken that one." He stood and reached for her hand. "And I hope we break it again. Until next time, Mrs. Jackson." He kissed her glove-covered knuckles, and it sent a shiver up her spine.

She stood and hoped the dim light covered the blush she felt creep up her cheeks. Picking up his cloak, she brushed it off and handed it to him. How tortuous to see him leave when she longed to spend more time with him.

With his greatcoat back around his shoulders, he turned as if to say something else, but instead he reached for her hand again and then squeezed.

Faith wished she could hold on to his hand, but that would be quite forward so she released it and gave him a smile.

He blew out the candle and slipped into the night.

"Yes . . . until next time." She whispered the words and hoped there would be another message very soon.

CHAPTER 5

Wednesday, March 1, 1775
Boston

Anthony looked around his office and tapped his fingers on his desk. Things were not progressing like he'd hoped. His recent visit to Governor Gage revealed a flaw in the British thinking. Gage was unsympathetic to the Patriot cause and the independence movement. He may have made great strides in diplomacy, but the one thing he should be paying more attention to would end up being his demise. Of that, Anthony was certain.

As of the moment, he wasn't sure which side would win. But one thing he was certain of. He would be on the winning side. He would make sure of it. Whichever that may be. The British had a massive amount of soldiers and supplies at their aid. But the Patriots were tired of the way things were. They were restless and prepared to do

118

whatever it took.

Understanding both sides was the only way to stay ahead of the game. For now, it behooved him to play the part to the British ruling class, and behind the scenes, he would find out all he could from the Patriot movement. He would get what he wanted. No matter how it played out, *he* would be the victor.

According to Governor Gage, the British were planning an attack on the rebellion's arms. Maybe he could use that information to get him into the good graces of those in leadership with the Patriots. He knew those silly women's meetings that Faith hosted were not just to make clothes for the poor. Maybe if he showed his own concern, he could convince her they were on the same side and should work together. If she truly was a Patriot. He'd have to investigate this further.

He just needed her attention. Once he gained that, he was certain he could convince her that theirs would be an advantageous marriage.

His masculinity and stunning clothes would certainly draw her inquisitive eye. She was smart and would know what was good for her.

Indeed — Anthony Jameson was the best for her.

It wouldn't take much time and then she'd be begging him to marry her.

And then her fortune would be his.

Monday, March 6, 1775

Faith sat in the red tapestry chair that was always her chosen spot in the parlor when she was alone. She'd read her Bible many times sitting in this very chair and had spent uncountable hours kneeling beside it in prayer. But most of the time for her meetings with the women, she liked to lead the meetings from the middle of the group. Today she needed the comfort of her favorite chair.

Lavonia entered the room in a lovely gown of silvery-blue that accented her white hair in a very becoming manner. The woman always had such style. She raised an eyebrow at Faith as Clayton announced her. "My dear, I can tell that something is amiss this evening." Her eyebrow almost met her hairline it raised so high with questions.

"Oh my . . ." Lydia gasped when she entered the room. "To what do we owe this change?" She tucked a curl of her brown hair under her lace day cap.

The other ladies made similar comments,

and it made Faith wonder if she had been so habitual that she became predictable. That wasn't her. At least it hadn't been. What had happened to her?

When the ladies were all seated and offered refreshment, Faith nodded to Clayton, and he closed the parlor doors behind him.

"I would like to do our reading today a little differently. Psalm 136 has really touched me. The end of each phrase is the same — like an answer to a difficult question, the answer will always be the same. His mercy endureth for ever. So as I read, let us all join in saying, 'His mercy endureth for ever.' "

Eager smiles answered her.

Faith began:

"O give thanks unto the Lord; for he is good:
for his mercy endureth for ever.
O give thanks unto the God of gods:
for his mercy endureth for ever.
O give thanks to the Lord of lords:
for his mercy endureth for ever.
To him who alone doeth great wonders:
for his mercy endureth for ever.
To him that by wisdom made the heavens:
for his mercy endureth for ever.
To him that stretched out the earth above

121

the waters:
for his mercy endureth for ever.
To him that made great lights:
for his mercy endureth for ever:
the sun to rule by day:
for his mercy endureth for ever:
the moon and stars to rule by night:
for his mercy endureth for ever.
To him that smote Egypt in their firstborn:
for his mercy endureth for ever:
and brought out Israel from among them:
for his mercy endureth for ever:
with a strong hand, and with a stretched
    out arm:
for his mercy endureth for ever.
To him which divided the Red sea into
    parts:
for his mercy endureth for ever:
and made Israel to pass through the midst
    of it:
for his mercy endureth for ever:
but overthrew Pharaoh and his host in the
    Red sea:
for his mercy endureth for ever.
To him which led his people through the
    wilderness:
for his mercy endureth for ever.
To him which smote great kings:
for his mercy endureth for ever:
and slew famous kings:

for his mercy endureth for ever:
Sihon king of the Amorites:
for his mercy endureth for ever:
and Og the king of Bashan:
for his mercy endureth for ever:
and gave their land for an heritage:
for his mercy endureth for ever:
even an heritage unto Israel his servant:
for his mercy endureth for ever.
Who remembered us in our low estate:
for his mercy endureth for ever:
and hath redeemed us from our enemies:
for his mercy endureth for ever.
Who giveth food to all flesh:
for his mercy endureth for ever.
O give thanks unto the God of heaven:
for his mercy endureth for ever."

There was something so beautiful about their voices raised together in unison. Even a few of the ladies had tears on their cheeks.

God's mercy would see her through. Even with the difficult matter she needed to discuss.

"Ladies, before we begin with our business for the evening, there's something that I must discuss with you all." She took a deep breath and released it in a very unladylike huff. "I have an annoyance."

Lavonia White leaned forward, her tea

cake held in midair. "I doubt you need to go any further. 'Tis a man, isn't it?"

Faith nodded and was shocked at the guess.

"Someone who pays you too much attention and you'd rather have nothing to do with this person?" Mary Wallace offered. Her new friend was the youngest in their group, her creamy complexion void of wrinkles or signs of worry. What it must be like to be able to look so untarnished by the sad world around them.

The thought made her realize her foolishness. Who cared what the women wore, the number of wrinkles on their faces, or the styles of their hair. "How did you all know?"

Several snickers were heard around the room.

Lavonia piped up. "Do not forget that we are your friends, Faith. We care about you. Besides, we've all been there. But I think we've also noticed that particular annoyance that is interested in you."

"Anthony Jameson." Mary shook her head.

Faith released another sigh and put a hand to her chest. "Oh, that makes me feel so much better, knowing that you all understand. His advances are getting quite irritating, and he won't take no for an answer.

Whenever I leave my home, he somehow finds me."

Lavonia's forehead furrowed. " 'Tis much worse than I was aware. Do you think he means you harm?"

"No. Well, I don't think he does. But he has become quite a pest. And with no father or any other man around to dissuade him, I am afraid he doesn't take my subtle hints."

"So you need someone to be straightforward with him. And you need to have other people with you so he cannot meet you unaware." Lavonia had gone into her mothering mode. And Faith didn't mind one bit.

Claudia Livingston nodded and walked over to Faith's side. "Ladies, I think we have another mission in front of us. I believe we need to schedule our meetings and outings with Faith so that she isn't out and about alone. If the man gets brash enough to start calling on her at home, well then, we will just plan meetings here more often."

Lydia stood as well. "I agree. There's enough of us to be able to schedule things to be attendant to Faith. I don't like Mr. Jameson. My husband had dealings with him a few years back, and the man was less than honest."

"You don't think he'd mean to do any-

125

thing . . . untoward?" Faith put a hand to her throat.

Lavonia shook her head. "But we can't be too cautious. We've seen how many men have been drawn to you because of your money. How many has it been over the years?"

Faith rolled her eyes to look to the ceiling. "Too many to count. But none of them have been as forward and . . . persistent as Mr. Jameson."

"Persistent is too loose a term for Mr. Jameson. When he sets his sights on something, he doesn't let it go." Lydia moved closer. "I am not saying you need to be afraid, Faith, but I am saying that I don't trust that man and I'm worried that he is paying all his attention to you. You need to be on your guard. And I think we should help you. You are doing so much for others. Goodness, you're risking your neck every time you go out to deliver one of those messages. The least we can do is be the protection that you need at a time like this."

Faith looked at each woman in the room. These friends had formed a bond they could have never imagined when they first started helping with the Patriot cause. Now she felt as if they were all her sisters. Especially after tonight. "Well then, thank

126

you all. I wasn't sure how to even broach the subject, but now I am confident that with your help I won't need to worry about Anthony Jameson anymore." She looked down at the list in her lap. "Let us get down to business. There are so many things we can assist with, that I don't believe we will have any issue scheduling extra meetings."

The ladies all gathered around her and hugged Faith and each other.

Anthony Jameson would be taken care of, and she would have the opportunity to focus on other things. Her heart gave a little lift when she thought of Matthew.

Lavonia tilted her head and studied Faith's face. "Ah, but what is this?"

"Whatever do you mean?" A moment of panic hit Faith. She hadn't told anyone about Matthew yet. Heat crept up her neck and into her face. They would all know soon enough.

"Let me guess . . ." Her friend returned to her seat and reached for her teacup. "The Patriot man you have been meeting has struck your fancy?"

Several gasps peppered the room, and a few of the ladies giggled.

"Perhaps." Faith sat back down in her chair and picked invisible lint off her skirt.

"Oh, do tell, Faith," Margaret prodded.

"We are all in need of some happy news."

While she was hesitant to share too much, Faith knew this was a safe place and the women adored her.

As she spoke of Matthew, one thought pushed to the forefront of her thoughts.

Prayerfully, she'd need to deliver another message soon.

Thursday, March 16, 1775
Mount Vernon

George scanned the letter for a third time. The details seemed to be unknown, and stories flew as fast as mouths could carry them. But the killing up at Westminster seemed to be the beginning of something.

Of what, he wasn't sure. But deep in his bones, he felt it.

"George, dear, are you all right? You are quite pale." Martha had come into the room at some point, and he hadn't noticed. The news had been too disturbing.

"I am sorry, my love, I am quite all right but am needed up in Philadelphia. I will probably need to leave in a day's time."

She moved closer and placed her hand on his. "It's news about what they are calling the massacre, isn't it?"

"How did you hear of it?" He should always talk to Martha about things — she had an uncanny way of knowing everything before him anyway.

"Mrs. Sidler mentioned it this morning at the market." She picked up her stitching and sat by the fireplace, creating another one of those lady's fire screens. "It's dreadful to hear that the British are becoming violent."

Indeed it was. And no matter which story was true, the facts were plain — people were dead. At the hands of British soldiers. Simple farmers who had only wanted to keep court out of session. Taxes had been outrageous, and many people couldn't pay. Didn't King George see that what he was doing would kill the Colonies and her people?

Did Parliament not understand that their ways were being seen as greedy and self-serving? How could people survive like this?

Martha sighed. "Why don't you talk about it, George. You know I am a good listener." She thrust her needle back into the piece she was working on. The screens were a popular gift from Martha. It was normally an elaborate needlepoint that could be set near the lady's chair at head height so she could still benefit from the warmth of the fire. Ladies never wanted their makeup to melt. Probably not unlike the men wanting their wigs to shift. Thus the reason why he powdered his hair rather than wear a stuffy wig.

"George?"

"I am sorry, my dear." At least the thoughts had distracted him for a moment. Martha was right. She was a good listener and great sounding board. *Lord, give us direction.* While he filled his wife in on the details that he knew, he also wondered how long he would need to be away from his beloved wife and home this time. With war imminent, he knew that he would be called up to serve in a higher capacity.

"It does indeed sound like they will be needing you. Sooner rather than later, I am afraid." Martha pulled the needle back through the screen. The lovely pink of the thread made him think of Faith. As a little girl, it had been her favorite color.

"My dear, this has been building for many years. I am afraid it will not end swiftly. In fact, Faith being so involved has begun to concern me."

Martha sighed and took her time with a few more stitches. "We both know that the best thing we can do for her is leave her in the Lord's hands." A small smile lifted the edges of her lips. "But we also know that perhaps we should start praying for anyone who stands in her way."

The remark broke the tension George felt in his shoulders as he laughed. Faith definitely could be an immovable wall when she wanted to be.

As the evening waned, he allowed his burdens to ease as his wife conversed with him about all he'd shared. Martha's insight was useful and encouraging . . . but he sensed she knew the same thing he did — even without her expressing it verbally.

War was upon them. The best they could do was pray and prepare.

CHAPTER 6

"It was quite invigorating, my boy! Quite invigorating!" Ben paced the room in the tiny upstairs of the home they'd hidden in. His hands waved around and animated his speech. "Patrick Henry stood there in front of all the Virginia Convention and convinced each county to prepare arms to defend themselves against the British. His words were like fire from heaven. Just like when he spoke at the Continental Congress and challenged everyone with his cry of not being a Virginian or Pennsylvanian or any other Colonial, but being an American."

"What do you think of it all?" Matthew wasn't sure what the outcome of the meeting had been because Ben was too caught up in reciting phrases from Patrick's short speech. The speech was several days ago, but it appeared that Ben could hear it as if

132

it were happening at that very moment. When his mentor asked for them to meet, Matthew knew it was important. They'd taken great risk to meet here in Boston, but the owners of the home were Patriot supporters and very trustworthy.

Ben raised a finger. "Ah, but you haven't let me get to the best part."

Matthew raised his brows.

Ben just smiled.

"Well, what was it?"

His mentor stood tall and placed his hands behind his back. He rocked back and forth on his feet. It must be for dramatic effect, because now Matthew couldn't wait to hear.

"Yes? What did he say?"

"He ended his speech with, 'Give me liberty or give me death!' " Ben lifted his hand and pointed to the ceiling. "I think even God Himself smiled down on us at that moment."

"What happened then?"

"The room erupted in applause and everyone rallied to Patrick Henry's call to arms. We all knew it to be the right thing to do, the Virginians just needed to be prodded along a bit. Like many others."

Matthew leaned back in his chair. *Give me liberty or give me death.* Powerful words.

133

Strong words. As they pierced his soul, he realized the depth of the truth behind the words.

Was he willing to lay down his life for liberty? That thought bounced around in his mind for several moments.

Yes. He was. And though it couldn't even begin to equate with the Savior's sacrifice, he imagined it was somewhat like Jesus giving His life for all of mankind. He suffered so that others may have life.

While Matthew couldn't save the world like the Messiah did, he could help pave the way for a better future — a free future — for those who came behind. Jesus did say that there was no greater love than to lay down your life for a friend.

Energized by Henry's words, Matthew knew what he had to do. The idea had been looming over him for weeks. It was time to immerse himself inside the Loyalists and stay there. The thought was a bit intimidating since he was hesitant to cut ties to all that he knew.

"Matthew? I see I have lost you." Ben waved a hand in front of his face.

He shook his head. "My apologies, Ben, I was lost in thought."

"I could see that." His friend chuckled and moved toward the fire.

"The time has come, has it not? For me to cut off from you — from all of you. That's why . . ."

The older man's faced drooped a bit as he gave a slow nod. "Yes. I figured you knew . . . but I was hoping to inspire you with Patrick's speech and to encourage you one last time."

"That's why you asked for the meeting?"

"Yes. I have never been too fond of farewells."

For a moment, he almost thought he spotted a tear in the old man's eyes. "Nor I."

Ben sniffed and pointed a finger in Matthew's face. "It's imperative that you get those messages delivered tonight. They are testing the coding skills of the women. We may not have much more time to prepare."

"I will." The thought of seeing Faith again made him eager for the time to pass.

"It's getting more dangerous for us to be seen together. Your position within the Loyalists has strengthened, and we are very glad for all your hard work."

"Thank you."

"But I am not sure when I will be able to sneak away to meet you again. Even though I would gladly risk life and limb for you, dear boy." He turned away for a moment and cleared his throat. "And I am afraid it is far too dangerous for you to come to my home anymore. If they found out the part you are playing, I fear your life would be on the line." Ben came to him and put his hands on his shoulders. The older man had to look up quite a ways to look at Matthew. "We are all so very grateful for all that you are sacrificing for the cause. I regret to say that one of my deepest fears is that you may feel very alone in this journey, but remember you are not — nor will you ever be — alone. You have the prayers and the hearts of many. And the good Lord above will always be with you."

The weight of it all pressed down on Matthew's shoulders. If he couldn't be in contact with Ben, then he truly would be cut off.

"God be with you, my son. I will send messages as I can."

"My prayers go with you as well." He breathed deep and stiffened his shoulders. The time had come to say goodbye.

Ben stepped forward and wrapped his arms around Matthew and then patted his back. "I am profoundly proud of you. Farewell for now, my friend."

"Farewell."

Old Ship Meetinghouse, Hingham

A little more than an hour later, Matthew stood outside the Old Ship Meetinghouse. Ben's words had echoed with him in the carriage ride, and he'd thought through his plans to make the rest of his facade fall into place. The foundation was laid. The relationships were there. William Franklin — the Royal Governor of New Jersey — was no wiser of the part he played.

Matthew never wanted to be an actor, but he found himself in that position. He had the part of his life, and he'd have to play it flawlessly.

With the realization of all that was laid on the line, Matthew thought of Faith.

He was such a blackguard for taking her time and putting her in danger. Yes, she'd volunteered for the job of messenger. Yes, she was a good friend of George Washington. Yes, she was braver than most men he knew. But she was also becoming dear to him. And the thought of anything happening to her struck real fear in his heart. He could handle it if anything happened to him. But to Faith? He wouldn't be able to bear it.

Faith was to meet him here in just a few minutes. He knew it had been asking a lot for her to journey so far from home in the late hours, but sometimes it would be the only way. Thankfully, she was willing, and no one suspected anything. But how long would they be able to keep up the ruse? Especially if things intensified?

She'd become very adept at sneaking around, all the while making it look like she was out for normal, everyday errands. Once again proving that she was up to the task.

Another thought hit him straight in the chest. She was now his only connection to who he really was. She was the only one he could see on a regular basis that knew Matthew Weber, the *real* Matthew Weber, the Patriot.

Soft footfalls on the snow made him go to the crook of the building to meet her. Excitement built in his chest to see her again.

As she rounded the corner, she gasped. "Gracious, Matthew. I was not expecting you to be right there."

He gave her a smile and put a finger over his lips. Tilting his head, he motioned for her to follow him.

Earlier, he'd found a door unlocked. Surely the Lord wouldn't be upset with them for sneaking into the meetinghouse for some warmth.

He made his way into the church and led

her into the far south corner. "Here. If we sit on the pew here, I do not believe we can be seen if anyone enters. We will just keep our voices low so they do not echo. Are you warm enough?" The room held quite a chill.

Faith sat and wrapped her cloak around her a little tighter. "I wasn't expecting to be able to meet inside, so I'm dressed for warmth." The smile she gave him made him feel special.

"I have several messages that need to be coded and sent on. This will be the final test of the women's skill. From here on out, everything will be in code."

She nodded and tucked them into her skirt. Faith pulled out a different folded note. "This one is of utmost importance."

Matthew sighed as he took the paper. "I am sure they *all* will be very soon."

She nodded again. "I have been given instructions on what to wear. Since I am a widow, it will not be a lie to say I am a widow, and whenever you and I meet, they want me to wear black. To aid in the cover of dark."

"That's a good plan."

She raised an eyebrow. "They also believe a veil might be a good idea so my face isn't recognizable, but I told them that it might draw more attention to me." She shrugged a shoulder. "Sometimes the men do not think about these things. Women will notice."

Smart. Very smart. Her comment about women noticing made him very aware that yes, women always looked at each other's clothes. Had the other men thought of this or only thought to try and disguise her as much as possible? "Do you agree that wearing black is a good plan?"

She leaned forward, a sparkle in her eye as she shook her head. "I have already set my maid working on several dresses that are all very dark in color. One is dark green, one a deep blue, and another a dark burgundy. That way you know the colors. I think that will suffice. If I am wearing all black and anyone recognized me, they would wonder why I would be bringing out my widow's garb after all these years. No reason to call attention to my movements because of what I wear. I will avoid wearing any lighter colors for when we meet. I also have a black cloak and scarf so that I can cover my face if need be. While the weather is cold, I think that is the best plan."

"I agree. Uh . . . that is, I think your idea is a better plan." Matthew moved under the window to catch some light from the moon. "Scoot over here — it's a little brighter."

He couldn't help it. He wanted to see her and know everything about her.

She did and he caught a look at her eyes. They weren't light brown at all. They had a greenish tint to them that was very charming in the moonlight. "Your eyes are green?" The question was out before he could stop it.

A light laugh left her lips. "Yes, why do you ask?"

" 'Tis been dark every time we have met and I am just now seeing the color. They are lovely."

She ducked her head. "Thank you."

"Have you journeyed to Plymouth yet?"

"Not yet. We have had a lot to keep us busy of late." She relaxed a bit against the pew, and placed her hands in her lap. "If you go, will you let my sister know I am in good health, just busy?"

"I would be most happy to. In fact, if you would like to write her a letter, I will gladly hand deliver it."

"That would be wonderful. Thank you. I am certain she will be very glad to hear from me. It's been too long." Watching her, Matthew felt a little thrill that she was completely focused on him. An awfully selfish thought, but he couldn't help it. "How have you gotten along lately? Well, I hope?"

"Yes, very." She looked down for a moment, but the smile that lit up her face couldn't be missed. "I have been so busy with the women's aid group that I have not had a lot of extra time on my hands. Which is good. I do not wish to focus on the difficult and possibly dangerous times ahead, I would much rather enjoy each moment and do my very best to serve the Lord." She tilted her head in a way that he'd learned signaled she was about to ask him a question. "And you?"

The air between them seemed charged, and Matthew hesitated. The moment was awkward and comfortable and terrifying all at the same time. Warning bells went off in his head. Her words came back to him. Dangerous and difficult times. What was he doing? What was he thinking? The longer he kept her, the more danger to them both. How selfish could he be? She tried to stay busy so she wouldn't have to think about all that was at stake, and here he was taking it all for granted. What kind of man was he?

Against everything within him, he made himself get to his feet. "My deepest apologies, Faith. It is quite inconsiderate of me to keep you any longer. I wish you no harm." He bowed and watched several expressions wash across her face. The stricken look she held transformed into a mask of uncertainty. Not knowing how to mend the situation, Matthew raced to the side door through which they'd entered. Outside, he strode to the next building and hid behind it so he could watch her leave and make sure she was all right.

Several moments later, she exited the building and slipped away into the night.

Matthew raked a hand through his hair, releasing the tie at the nape. He longed to spend more time with her, but that conflicted with everything he knew he had to do.

Immerse himself with the Loyalists. Cut all ties.

But that didn't mean Faith, did it? She was the only one he could meet. The only one with whom he could have any semblance of normality. The only one he could be real with.

All the feelings and thoughts he'd had on the way to meet her were now in conflict with his logical processing of the future. She'd even expressed it — she had to stay busy so she didn't think about the difficult and dangerous times ahead. And they were indeed facing the unknown. Who knew what they would face? The dangers that were possible? The war that was inevitable. He couldn't risk her.

But could he risk *not* spending time with her? He found himself thinking of her many times each day. And she was his lifeline to the reality of who he truly was.

The look on her face when he'd dashed out of the meetinghouse replayed over and over in his mind.

What had he done?

CHAPTER 7

Monday, April 10, 1775
Boston

Anthony commanded his driver to take him to Mrs. Jackson's home. These playing at niceties and following the rules of etiquette were inconceivable. He was a man. It was time for him to *be* the man and take charge of the situation. Mrs. Jackson had an exemplary reputation, so he was certain that she played coy and kept her distance so that society would approve.

Well, what could it hurt for him to take the next step? He would call on her at her home. There was no harm in that. They were both older and more mature. It wouldn't be imprudent for him to visit. Besides, he needed to move things along.

Taxes were up and supplies were down. As much as he tried to build his own little empire, it was becoming increasingly difficult. And as soon as he depleted his own funds, he'd need another source of income. Mrs. Faith Jackson's would do nicely.

She was also quite pleasing to the eye. Still of childbearing age, she would be the perfect choice to bear him heirs and mother his children.

The plan was perfect. If only this blasted conflict weren't taking place. But then, he needed the conflict. He needed for the Colonies to get out of British clutches so he could show the King exactly who he was. How dare the man decline his request again. It didn't make sense.

Of course, if the Colonies couldn't defeat England, then Anthony would have to pay homage to the King once again — except this time, his worth would be far greater and good ol' George His Majesty would have to see that Anthony was well deserving of title and station.

But only if it came to that. Right now, his plan was far better the way it was. He rather liked the idea of not having to answer to anyone, and wasn't that what the Colonies wanted?

The carriage jerked to a stop, and Anthony hit his head on the side. Blasted driver. The man obviously needed training in how to carry a man of means without jostling him about unnecessarily.

When the door opened, he held his head high and stepped down. He checked his appearance and picked a piece of lint off his velvet breeches. The attire might be a bit ostentatious for an afternoon visit, but Anthony had an impression to make. Besides, he liked formal attire. His green coat and waistcoat were made of the same luxurious fabric with gold embroidery lavishly displayed, and his new powdered wig was of the finest design. Mrs. Jackson should be thrilled to see him and the effort he'd made. What lady wouldn't?

He made his way to the front door of her massive home and smiled. This would all be his soon. Another wonderful home to add to his list of properties.

The door opened before he even reached the top step. What service! Now this was a servant who knew how to do his job well.

"Good afternoon." The butler raised his brows but blocked the door.

Ah. Also a good guard of the premises. Well trained indeed. "Good afternoon." Anthony pulled off his gloves and moved forward, daring the man to refuse him entrance. "Mr. Anthony Jameson for Mrs. Jackson, please."

The butler eyed him for a moment and didn't move, stopping Anthony's forward motion. "Is Mrs. Jackson expecting you, sir?"

"Not at this moment, no. But we are well acquainted." Anthony used his large size to move forward and stepped over the threshold. If the butler didn't move, he'd have to run him over. "She will be most happy to see me, of that I am certain."

The servant's eyebrows lifted as he stepped back mere inches, watching Anthony the whole time. How rude. The man should know his place and not prolong eye contact with someone well above his station in life. Maybe he wasn't as well trained as Anthony had thought. He gave a disgruntled humph just to make sure the man understood his displeasure.

The butler finally moved and closed the door behind him. "If you will allow me, sir." He held out his hands.

Finally, some respect. Anthony handed over his tricorn hat and gloves, and the man helped him out of his cloak.

The butler then led him to the parlor. "Mr. Jameson, ma'am."

The man slowly moved away as Anthony bowed. When he raised his head, he found himself looking at several women. Not just Mrs. Jackson. This was *not* as he planned.

Mrs. Jackson's face appeared a bit

pinched. She raised an eyebrow and greeted him. "Is there something I can help you with, Mr. Jameson? I was not expecting you."

Every lady sitting in their circle held a bit of a frown. What was going on here? Why did they all look sour and a bit put out? "My apologies, Mrs. Jackson. I was hoping to entice you with an invitation."

"As you can see, we are in the middle of a meeting, Mr. Jameson." Mrs. Jackson gave him a slight smile. Ah, just as he suspected. She was glad to see him. "But you may leave your invitation with Clayton."

Dismissed? Without even an invite to tea. What poor manners. When they were married, he'd have to work with her on the appropriate way to greet guests. "I shall come back tomorrow, then."

A lady with white hair stood. "I am afraid we have another important meeting tomorrow. It will take most of the day."

The butler — who he assumed must be Clayton — showed up at Anthony's side. Perhaps he'd never left. The man was everywhere it seemed. "Sir, allow me to see you to the door." Clayton turned back to the ladies, "I apologize for interrupting your meeting, ma'am. It will *not* happen again."

"But . . . I . . ." Anthony found himself

149

prodded along to the door like a lowly cow being led to the barn. "Well, I never." He cleared his throat and lifted his chin.

Clayton handed him his things. "Thank you for stopping by." He held the door open, and Anthony had no choice but to walk through.

It closed firmly behind him.

As he stood on the stoop, Anthony went through everything in his mind. Perhaps another day would be better. Mrs. Jackson was a very charitable woman and was probably deeply involved with a cause. Poor Clayton had just been doing his job, and Anthony probably got him in a bit of trouble with his mistress. That's the only account Anthony could see from the brief time he was inside. He'd just have to try a different tactic next time. And make sure he didn't put the butler in jeopardy of losing his job. The man *had* been very attentive. And good servants were so hard to find these days.

Yes, he'd just have to plan better next time.

The gnawing, worrisome feeling in the pit of Faith's stomach could only be because of one thing — or more precisely, one man.

Anthony Jameson.

She was feeling fine as their meeting

began. It was ludicrous that his short visit could cause such turmoil within her, yet it came upon her regardless of what her mind and logic told her.

Lavonia walked over to her. "Faith?"

She looked up at her friend. "Hm?"

"You have been sitting here all too quiet for several minutes."

"And she is very pale. Have you noticed how pale she is?" Lydia squeaked.

"Indeed. She is white as a sheet." Claudia nodded and took a sip of her tea. "Maybe she needs some liquor added to her tea."

"Claudia!" Lavonia put a hand to her chest.

"What?" Claudia stirred her own cup of tea. "My doctor prescribes it all the time." Lifting the cup to her lips, she sipped.

A chuckle started in Faith's stomach and bubbled up. "My friends. I am fine."

"Do you need some liquor?" Again, Claudia with her liquor.

"No, thank you, but I do appreciate all of your concern. And actually, laughter truly is good medicine. I allowed myself to worry there for a moment when I really needed to be thanking you all." She reached over and grabbed Lavonia's hand. "I am certain that we will be able to figure out how to handle

Mr. Jameson if we just put our heads together."

"Well!" Lavonia sat back and stiffened her shoulders. "We cannot abide that man. It's worse than we thought, is it not?"

Faith shook her head. "This is the first time he has come without an invitation. And to my home. So I do not know what to think about what his intentions are, but he did seem quite put out that I gave him no invitation to sit or stay."

"The man *needs* to be put out." Lydia *tsked* several times. "He has no idea whatsoever how bothersome he is. He thinks that the world loves him and should love and adore him even more. *And* he thinks that he is entitled to more than anyone else. He told my husband as much on several occasions. I know this may shock you, but he is not above lying or cheating to get his way either." The time she huffed. "I cannot abide the man." She covered her mouth with her hand. "My apologies."

Lavonia stood and placed a hand on Faith's shoulder. "No apologies necessary, Lydia. I think we all get the picture, and we are in confidence together. We should — every one of us — feel safe to share our thoughts with one another as this is probably our only such place." She cleared her throat and took a long, deep breath. "I think we all agree that this is serious. And with all that Faith is doing for the cause, it is of utmost importance that we protect her. Are we in agreement?"

Every lady stood and nodded.

"Good. Then let us resolve to make a plan. How do we help Faith avoid Mr. Jameson?"

CHAPTER 8

Tuesday, April 18, 1775

Sleep eluded Faith as her mind deliberated over all the complicated facets of her life. Giving up on sleep, she climbed out of bed and went downstairs to pray about it all by the fire.

First, there was the unwanted and disturbing attention of Mr. Anthony Jameson. Second, her new job as messenger. Third, that new job entailed meeting with Mr. Matthew Weber. A man whom she thought very highly of and hoped to get to know better. She'd thought he felt the same way. But now? Their next meeting was already scheduled for the coming Friday with instructions for them to meet every other day after that.

Things were moving at a rapid pace, and the stakes were much higher.

To deal with her first problem . . . well, the ladies agreed to help her with that. But it still annoyed her. And if she were honest, it worried her as well. More than she cared to admit. For the first time in all these years of living alone as a widow, she felt afraid of what a man would try. What if he got it into his mind sometime to follow her? What would he do if he discovered her mission as a messenger?

She banished those thoughts. Anthony Jameson wasn't smart enough to keep up with her. He was an annoyance, yes, but now she was aware of his attention to her. She was an independent and smart lady. She could outsmart him.

Besides she could outrun him, that was for certain.

She nodded. Independent and capable had always been how people described her. Yes, she was considered to be old and set in her ways because she had turned down uncountable suitors. But they had all been after her money! And she refused to marry again for convenience. She had plenty of money and could take care of herself. Besides, she liked having her own mind.

Her second problem was silly. It was simply fear of the unknown. But if she readily admitted her true feelings, her only fears stemmed out of the fact that Matthew had stepped away so abruptly the last time they met. So when she really analyzed it, problems two and three were inexplicably tied to each other. Would she have a second problem if she felt as comfortable as she had with Matthew from the beginning?

Probably not.

The answer didn't startle her or amaze her. But it did hurt. If Matthew chose to keep his distance from here on out, then would she change her mind about being the messenger?

No. She couldn't. She'd made a commitment and would see it through.

As she paced the parlor in front of the fire, she realized a number of things: (1) She really wasn't afraid of being the messenger. (2) She *was* afraid of rejection by Matthew. (3) Anthony Jameson made her skin crawl. (4) If he were out of the picture, her life would be much easier.

And five? She loved helping out the Patriot cause. It was more important than her silly feelings on any matter, and she should just buck up and tackle the job ahead of her.

If Matthew ignored her from now on . . . well, so be it.

If Anthony continued to annoy her? She'd have to set him straight. If she could manage to get the man to listen to anyone other than himself.

If she had to put her life on the line for the Patriots? She would gladly lay it down.

Decisions made, her heart felt lighter. She knelt beside her favorite chair and prayed. *Lord, I should have come to You first with all this mess. I am sorry. But I am laying my burdens down at Your feet now. I am sorry for my doubt. I am sorry for my fear. Forgive me where I have failed, and help me go forth in Your strength and Your peace. In Jesus' name, amen.*

A banging on the outside door made her jump to her feet. Who would be there in the middle of the night? If it was Anthony, Faith just might skin the man alive. What a pest.

Clayton was at the door in such swift strides that Faith wondered from which direction he'd come.

As soon as he opened the door, a man stepped inside. "Are you the lady of the house?"

She straightened her shoulders. "I am."

"Paul Revere has been riding through the night to alert everyone." The man was still out of breath.

"Alert us of what?"

"The Regulars are coming out."

She took a deep breath. Exactly what they all were expecting. "Thank you, sir. Would you like any refreshment before you continue on your journey?"

"No, thank you, ma'am. I best be on my way." And with that, he was out the door.

Clayton closed the door and looked at her.

Faith could only shake her head and sigh. "We knew the British troops were planning something. It appears they are on their way."

"I shall prepare the house, ma'am." Clayton walked away, and Faith knew that he and the staff would bar all the windows and keep the house locked up.

But it wasn't her house or even herself that she was worried about.

Matthew was in even more danger now.

Things just got trickier.

For the rest of the night, sleep proved to be impossible. Faith dragged herself to a sitting position on her bed and watched the sunrise. She hadn't bothered to draw her curtains last night, thinking that if fighting or a fire or anything else started, she wanted to be able to see it.

There must be news somewhere about what was happening. Had the British army attacked? Had they captured the Patriot weapons cache? That had been the goal — they all knew it. But had they succeeded?

Marie entered her room with a tray. "Are you ready to eat, ma'am?"

Faith nodded. "I would like to get dressed

as swiftly as possible, though. There's things I need to check on."

"Aye, ma'am. I'll get your clothes ready, right now. How's the blue silk for today?" Marie brought her the tray and headed for the door.

"That is just fine. I will be done by the time you return."

Marie curtsied and exited the room.

She ate a few bites and realized nothing sounded appetizing. Not until she knew more. Food could wait. Getting out of her bed, Faith hoped that Marie would return in the next few moments. She went to the dresser and picked up her brush and ran it through her dark blond, curly hair.

Several thoughts niggled at the back of her mind. Was Matthew all right? What about George and Martha? Would they have heard yet? Mount Vernon was a good distance away, and it took a good deal of time for messages to be delivered. Since George wasn't currently serving in any military capacity, Faith realized that when they did hear, they would be quite worried about her. And then it probably wouldn't be too much time before George had to leave his beloved farm again.

Marie entered with gown and petticoats, shoes and stockings, in tow.

Without waiting for her maid to start, Faith slipped on her stockings and tied the ribbon garters above her knees. Marie handed her the dicky petticoat next, and it went over her head and shift. Dressing was such a tedious job sometimes.

Her maid then tied the pockets around her waist, taking the time to knot them and pin them the way Faith had instructed. It took several minutes to then wrap the stays around her and lace them up the back. She must have sensed Faith's hurry because she had the next two petticoats ready in an instant. Over that, she began to pin the stomacher to her stays and had the open robe gown draped over her arm, ready for the next step. Helping Faith ease her arms into the gown, Marie then pulled the sides together over the stomacher and pulled more pins from her apron to attach the dress.

"Let me fasten your shoes, ma'am, and then I will tie the gown skirts."

"That is fine, Marie. Thank you for being so swift."

Her maid buckled her shoes and then tied the ribbons of the skirts to create the polonaise puff. She circled around Faith and tucked here and there. "I think everything is in order. Let me grab your apron."

The beautiful — but completely useless — white apron was thin enough to see through, but was expected for someone of her status. Faith looked forward to the day when simpler clothing could be worn, but for now, she had to continue to dress the part of the wealthy widow that she was. She could do nothing different that would betray Patriot leanings to Loyalists. But if God needed to use her fortune to help see to the freedom of the Colonies, then so be it. She was fine with that. If only she could wear the simpler dress — like Marie.

This whole social status and extravagance wore on her day in and day out. But she would be thankful. She would. The good Lord had seen fit to bless her with it, and she would use it for His glory.

Marie dressed her hair a bit backward from normal, but Faith had been in a hurry and her maid obviously picked up on her eagerness to be about as soon as possible.

"Something simple is perfectly fine for today. I'm sure you can cover it up with my day cap anyway."

"Yes, ma'am."

Within a matter of minutes, Marie was done and stepped back. With a curtsy, she nodded.

"Thank you, Marie."

"I will be downstairs if you need anything else." Her maid made a swift exit, and Faith wasn't far behind.

Fully intending to take the carriage into town and see what she could find out, she found herself brought to an abrupt halt at the top of the stairs.

Clayton's face frowned down at her.

She raised her eyebrows. "Is there anything you need to tell me, Clayton? If not, I really must be going."

"Mr. Jameson is in the parlor awaiting you, ma'am."

Letting her shoulders droop, she threw her head back and looked at the ceiling. Would the man never leave her be? An idea took root. "Please sneak back and ask Hobbs to get my carriage ready at the back door. You may then go to the parlor and serve Mr. Jameson some tea or whatever other refreshment he might want and inform him that I am unavailable at the moment — which I am not, so it is not a lie. Then tell him you will come check on me and see how long it will take. By then I will be gone, and you can let him know that one of the other servants informed you that I left on an urgent errand."

"Yes, ma'am." Clayton's lips lifted in the slightest of smiles — which for him was quite something. "I will enjoy this."

"Good. I am most glad and grateful for your help." She smiled back at him. "It's almost like we are in a conspiracy together, isn't it?"

"Quite, Mrs. Jackson. One I am glad to be a part of. Very glad."

Faith pressed her lips together so she wouldn't laugh aloud. "I must admit, I admire this side of you, Clayton. I hope we can do more of this in the future."

"Anything for you, ma'am." He bowed and turned to go back down the stairs.

She shook her head. Who knew? After all these years, it was refreshing to see a different side of her most beloved butler. And it was perfect timing to find it out.

Now she was certain that he would aid her in any of the *activities* she might need to do.

She just might enjoy being a spy after all.

Thursday, April 20, 1775
Perth Amboy, New Jersey

The roaring fire in the fireplace couldn't ease the chill in Matthew's bones. He'd been in New Jersey for several days meeting with Loyalists that William Franklin wanted him to see. For hours, he'd tried to get any word that he could about the troops that

163

headed into Boston but to no avail. Then he'd been summoned to William's home. Hopefully he had some news.

William strode into the room purposefully — his face stern. "Thank you for coming so quickly, Matthew."

"Of course. How may I be of assistance?"

The chair behind the desk creaked as William took a seat. "Somehow our troops have failed."

"What?!" While he put his best effort into appearing shocked and angry, Matthew couldn't help but feel a sense of relief.

"The so-called minutemen — those untrained Patriot ruffians — knew we were coming. I don't know how. But they knew. We won a small skirmish in Lexington and then marched to Concord. Even though we were able to find their weapons and destroy some of them, those colonists overtook us at North Bridge." William sighed and shook his head. "Our men retreated to Boston and suffered several casualties along the way."

"What does this mean for us?" Matthew stood like he was upset.

"It means that the war has begun." William looked up at him, his face indecipherable. "And we did not win the first battle."

Later that afternoon, Matthew sat in a carriage and went over everything William had said during their meeting. It was a long ride back to Boston, and he doubted he'd be able to sleep as they raced down the rough road.

The fighting had begun. But at least the colonists had held their own. That didn't mean they'd be able to handle future battles, but maybe the Brits would realize they couldn't just come marching in and win every fight. They had a real opponent.

Not that Matthew even wanted to think about how many might be killed.

So far, William appeared to believe the story of Matthew's switch over to the Loyalist side. He'd brought him into deeper confidence and relied on him. Which was good for the cause. But also made things a lot more dangerous.

The recurring thought that kept pounding his brain though was of Faith. Was she safe? Was she all right?

After their last meeting, he feared she might not even speak to him next time they met. And he deserved it. He was supposed to meet her tomorrow, but that was only if he could be back in time. His driver knew that time was of the essence, but would the horses hold out?

Exhaustion seeped into every inch of his being. He needed — wanted to sleep.

It'd been too long already. But he couldn't stop thinking about Faith.

He had to make things right.

With new resolve, Matthew thought about what he would say to her — if she showed up.

The only consolation he had was that Faith's personality was one that never gave up.

He prayed that she hadn't given up on her commitment . . . or on him.

CHAPTER 9

Friday, April 21, 1775
Old Ship Meetinghouse, Hingham

The snow was deeper outside the meeting-house this time, but at least the same door was unlocked. As soon as Faith arrived, Matthew would offer to go inside out of the cold. At least he'd made it in time. Every bone and muscle in his body ached from the long journey.

The moon above was covered in clouds. Too bad he didn't have a candle with him. He wouldn't be able to see Faith's face very well.

Her soft footfalls — now familiar to him — sounded to his right.

When she appeared, she didn't say anything. Just stopped in front of him and held out a packet.

"Faith?"

She shook her head. "I need to give you this. Do you have anything for me?"

167

He took it and then pulled several notes from his coat and handed them to her. "Please. Would you step inside with me for a moment?"

"I do not think that is a good idea." She turned as if to go.

"Faith, please. I need to apologize."

Her shoulders rose and then fell. "All right."

In silence they entered the building and walked to the same pew they'd sat in last time. The air around them was stale. Just like their relationship.

She sat with her hands folded in her lap. Rigid. Unwelcoming.

He'd done that. Wiping a hand down his face, he released a long sigh. "Faith, I am deeply sorry for my behavior last time."

She simply watched him.

Obviously not going to make it easy on him. "I allowed my fear to rule my mind and my heart. I was so worried about what might happen to you that I slammed the door of my heart and I am afraid it hurt you."

"Slammed the door of your heart?" She tilted her head.

He wasn't a wordsmith, a man of poetry, or really anything else relating to how to woo a woman. Of course she would question his words. How did he get out of this one? "What I meant was that I had begun to care for you and looked forward to *nothing* more than seeing you again. But when the reality of the dangers hit me, I feared I had made a grave mistake."

"It did hurt me." She lifted her chin, paused, and then gave him a slight smile. "But that does not mean you cannot be forgiven."

Her words gave him hope. He inched toward her on the pew, still keeping an appropriate distance — or at least a small amount of space — between them, but he longed to gaze into her eyes and the light was so dim. "I am very sorry, Faith. Will you please forgive me?"

"Of course, I will forgive you." She shook her head. "Men can be so difficult sometimes."

He frowned. "What is that supposed to mean?"

"Most men think that females are weak and emotional and incapable of handling anything of a weighty nature. Men also think that things have to be much more complicated than they actually are."

He hadn't given her enough credit. "I am afraid you are correct."

"Well, let us just get that out of the way

169

right now, shall we?" She raised that one eyebrow in a very becoming way. "I am capable of handling the truth, Matthew. Plain and simple. I simply want the truth. So if you care about me, I expect you to tell me. Neither one of us is young anymore. We both know our minds. We both know the dangers and risks. We are at war in America now. Just be honest with me." She gave a little huff, and he watched her shoulders relax a bit.

"All right then. I freely admit that I would like to get to know you better, Faith Lytton Jackson. But I cannot say that I will not be concerned for your well-being . . . or afraid that George will skin me alive if anything happens to you." He couldn't help but smile at her.

She scooted her small frame closer to him. "I would not expect anything less. And I would like to get to know you better as well."

That feeling was back — like the air around them was alive and sparking with . . . something he couldn't put into words.

She tilted her head again. "So where do we begin from here? Do you have any questions for me?"

His mind spun in a million different directions. There was so much he wanted to know — everything about her. He laughed. "Well, there is something I have been wanting to ask you since our very first meeting all those months ago. . . ."

"Go ahead. What is it?"

"When you first came, I heard your footsteps in the snow. They were very quiet, but I had been waiting in the silence and heard every sound." He paused and smiled at her.

"I do not believe I heard a question in there." Her brow furrowed like she was trying to figure out a puzzle.

"You hesitated that night. And then you let out a tiny breath. I have been most curious why. Did you second-guess yourself? Did you see something?"

Bell-like laughter echoed through the meetinghouse. She covered her mouth to stop the sound, but her shoulders continued to shake. The clouds moved for a brief second, and silvery moonlight shone through the window, making her eyes sparkle. He saw her merriment.

"Whatever is so funny?"

She put a hand to her chest and composed herself, but the smile didn't leave her face. "I did not hear anything, and no, I was not about to back out."

"What happened then?"

"I got snow in my shoe, silly, and it was

171

quite cold. I huffed at myself for not being more careful and realized I would simply have to endure a wet foot."

Her spunk really was quite amazing and endearing. Of course she wasn't afraid. This was Faith. George Washington's braver-than-ten-men Faith. He shook his head and they laughed together.

Watching him listen to her talk about how she got the melted snow out of her shoe after their meeting, Faith realized that she cared quite deeply for Matthew Weber. In the midst of the tough times around them, they were able to share in some much-needed laughter, and just like the Bible said, it was good medicine.

His face turned a bit more serious. "Were you all right? When the British came through?"

"Yes. Although the knock on the door in the middle of the night to inform of Paul Revere's news kept me from more sleep."

"But your home? It is in a safe area?"

"Yes, quite. Clayton has barred all the windows and keeps the doors locked, but I assure you, we are quite safe. The skirmishes were many miles from my home."

It was his turn to put a hand to his chest. "That is a relief. I cannot begin to tell you how worried I was for your safety when I heard. But I fear it will only get worse. The Brits want to take firm hold of the city of Boston. They believe they already do."

"We are quite safe, I promise. Besides, I am very useful in Boston. Our ladies are accomplishing a lot. And you are here. I want to stay as long as I am needed."

Matthew looked out the window toward the moon. "It is getting quite late." He gave her a long look. "Promise me you will stay safe."

Her heart fluttered at the intensity of his gaze. "I promise. But I am not afraid."

"Well, I *am* afraid I have kept you far too long." He stood. "My apologies."

She stood as well. "Our time together has been quite enjoyable, and I look forward to seeing you on Sunday."

"Until then." He bowed. "I will go outside first and make sure that there isn't anyone around."

She nodded. "Thank you."

He left her side and went out the door. Several seconds later, his silhouette appeared and she heard him whisper, "It is safe."

For several moments, she stood inside the building and thought about all that had transpired. He cared for her. The thought made her heart race.

As she made her way through the streets back to the corner where her carriage awaited, Faith couldn't help but smile. Perhaps love came to old widows as well.

When she arrived home, it was quite late, but Faith couldn't even think about going to sleep. She asked Marie to help her out of her gown and then to bring her a cup of hot tea. Perhaps she should write to George.

So many things ran through her mind. First and foremost was Matthew. Then there was the fighting that had begun. What would happen next? She also longed to go see her family in Plymouth, but the thought made her quite nervous. She needed George's advice on it all.

Mind made up, she sat down with paper, ink, and her quill:

April 21, 1775

Dear George,
I find myself in need of your advice once again. Since you are not here in person, which you know I prefer when I discuss my thoughts, I figured to write you a letter.

My list will be quite long, so please feel free to respond when you have time to truly think it all through. That being stated, I will anxiously await your reply because you remember my lack of patience. My poor mother always told me I tried her patience and that was her Christian name!

I believe I can hear your voice in my head, and you are telling me to get to the matters at hand.

First, I would like to discuss with you the suggestion you have made several times: me going to Plymouth and trying to reconnect with the Lytton family. Our mutual friend has also informed me that his sister lives in Plymouth and knows some Lyttons. While the thought of reconnecting with my family is wonderful and exciting, it also makes me very nervous. I do not know these people. What if I am not good enough? The loss of Mother and Father was quite a blow to them, I am sure. What is your advice for me in this matter? Is it safe in Plymouth? Do the British have troops there? Or do you think I am making excuses for why I should not go?

Second on my list of questions needing your infinite wisdom is about the fighting . . . dare I say war? I will continue to stay in Boston, where I promise

I do feel quite safe right now, but nevertheless, I am worried about others. Families and such. And the servants. Should I release them to go home? Should I instruct my ladies' group to evacuate to a safer location? Do you think the war will continue to grow? These are the things that keep my mind spinning at night. Yes, I hear your advice: drink a cup of tea and go to bed. But I will still await your word on this matter as well.

Third, well . . . I am hesitant and do not even know where to begin. It was actually the thing most prominent in my mind, but I was nervous about discussing it with you and had to get up the nerve. You know me well, so you know exactly how I am feeling at this moment. If you were here, I would pace the room and chatter on about the subject while you graciously listened and propped your feet by the fire. Yes, I hear your voice again: get on with it.

Here it is: I believe I am beginning to care a good deal about our mutual friend. I know you are well acquainted with him and have known him many, many years. You once told me that he was an old friend. What do you think?

Would he be a good match for me? I know you and Martha have wanted me to remarry and settle down for some time, but you also know that no one has interested me. That is, until I met him.

I am seeking your honest opinion and advice in this matter. I will respect your wishes if you will only grant me the true response from your heart. You have always looked out for my best interest, and I trust you with this. I have prayed much over all of these items, but especially about our friend.

Please give Martha my love and reply as soon as you are able.

Faith

CHAPTER 10

As much as Matthew loved seeing the colonial troops camping around Boston, the level of danger for him had just increased exponentially.

Word had come that the Provincial Congress of Massachusetts had ordered more than ten thousand troops to mobilize and head to Boston. Colonial volunteers from all over New England were now camped around the city.

The siege on Boston was good for the Patriots. But as a spy for the Patriots, posing as a Loyalist, he was now in danger from both sides.

If Patriot soldiers grabbed him, he couldn't give away his cover. He would probably be imprisoned and beaten.

If the Loyalists found out he was actually a spy . . . Well, they would probably tar and feather him — or possibly even kill him.

Either way, he was going to have to be more careful.

That meant he'd have to make sure Faith was aware of all that was going on as well. Neither of them could risk getting caught.

As he headed to the new designated meeting location, he realized he would have to suggest that they rotate amongst the three each time they met. He and Faith could be the only ones aware of where the handoffs were taking place.

The thought of putting her in danger made his heart ache. But she was the only way he could feed the Patriots information and the only way instructions got back to him. Everything hinged on the brave widow from Boston.

Especially his heart.

They'd met many times over the past few months. But now they saw one another every other day. It was wonderful. And not enough.

He wanted to see her every day. But he couldn't be so selfish. He shouldn't even be thinking about pursuing a relationship with the beautiful Mrs. Jackson. Now was not the time. Nor the place.

They were at war.

But then . . . would there ever be a good

time? Hadn't God put them together for such a time as this?

His mind went to the book of Esther — where those words had first been written. Esther had been placed in the King's palace in the midst of very tumultuous times. And God had used it for His glory.

Could He use Matthew and Faith together?

He shook his head. Of course God could do that, but how selfish could Matthew be? All these years, he'd never fallen in love. Even though his mentor — good ol' Ben — had fallen in love at seventeen and loved Deborah all his life and tried to convince Matthew on numerous occasions that he should settle down and start a family. It had never happened. There had never even been a spark other than boyhood attractions. Until now. During the most dangerous time of his life.

It couldn't have happened when things were calm and quiet. No. It had to happen while he was a spy. And America was at war.

The heaviness weighed him down. But the thought of seeing Faith lifted his spirits.

What a mess! To be so excited to see her and feel horrible about placing her in danger all at the same time.

When he rounded the corner, he spotted

her with her basket, her shawl covering her head. He gave her a nod, and they headed into the barn together.

"Oh, Matthew, it's so good to see you are well." Relief gleamed in her eyes.

"And I you." He moved closer to her and wanted to drink in those green eyes. Her face was framed by her dark blond curls. He closed his eyes and tried to memorize the ways her eyes smiled at him, the lines of her face.

"What are you doing?"

He opened his eyes and chuckled. "Just wanting to remember this moment."

"That is sweet of you to say." She tilted her head and pursed her lips — a look that was becoming quite endearing to him. "But something is bothering you."

"Come. Please. Let us sit together for a moment." He took her hand and led her over to the hay bales. When she had settled herself, he took a deep breath. "I just want to make sure you are aware of all that is happening around us."

"Of course. Go on." Her brow scrunched when she was serious about a topic. It was adorable.

Matthew shook his head again. Focus. He needed focus. "Two days ago, the Provincial Congress of Massachusetts ordered for thirteen thousand soldiers to be mobilized." As he filled her in on every detail he had, she nodded several times.

With a sigh, she touched his hand. "That puts us in a different place, does it not?"

"What do you mean?"

"The level of danger has increased — especially for you, Matthew. While this information actually makes me feel a bit more safe in my own city, I cannot imagine what this is going to entail for you and your safety."

"I am more concerned for you, Faith."

She sat up a little taller and raised her eyebrows at him. "Honestly, Matthew. You and George are all worried about me when it is the two of you who will have your lives on the line."

That information was new. "Has George been asked to command?"

"Not yet. But you and I both know that it is coming. And he does as well, I am sure."

"But that still does not mean that you should take this lightly. I am quite worried for your well-being, and I think we need to plan accordingly."

Faith cocked just one eyebrow at him this time. She may be small in stature, but her looks could level a man. "I am taking this seriously, Mr. Weber. But you need to please have the courtesy to remember that I am good at this. I am just a messenger. And I will be very careful."

Friday, May 5, 1775

Lifting the knocker on Mrs. Jackson's door, Anthony was disappointed that Clayton hadn't opened it upon his arrival. Was the man slacking in his duties? He'd been spoiled by the man's astute attention to detail.

A clicking noise sounded. Ah . . . so that was it. They'd kept the door locked. Probably because of the skirmishes of late. Good, good. That explained it. At least the servant was keeping his mistress safe. That was excusable.

The door opened about a foot. Clayton frowned at him. "How may I help you, Mr. Jameson?"

"I have an appointment with Mrs. Jackson."

The butler's eyebrows shot up.

"Yes. I sent her a letter last week, and she responded quite rapidly, I might add." He pasted on his best smile. It appeared he'd have to win over the butler before he could win over the lady of the house.

Faith's voice echoed from behind Clayton. Anthony didn't understand the words, but

183

in the next moment, the door opened and he was admitted. Finally.

Clayton took his hat and gloves and led him into the parlor. "Mr. Jameson, ma'am." He bowed and exited.

Anthony took a moment to offer a deep bow of his own. "Mrs. Jackson, you look lovely today."

Rather than offering him a chair or even sitting herself, she stood in front of the empty fireplace with her hands clasped in front of her. "I have a rather full schedule, Mr. Jameson, so what is it that you would like to discuss?"

"I was hoping we would have a bit more time. Since after all, you did invite me." He used his smoothest and calmest tone. Like he did with his dog when she got feisty. Appealing to Mrs. Jackson's sense of social etiquette should help her to relax a bit.

"Mr. Jameson, while I quite apologize if I led you to believe something different, we are in the midst of a war, and I have things to do." Agitation was etched all over her face.

Not the best way to gain her attention. Anthony gave her a full smile and sighed. "Yes, the war. You are helping the poor souls who are displaced, are you not?"

"Mr. Jameson, I appreciate your wish to

create ease of conversation, but as I stated before, I am quite busy. Was the purpose of your letter simply to get together and visit?"

The lady was not at all like the submissive and quiet women with whom he was accustomed. But he admired her spirit. He tried another tactic. "I would never wish to waste your valuable time, ma'am. I am merely here to speak with you about how I may be of service. You see, I would like to help."

"Help?"

"Yes. I would like to help you save people. Together we can be the backbone for the Colonies."

Her brow furrowed. "Together? Backbone?"

"My fine lady, I am sure you have noticed my attention all these months, and I appreciate that you have wished to follow the rules of propriety. But certainly you see that enough time has passed. We are both mature adults who know our own minds. I envision us working quite well together to aid this great cause."

She blinked in rapid succession, which he took as permission to continue. While he had her undivided attention, he might as well get to the point.

"I have been buying up property for some

time now and have created quite a small empire for myself. Estates and land . . . Well, you are aware that many have suffered and struggled for some time with the taxes and lack of supplies because of the boycotts. I have helped a great many families by paying them substantial amounts for their property."

She had her hands on her hips now. An unusual posture for a lady. "Helped?" Her voice sounded almost like a squeak.

Anthony puffed out his chest. "I see you are impressed with my help to the cause. You see, I believe with your fortune combined with my own sizable one, we can assist a great many more. Think of all the good we could do. We can be the foundation for this new era. Possibly this new government the Patriots seek to create. With you by my side —"

"I need to ask you to stop right there, Mr. Jameson." She lifted a hand from her waist and pinched the bridge of her nose.

She must be overcome with emotion as she understood what he was proposing. There was no need to tell her of his deep debt from all those purchases, her coffers would cover that and more. He paused and allowed her a moment. He smiled as he waited for her response.

"Mr. Jameson. I hardly know you. And while I am certain you are a well-bred gentleman, who would strike the fancy of . . . some wonderful lady, somewhere, I am *not* that woman. I must ask you to leave now." She moved from her spot by the fire. "Clayton!"

The butler appeared in an instant.

"Please escort Mr. Jameson outside." She turned back to Anthony. "Thank you for your visit, but I am afraid it has come to an end. There will be no further invitations from this house. Thank you." She gave him a look that almost bordered on angry.

What had he done to invoke such a response?

Before he could do anything to stop it, Clayton was ushering him out the door. The butler didn't even help him, he just handed Anthony his things and shut the door.

And locked it.

He narrowed his eyes. That did not go as planned.

Anthony's driver looked at him.

Walking down the steps of the Jackson home, he straightened his waistcoat and lifted his chin. "We have many errands today. Let us get on with it."

After he'd climbed into the carriage, he thought about Mrs Jackson's words. She

187

was just nervous. Confident she would come around, he allowed himself to smile. It wouldn't be long now.

She stood at the bottom of the stairs and shook. The nerve of that man!

"Madam?" Clayton's voice was soft behind her. "May I get you anything? Perhaps you would like to sit for a few moments?"

"Is he gone?"

"Yes, ma'am."

"And the door is locked?"

"Quite soundly."

She closed her eyes for a second. "Perhaps a cup of tea would be good. I am quite upset from that . . . that man." She wanted to spit his name or, even better, punch him and wipe the smug smile off his face. She'd had plenty of practice when she was younger, and she knew she could knock the man off his feet if necessary. She should probably ask forgiveness for such horrid thoughts, but it was the truth. Even if ladies weren't supposed to go around punching gentlemen in the face.

Putting a hand to her forehead, Faith prayed. *Lord, please keep that man away from me so I don't resort to violence. You know it's for his sake and not mine.*

Even as riled as she was, she had to admit

that his oily demeanor made her skin crawl. She would go so far as to say that it struck a chord of fear within her. What would the ladies say if they knew what the man had come to say today?

Clayton appeared at her side. "Let us go into the parlor, ma'am. Sylvia is preparing you some tea."

His gentle hand behind her back led her like she was a small child. Once she sat in the chair, he hovered over her. "Would you like me to call for Mrs. White? Or perhaps all of the ladies?"

Faith looked down at her hands. They were white from being clenched into balled fists. And they shook. She took a deep breath. "I think you better, Clayton. It will take them a bit to get here, and after I have had some tea and a chance to calm down, I will need them here to help me decide the best way to proceed."

"Good, good." Clayton headed out of the parlor, and Faith was sure she'd see the women begin to arrive within the hour.

Sylvia brought in a serving tray with a pot of tea and a cup and saucer. Her favorite china to boot. Her staff knew her well. After several sips, she felt her racing heart calm to a normal rhythm. It was then that she dissected Anthony's words.

The man had had nothing to do with the Patriot cause before now. If he had, she would have known about it. She also knew from one of his first visits last year that he had boasted about his close relationship with King George. So how could a man that was granted land from the King of England now say that he was loyal to *her* cause — that of the Patriots. What did the man know?

If she didn't know better, she'd think the man was a spy for the Loyalists. But it was clear that he was all bluster and smoke. Seeking to make himself look better in her eyes to win her attention. But even if that was all there was to it, he could still be dangerous. Something wasn't right about Anthony Jameson.

Either the man was a fool, or he would get caught in his duplicity.

And Faith did not want to be anywhere near the man. Ever again.

The ladies soon began to arrive, and after several cups of tea and a lengthy retelling of all that had transpired, Faith was exhausted. Lydia, Claudia, and Mary appeared shocked, but Louise, Ruth, Sally, and Esther all looked afraid. When Faith looked at Lavonia . . . Well, the only word to describe her friend's expression would be horrified.

At least Faith knew she wasn't alone in all

this. And that her feelings weren't an over-reaction. But what could she do?

Lavonia set her teacup down and wiped at her skirt. "I cannot begin to tell you how much this disturbs me, Faith. And while I think it is imperative that we all remain calm and sensible about this matter, I do believe that actions need to be taken to protect Faith. And the cause. Mr. Jameson does not seem to be trustworthy on any count."

The room erupted in chatter as all the ladies began speaking at once. Overwhelming weariness washed over Faith. More than anything she'd ever felt. Why on earth was Anthony Jameson so fixated on her? She didn't have time for this.

Lavonia jumped from her seat. "Faith, you have gone completely white."

"I do not feel well all of a sudden. I think I need to lie down." Faith stood, the room spun, then everything went black.

CHAPTER 11

Wednesday, May 10, 1775
Philadelphia

Matthew snuck into Ben's house after midnight. Thankfully, Charles — the butler — knew him well and didn't raise a ruckus. As he made his way up to Ben's room, he felt bad for having to wake the old man.

"Ben?" Matthew tried to keep his voice to a whisper.

"What?!" Franklin sat straight up in his bed. Blinking rapidly, he reached for the candlestick by his bed and raised it over his head. "Who is there?"

"Put the candle down, Ben. You are not being robbed. It is me. Matthew." He took off his cloak and hat and slouched into the chair by the bed.

"Good gracious, Matthew. You about scared me to death." Ben wiped a hand down his face. "Has something happened to William?" A bit of sadness covered his features.

"No. Do not worry, my friend. William is fine. But I find myself in a serious quandary."

Ben fluffed his pillow behind him and sat up a little straighter. "Go on. How may I help?"

"First, I must warn you, it is about Faith."

"Your messenger?"

"Yes."

"Ah. I see." Ben put on his glasses. "You care for her a great deal, do you not?"

How did he know that? "Yes. That is why I am concerned."

"For her safety?"

"Yes, but no. If I may continue, please." Matthew quirked an eyebrow at his mentor.

"Of course. I will remain silent." Ben closed his mouth and sucked his lips in.

He couldn't help it, the silly face made him laugh and tension eased from Matthew's shoulders. "We are scheduled to meet every other day now, and we should have met five nights ago."

Ben held up a finger. "Excuse me. You need to clarify. Five nights ago, meaning what day exactly? It is the middle of the night you see, and thus we have already begun the day of the tenth."

Matthew looked to the ceiling. "It would

have been the fifth. We were supposed to meet on the fifth."

"All right. Now that it is clear, you may continue." Ben waved a hand at him.

"Thank you. How kind." His mentor might want to smack him for his sarcastic remark, but Matthew was thankful for the keen mind and listening ear. "Faith did not show at our appointed time."

His friend's eyebrows raised. "What did you do?"

"I waited for two hours, and she never came. That has never happened before. The rule is that if the other does not come, we still continue to meet at the designated times and places just in case there was some mishap. But now I have missed a meeting, and I am worried about her, and she will most likely worry about me."

"So exactly why are you here? In Philadelphia?" Ben tried to sit up straighter. "I am not sure I understand the chain of events."

Matthew leaned forward and put his elbows on his knees. "She did not show up on Friday — the fifth. Then the next morning, the sixth, I met with the group of Loyalists — William's group — and they gave me a new task. Since I have a history with George Washington, they have asked me to attempt to come and get into his good graces and attend the Continental Congress or at least get them information about it. In essence, they want me to spy."

"Oh, gracious." Ben slumped. "That is very ambitious of them, thinking you could attend the Congress. That is, of course, since you are a Loyalist — er, pretending to be a Loyalist." He shook his head as if to clear it.

"Exactly. They had a carriage ready for me immediately, and I have been traveling here ever since. Of course then I missed our scheduled meeting on the seventh — Sunday — and missed last night's meeting as well. Faith will most certainly think that something horrible has happened to me. That is, if she is all right and something horrible has not happened to her!"

"Lower your voice, Matthew. No need to alert the neighbors." The older man straightened up in the bed again and smoothed the covers. "I understand your concern. First, for Faith. And then for this position you are in. You are in essence a spy being asked to now act as a spy for the side you are spying on. It's confusing just to wrap my mind around it."

"What should I do? I mean, somehow I have to get word to Faith, but how should I do it without anyone finding out?"

"I have an idea." Ben smiled. "I have this friend. You could say she is a middle-aged widow — or at least she was. Perhaps she could have her daughter write Faith a letter?"

Matthew shook his head. "Dogood? Really, Ben?" He had read all of Ben's letters to the paper that he wrote under the name of Silence Dogood — the middle-aged widow.

"Well, it was just an idea. You have to admit it worked before."

"But I doubt Faith will even know anything about those letters. So she will have no reason to recognize the name."

"Humph. Well, that just goes to show how old I am." Ben shrugged his shoulders.

Matthew snapped his fingers. "But you are a brilliant old man. You have just given me an idea. I am going to need you to go see someone very special."

"Anything for you, my boy." Ben rubbed his hands together.

Wednesday, May 17, 1775
Boston
Faith paced in her parlor. After seven days bedridden from some horrific illness the doctor wanted to call influenza, she was beside herself. Forever thankful that it

196

wasn't the dreaded smallpox, she'd still prayed in earnest about her plight.

She'd missed four designated meetings with Matthew. As soon as she was strong enough, she went to meet him, but now he'd missed two. But did he think that something had happened to her and so he hadn't tried for a while? How could she contact him and let him know that she was all right?

They were supposed to meet again later that evening, and she began to wonder if he would be there. What if something horrible had happened to him? What could she do?

The more she thought about him, the more she realized that she was more concerned about the man than the mission. Dare she call it love?

Putting a hand to her chest, she drew a deep breath. It'd been so long since she'd felt romantic love. She'd been so young when she fell in love with Joseph. Their courtship was full of dances, fancy parties, and festive occasions. He sent her gifts and flowers and showered her with compliments. They'd never even had a fight — which was quite miraculous since Faith knew she was far too opinionated. But they'd never had a chance to argue since their week-old marriage ended with his death. He'd been sent back to battle the day after their wedding.

The memories were lovely. Much like a fairy tale.

But life wasn't a fairy tale. This she knew all too well. Loss had been a large portion of her life — thank the good Lord it had made her stronger.

Matthew's face came to mind again. *Oh, Matthew.*

What had happened to him? Wracking her brain, she wondered how to contact him. Should she get a message to George? Mr. Lewis? Or would that compromise the mission at hand? No. She couldn't be so careless. Both of those men had too much at stake as well.

A knock at the front door stopped her pacing. If it was that odious Mr. Jameson again, she would run away. Or throw something at him.

Neither option was befitting her station or her age. Which was sad. The man might benefit from something hitting him in the face.

She put a hand to her forehead. If Matthew knew the thoughts that sometimes went through her head . . .

Clayton entered the parlor with a lady following behind. "You have a visitor, ma'am. Mrs. Elizabeth *Dogood.*"

Dogood? That was odd. Where had she heard that name before? And why did Clayton pronounce it in such a way? "Good afternoon, Mrs. Dogood."

"Good afternoon." The lady curtsied.

Clayton gave Faith an interesting look over the visiting lady's head before he backed out of the room and pulled the door closed.

"Mrs. Jackson." The woman walked up very close to Faith and then looked around. "There is no one else in here?"

Faith narrowed her eyes. "No."

"So it is safe to speak?"

"Yes." She tilted her head. What was this lady about?

"I am Matthew's sister."

Faith gasped and grabbed the woman's hands. "Oh, praise the Lord above."

"And my name is not Dogood, but that is the name I traveled under, and I was told I must keep up my ruse."

Faith nodded. "So Matthew is well?"

Elizabeth — or whatever her name was — nodded and smiled. A smile very similar to her brother's. "Yes. Quite. But it is a long story to tell. He is extremely worried about you."

Faith let out a heavy sigh and put a hand to her chest. "I had a horrible illness for the length of a week. And I missed . . ." Wait. Could she trust this woman? What if it was a trick? She clamped her mouth closed and stepped back.

Her guest nodded. "I understand. Perhaps this will explain." She pulled a letter out of her pocket.

Faith took it and opened the seal. The handwriting wasn't familiar. But the code within the letter *was*. After she read through it twice — making sure that she understood and didn't miss anything — she hugged her visitor. "My apologies."

"There is nothing to apologize for, Mrs. Jackson." She looked weary.

"Goodness, yes, there is. You must be dead on your feet. Let me get you some refreshment." Faith pointed to a chair. "Please have a seat. I will ring for Sylvia."

After her guest had been seated, Faith rang the bell. Clayton appeared immediately. "We would like some tea, please. And perhaps some sandwiches and teacakes? Let Sylvia know we have a guest."

"Of course, ma'am." He closed the door again.

"Now please, tell me all about Matthew." Faith scooted her chair closer.

"I cannot say much, but he is fine. He is in Philadelphia at the Continental Congress

200

meetings."

That puzzled Faith. "I am sure I do not understand. Those are . . ."

Mrs. Dogood nodded. "Yes, they are Patriot — Colonial meetings." She leaned in and looked around again. She motioned for Faith to get closer and whispered, "You see the Loyalists sent him on a mission to spy on the Congress."

Faith raised her eyebrows and began to laugh. The irony of the situation.

"I may not be able to speak much about Matthew's current condition or work, but I can tell you all about him from a sister's point of view." She raised an eyebrow and gave Faith a smirk.

"Now that sounds very interesting indeed. Can you stay awhile?"

"I would love to. I hear my brother is quite fond of you, Mrs. Jackson."

Faith felt a blush creep up her neck and into her cheeks. "Truly?" She cleared her throat. "And please, call me Faith."

"Then you must call me Amelia. That's my real name, and I hope that we will know each other for a long, long time. Because my brother is quite taken with you."

The rest of the afternoon passed in a blur. Matthew's sister was a delight. Once Faith discovered that her name was actually

Amelia, she realized it fit the sweet woman perfectly. Small in stature — especially in comparison to the broad shoulders and exceptional height of Matthew — but with the same coloring as her brother.

"Do I need to call you Elizabeth in front of Clayton?"

"Yes, please." Amelia took a sip of her tea. "That way if any of the staff talk with others, they can say that your visitor was Elizabeth Dogood."

Faith narrowed her eyes again as she lifted her own cup to her lips. Where had she heard that name? After a long sip of tea, she was still puzzled. "Why does the name Dogood sound oddly familiar?"

Amelia laughed. Setting down her cup and saucer, she leaned in again. "You really do not know?"

Shaking her head, Faith smiled.

"Benjamin Franklin wrote letters to be published in his brother's paper decades ago since his brother would not allow him to write anything. He used the name 'Silence Dogood' and stated that she was a middle-aged widow." Amelia chuckled. "In some circles they still receive quite the chain of gossip."

It didn't make sense. "I am still confused, I am afraid. What does that have to do with

Matthew?"

"Ben has been close to Matthew for many years. Matthew looks up to him like a father figure — a mentor."

Faith blinked. What was she missing?

"*Ben* is the one who sent me." Amelia looked puzzled. "Benjamin Franklin. Have you never read any of his writing?"

"Oh my! Goodness, that explains it. I was wondering how on earth Matthew had gotten word to you. Well, Benjamin Franklin . . . *the* Benjamin Franklin. Of course, my father loved *Poor Richard's Almanack* and . . . um . . . whatever that magazine was that he wrote for the plantations." She took a deep breath. "I just had no idea that Matthew was close to him. My apologies. I had not put the pieces of the puzzle together."

"Ben is eager to meet you, my dear."

She put a hand to her throat and raised her eyebrows. "Really?"

"Indeed. He said that whoever has caught Matthew's attention must be very special."

Dare she hope that Matthew cared for her as much as she did him? The hope that had begun to grow in her heart now blossomed into a great swell.

"I do not mean to embarrass you. But I do want you to know that I am very pleased with his choice." Amelia patted Faith's hand.

The feelings that rolled through her were new and exciting. What she wouldn't give to be able to see Matthew today. But she had to wait. Neither one of them was safe to declare anything until this horrible conflict was over. "Did he say when Matthew will return? When I should look to meet with him again?" Three messages were waiting to be delivered. She never knew how they got there or who brought them, but they showed up in her sewing basket by the fire, waiting to be coded and delivered. When she'd taken on the job, one of the rules was not to ask questions. While it was a bit eerie at times to think of someone coming into her home to deliver the messages, she knew it was for the cause.

Faith was the only one allowed to code the messages sent to Matthew. There were plenty of other missives that the other ladies coded. But they were all notes going to known Patriots. Not a Patriot spy posing as a Loyalist. She knew that her job was the most dangerous, but that never made her want to quit.

"On the twenty-fifth of this month."

Only eight more days. Faith could wait that long, now that she knew Matthew was all right.

Amelia invited her to Plymouth and said she would love to help Faith connect with her family. Then she shared some comical stories of Matthew from their childhood.

All too soon, Amelia stood. "I am afraid, it is time I bid you farewell. It is a good distance back to Plymouth, and my driver will be anxious to get back tonight. It takes awhile to cross the barricade outside the city. But I have special papers to give them." She winked. "Good to have friends in high places."

Faith stood and walked her new friend to the door where Clayton waited. "I hope to see you soon . . . Elizabeth."

"And I you."

CHAPTER 12

The Continental Congress had discussed more than George had anticipated. But that's what had to be done since the British forced the Colonies' hand. As he sat in his uniform in the back of the room, he thought ahead to what was to come. It would probably be some time before he would be able to return to Mount Vernon. That dealt a harsh blow to his heart, but it was what had to be done. The path before them would be harsh. Up against the strongest army and navy in the world.

But it had to be born. On the shoulders of farmers and carpenters and every man, woman, and child who loved this land and called it home. The Colonies weren't made for the monarchy. They were built on the quest for freedom. Granted the Separatists who'd come on the *Mayflower* simply

206

wanted religious freedom, but didn't freedom cover it all? Freedom to all for worship, work, and trade. What they needed was a good form of government. That was *for* the people. Made up *by* the people. Not a king or a queen or prince who'd only ever known a life of ease. Regular, ordinary, hardworking people.

His thoughts turned to Martha. Strong and capable, she would handle things at the farm, along with his servants. He would miss her greatly, for certainly this conflict would keep him away, but she knew that. She supported him, and a husband couldn't ask for anything more.

Then there was Faith. If he wasn't careful, he'd find her out on the battlefield beside him. And she could probably win the war too. He shook his head and smiled. It was already dangerous enough that she was carrying messages in Boston when the British troops had control. But deep down, he knew she could handle herself.

As the president of the Congress — John Hancock — pounded on the table to gather everyone's attention, George sat up straighter.

"Gentlemen, we have received news that is disturbing, but not all that surprising considering everything that has transpired in recent years." He stepped around the table and continued. "A new Act has come down from England. It goes into effect as of July the first. The Colonies will only be allowed to trade with England. It is a new law, which means there will be punishment for not abiding by it."

Many of the men shook their heads, and whispers filled the room.

"Gentlemen." He held up his hands. "There is more. As of July the twentieth, the Colonies will no longer be able to catch fish in the North Atlantic."

That prompted a lot of gasps, and voices raised in agitation.

"They cannot do that! Do they believe they own the ocean?" One of the delegates stood from his desk.

"Apparently they do. King George believes he owns it all from how it appears. And the Act is in place. So, gentlemen, how do we wish to respond?"

A cacophony of sound rose throughout the room.

Discussions were had.

Options laid out.

But George knew that their path was to fight for their freedom. It was indeed their *only* path.

That . . . or be enslaved by the King.

■ ■ ■ ■

Sunday, June 4, 1775
Hingham

Matthew paced inside the odious barn. It wasn't his favorite place to meet, but any time he could have with Faith was worth it. He couldn't wait to see her face again — it was what kept him going each day.

The longer he was with the Loyalists, the harder it became to bite his tongue. There seemed to be so much arrogance among the men he had the so-called pleasure of knowing. They all wanted power and for the Crown to rule it all. It didn't make sense to him. Not one bit. Didn't those men long to make decisions for themselves? To build something with their own hands? Or were they so concerned with their titles and positions that they didn't care?

Breathing out a huff, he realized he couldn't lump them all into the same group. Not every Loyalist was a bad person. Or arrogant. Or lazy. He cringed at his own thoughts. Yes, he'd begun to lump them all together and formed opinions about them because of their political leanings. That wasn't the way things should be. That wasn't how the good Lord showed them in the Good Book either. But it was so easy to judge and become prejudiced. Especially in the middle of a war.

Hate could do horrible things to one's mind. And Matthew was determined not to let it go there. He had a job to do, and he would see it through. Thoughts of a bright future with Faith indeed spurred him on and kept him on track. Even when exhaustion and frustration overwhelmed him.

Faith.

She was beautiful. And feisty. And full of life. She also had a good mind and strong opinions. It didn't bother him one bit that she could think for herself, manage her estate by herself, and everything else she did so remarkably by herself.

The barn door creaked, and his heart picked up its pace. He watched from the corner to make sure it was her, and when he saw her sweet face, he came out of the shadows to greet her. "Faith. It is so good to see you again."

A huge smile split her face. "It is good to see you as well." She looked up at him as she stepped closer. "I have been looking forward to this all day."

His heart felt like it skipped a beat with a declaration like that. "You are my one bright spot, Faith."

She didn't look away or down. Not at all skittish or coy like so many other women he'd seen. Maintaining eye contact, she licked her lips. "I believe God has given us something special. Do you agree?"

"Yes." He took her hand and led her to where he had lit a lantern. In a relatively clean stall, he'd placed two milking stools he'd found, and they sat together in the dim light. He reached into his waistcoat. "This is for you." He handed over the letter.

"Aye. Thank you. I have several for you as well." She reached into her skirt to pull out a packet she'd tied with a ribbon. "Tell me about all that has been happening. Are you doing all right? Is it difficult?"

Her curiosity made him chuckle. "I love your quick mind. The happenings are not all that interesting. Frustrating is more the word I would use. Mainly because it is difficult to watch what they are planning and deciding with no regard for the common people. I have to keep my mouth shut and play my part. Which is not always easy."

She made a scrunched-up face. "I would have great difficulty keeping my mouth shut, I assure you."

Oh, how she brought joy to his heart. Before he could think about it and stop himself, he plunged on ahead. "Faith, I

211

know this is not the appropriate time nor the place, and I do not want to put you at any more risk than you already are, but —" He took a deep breath and paused. The green of her eyes enchanted him. And he wished he could stay right here . . . forever.

"But . . . ?"

All right, maybe not forever, but it was wonderful simply to bask in her presence. "I am hoping that you will wait for me. After all this is over. The war. All of it."

She sat up a little straighter and lifted her eyebrows. "I believe that you need to be a bit more specific, Mr. Weber."

He furrowed his brow. "What do you mean?"

Closing her eyes, she shook her head. "Men. You all can be so daft sometimes." Small as she was, sitting on the tiny stool, she put her hands on her hips. It was adorable. "If you are asking me to wait for you, kind sir, I believe that means you should at least admit that you care for me in some way." She lifted one of those pretty little eyebrows and smirked.

"Oh, Faith." He reached for both of her hands. "You must know that I care a great deal about you. I cannot get through the day without thinking of you a hundred times. And I would not wish to. I thank the

Lord above for giving me the opportunity to know you. You have brought joy into my life that I have never experienced before."

"Truly?" Her voice was soft.

"Truly."

She sighed. "I care for you a great deal as well." Light laughter lifted her lips. "I do not think I told you, but your sister told me several stories. They were quite endearing."

Lifting his eyes toward the ceiling, he wondered what *endearing* stories Amelia could have told. "I can well imagine."

A gust of wind rattled the sides of the barn and whipped up the smell. Faith put a finger under her nose. "You never told me how well you were acquainted with Benjamin Franklin." Her voice sounded pinched with her hand there. Probably trying not to inhale while she spoke.

"Ben? He's a great fellow. I know Amelia told you that I had sent Ben to her with the message for you. It was the only way we could think of to keep my cover."

"What is he like?"

"Who? Ben?"

Faith nodded.

"He is a very amiable man. Short and stout. Brilliant and a wonderful mentor to me. It's just such a shame that he and his son are at odds."

"What do you mean?"

"You don't know?"

As she shook her head, her blond curls bounced.

"His son is William Franklin, the Royal Governor of New Jersey."

Her eyes widened. "Are you saying that they are on opposite sides?"

"Quite irrevocably. And it has put a great strain on their relationship. So much so that I fear it may never recover."

"That is so sad. Family should always come first, do not you agree? I mean, even if they disagree politically, should not they always put the other first and seek to maintain peace within the family?"

"That, my dear, is much easier said than done."

She put a hand to her chest. "It is heartbreaking is what it is."

"I agree. But Ben refuses to contact William, and William is too caught up in everything around him to realize that he may very well lose his father over this."

Watching the pain wash over her face, Matthew reached out a hand to cover hers. "Let us talk about happier things, shall we? While we have a few moments."

"Agreed."

"As much as I want to tell you how I

worry about you, I can see you are doing very well." He lifted one of her hands to his lips and kissed the top of her lacy glove. "You look absolutely beautiful this evening."

She didn't break eye contact and leaned an inch closer to him. The deep green of her dress made her eyes even greener in the lantern light. "Thank you for the compliment, Mr. Weber. You are quite handsome yourself."

In that instant, he could imagine the stinky barn was gone and they were out in the fresh air under the stars together. She made everything brighter. What was this feeling? Was this what true love felt like? Many men had talked to him about it over the years. Some in boasting, some in earnest awe of the emotion. But he'd never felt it. Never.

A horse whinnied behind him, and Faith laughed.

As much as he wanted to take her in his arms and kiss those lips until the war was over, he prayed for control. He wanted to do the honorable thing by her. Oh, but how he wanted to kiss her. He gripped her hands again. So this is why most men married young. The yearnings and feelings that had taken over the past few months with Faith were quite intense. But he was a soldier.

And now a spy. He could conquer this and keep control.

The horse whinnied again.

It was his turn to laugh. "Not very romantic, is it?"

"You are all the romance I need, Matthew Weber." With that she stood and leaned over him. Placing a kiss on his cheek, she smelled of roses and lilacs. "I will see you in two days."

He longed to pull her back into his arms, but she dashed out the door.

Good thing too. He'd have to do a lot more praying.

CHAPTER 13

Monday, June 5, 1775
Boston

Too many sounds in the night had kept Faith from sleeping well. That and her thoughts of Matthew.

She'd been so young and naive when she'd married Joseph. He'd been a very handsome and strong man, and their attraction had been strong. Their affection for one another had been sweet and tender. But the marriage lasted only a week. Really a day, if you counted the fact that he went off to battle the very next day after the wedding. But she had adored him. As much as her twenty-year-old self could.

Now time and experiences had shaped her. Matured her. Gained her much wisdom. And while she held Matthew in great esteem for his bravery and his hard work, she had to admit that she was very drawn to him physically as well. It did strange

217

things to her heart.

He was so tall. Trim but very strong. His cutaway coats accentuated his broad shoulders. But it was his eyes that drew her in every time. As much as she wanted to be held in his strong arms, she longed to look into his eyes even more. The man was a commanding presence — much like George was — but she never felt any fear around him. Only great respect and a strong sensation of being . . . safe.

Then there was her attraction to him. She longed for his touch. Longed to be kissed by him. Loved by him. She shook her head. *Lord, keep my thoughts pure.*

She was incredibly thankful for the opportunity to get to know this dashing man.

So many gentlemen nowadays were all absorbed in themselves or their work. They loved mirrors and to look at their reflection. They wanted women to swoon and fall at their feet and to think that they were the greatest gift from God above. They gave more attention to their hair, clothes, and shoes, than they did to their character and reputation.

Joseph hadn't been that way. George wasn't that way — his care for Martha was a wonderful thing to behold. And from what she could tell, Matthew didn't appear to be that way either.

The thought of having a future with him thrilled her and sent tingles down her spine. How long would the war last? She truly hoped that King George would see the error of his ways sooner rather than later, because Faith desperately wanted children. Lots of them.

Making her way down to the parlor, Faith pulled her dressing gown closer to her. There was quite a chill before the sun rose. Even though it was summer, she almost wanted to ask for a fire to be lit, but she would settle for a blanket and her comfy chair to watch the sun rise since there was no chance of sleep.

It must be getting close to four in the morning. Last time she'd looked at the clock it was past three. The kitchen staff would begin their work for the day soon, and she could ask for a cup of tea to warm her bones. She turned her chair to face the window. The quiet was one thing she loved most. In Boston there was very little of it.

Wrapping herself in a blanket, she sat in her chair with her feet tucked up under her. Not a position she could manage in her stays and full dress. But she'd done it since she was a child and would climb up onto the settee with her mother and they would make up stories while she embroidered pillows. As an adult, her short stature made it a comfortable and cozy way to curl up in her chair, and she would enjoy the time she could relax even if she couldn't sleep.

Faith leaned her head back and thought of Matthew. How she wished the time would fly until their next meeting. Thoughts of him gathered in her mind more often each day. She could see his face, his dashing figure, those twinkling eyes, and could almost smell his scent. His very intoxicating and manly scent.

Gracious, time to pull herself together. Giving a little huff, she promised herself to keep her mind in check.

In the silence of a sleeping house, that was more difficult than she'd hoped. But she could do it. So she turned her thoughts to their subsequent conversation. What would she say to him next —

The floor creaked behind her and brought her lovely thoughts crashing to a halt. Someone was coming into the parlor.

Afraid to move or even breathe, Faith looked to the tools by the fireplace. Was she within reach of the poker? It was the only defensive weapon she could think of within easy reach.

A slight shuffling sounded, and she wished

she could disappear under the blanket. With the back of her chair to the entrance of the room, she couldn't see anything. Did anyone know she was there? Maybe she could stay hidden.

Unless the intruder was after *her*.

Whoever it was moved to her right and headed toward the fireplace. She could almost feel them next to her. There was nowhere for her to hide. Sending a quick prayer heavenward, she hoped she would be able to move quickly if she needed to, but the numb feeling in her feet and legs warned that they had fallen asleep underneath her.

A shadow emerged.

As soon as she recognized the figure, relief flooded her whole being. "Clayton! What on earth are you doing?"

He moved very slowly and held up a packet. Ah . . . it all made sense now. In his hand were letters. Like the ones she always found in her sewing basket. "I am very sorry to startle you, ma'am."

She put a hand to her chest and eased her feet to the floor. One of the rules was not to ask questions about how the deliveries were made. The less she knew about some of the details, the better. Another wave of relief washed over her. "You are working for the cause, aren't you?"

"Indeed, ma'am." He stood up straight. "I did not wish you to think that I took time away from the house, so I kept my mouth shut and snuck out in the middle of the night to ensure these were delivered safely."

Did the man never sleep? To think, she'd known him all these years, yet she knew so little about him. "Is it dangerous work?"

"Not much of it, ma'am. Not any more dangerous than what you do." His expression was very fatherly and protective.

She gave him a sheepish smile. "Clayton, you amaze me. Thank you for all that you are doing."

"Indeed. 'Tis my duty. But I appreciate your support." Instead of placing the packet in her basket, he handed it to her. "Is there anything else you need, ma'am?"

"Why don't you join me for a cup of tea, and we could discuss all that has transpired so far. I am sure you have quite a few stories to tell, and I would love to hear them." Light laughter bubbled up. "Besides, I need to sit for a while and wait for my heart to calm down. You gave me quite a scare. I thought you were an intruder."

"An intruder? But the doors and windows are barred, ma'am." He tilted his head.

She leaned forward. "Yes, an intruder. Someone who found out who I was and came after me to stop the messages from getting delivered." In all seriousness, her mind had gone there. But saying it in front of Clayton made her feel ridiculous. No one knew who she was. "I know . . . you think it is silly of me."

"No, ma'am. Not at all. 'Tis good that you are taking the danger seriously." He smiled at her. Actually smiled. "And yes, ma'am. I will gladly join you for tea."

"I cannot wait. My butler — the man I thought led such a boring life since all he does is take care of little old me all the time — has secrets. This I simply must hear."

After sharing stories with Clayton for almost two hours, they both went about their days and promised to keep the other's secrets. Faith shook her head. It still amazed her. Clayton. Stiff, stoic Clayton. To think of him slinking about in the night, jumping fences, and darting between buildings. It made her chuckle.

The ladies would soon be gathering, and she needed to prepare herself for what was to come. Most of them would be leaving the city with their children within the next few days. The dangers were just getting too high. Most of the other women and children had already left town, but her ladies had been invested in the cause and wanted to see it through and do as much as they possibly could. It was hard to think about this being their last chance to see each other for an unforeseen amount of time. Goodbyes were one of her least favorite things.

Marie came in with her gown for the day. "Are you ready, ma'am?"

"Quite."

As Marie quietly went about their normal morning routine, Faith realized that if things continued to escalate and she was forced to leave Boston as well, she would need to make provisions for her staff. It might do well for her to see if there were people — especially other women and children — who might need assistance. Maybe that was something she and Clayton could look into together. Now that she knew about his extra activities, it would be fun to have a coconspirator.

Marie tightened the laces on her stays a bit too much, and it made her gasp.

"Oh, I am sorry, ma'am. I guess my mind is elsewhere." Her maid sniffed.

"Is everything all right?" Faith turned and looked at her maid's teary eyes.

A shake of the girl's head was all Faith needed.

"Please. Tell me. Let me help."

Marie wiped at her face. "My parents were

kicked out of their home yesterday to make room for redcoats — not even officers, mind you, just some stinky soldiers." She sniffed again. "I am sorry. That was unkind." At tear dropped from her chin. "Oh! I am so sorry, ma'am. I do not wish to get anything on your gown."

"Don't you worry one little second over my dress." Faith grabbed Marie's hands. "Do they have anywhere to go?"

"No, ma'am." Marie lifted her chin. "But I am working to find a place. I am sure the Lord will provide."

"You must tell them that I insist that they come here. I have plenty of room."

Marie's eyes widened. "But, ma'am."

"There are no *but*s. They will stay here. As soon as you are done helping me this morning, go and fetch them." She narrowed her eyes. "But you must be very careful, and you must also ask your parents to keep the secrets of all the Patriot duties of the house. We cannot afford to put any of us at risk."

"Aye, ma'am. I am sure they will aid in any way they can, and they will work for their keep."

"Don't you worry about that." Faith turned back around so Marie could finish with her dressing. "Now let's hurry so that you can go quickly. Sometimes the soldiers

225

aren't too kind to the people they have booted out of their homes."

With a firm hand on the knocker, Anthony determined that he would *not* be denied entrance again. Today would be the day. Mrs. Jackson could play hard to get all she wanted with other men — but it was unacceptable with him. She was to be his bride, and he wouldn't take no for an answer.

The door unlocked, and Clayton's face peered through the inch-wide opening. "Mr. Jameson. I am sure you understand —"

"I will not be denied, Clayton." He pushed his full weight against the door and gained a foot. "Mrs. Jackson will see me immediately."

The much smaller man had more strength in his wiry frame than Anthony had given him credit for. He had to push a lot just to keep the door open.

"Mr. Jameson, while I am sure we are all impressed with your fervor, Mrs. Jackson offered you no invitation to this home. Now if you will kindly remove yourself before I have to do it for you."

"I will not be spoken to by a servant in such a manner!" No one got away with that. No one. Anthony wasn't even denied an audience with the King when he wanted it.

"Mr. Jameson!" Clayton yelled and pushed back.

"I warned you!" Anthony leaned with all his might when all of a sudden the door gave way and he found himself with too much momentum. In less than the blink of an eye, he was floundering and falling toward the floor. He hit and bounced a few times before landing face-first on the marble floor.

Clayton sighed beside him.

Heat warmed his cheeks. "How dare you! Why you —"

"Mr. Jameson, that is quite enough." A gown of golden yellow with matching shoes — that were quite exquisite — were inches from his face. He recognized the voice. The object of his affection must have given him entrance. And look at the spectacle he'd made! Gathering every ounce of pride he could muster, he rolled to his side and then his back to attempt to gain his feet. But his breeches were laced a tad bit too tight. He shot a look to the butler for help.

The unhelpful man crossed his arms.

"Clayton, please assist Mr. Jameson to his feet."

"As you wish, ma'am." The butler leaned down with an arm. He whispered into Anthony's ear. "Not — one — wrong —

move." The threat was accentuated by a steely and forceful grip of Clayton's hand.

Once he was back on his feet, Anthony lifted his chin and cleared his throat. He tugged his waistcoat down and straightened his coat. The cravat at his throat felt increasingly tight. Dignity. He must show Mrs. Jackson his supreme dignity. Remembering he had been a dear friend of the King, invited to every special occasion and event at the palace, helped him to put on the same appeasing expression he'd used to woo subjects to the King's wishes. He adjusted his neck's adornment and turned to face her with a bow.

"Mr. Jameson. I believe I informed you last time you were here that there would be no more invitations from this house. I hate to be rude, but you simply are not welcome here." Hands on her hips, Mrs. Jackson actually looked perturbed. Her eyes held a fire he hadn't seen before, and it was quite lovely.

"Mrs. Jackson, if you would but grant me a moment of your time, I believe I can get you to see my undying admiration for you and that you and I were made for each other by the gracious Lord above and —"

"Mis—ter Jam—e—son!" Her voice raised several tones as her face flushed a deep crimson. It brought out the beauty of her emerald eyes. "You will leave. Now. And not return."

"But you will marry me, Mrs. Jackson. You will. I will not take no for an answer. There is no need to play these games."

Clayton pushed his shoulder and turned him toward the door.

"Unhand me, my good man! I am not finished!"

"Oh, yes you are." Clayton's words were deep and harsh.

As the butler pushed at his back, Anthony leaned onto the man to stay within his beloved's presence as long as possible. She needed him. He needed her money. And her beauty. He deserved it. He did.

"Mr. Jameson, let me assure you one last time. I am not playing games. Nor do I wish to speak to you again. Good. *Day.*" There was a note of finality in her voice that simply didn't make sense. What was she up to? Surely this was all a ruse to convince her lady friends and staff that she was the purest and saintliest of women.

The wiry butler succeeded in shoving him out the door. It slammed behind him followed by a resounding click of the lock.

Anthony turned and studied the door. Something was amiss. He couldn't put his finger on it. But he would.

He would have Mrs. Jackson.

Or no one else would.

CHAPTER 14

Tuesday, June 6, 1775
Hingham

The long daylight hours made it difficult for Faith and Matthew to make their drop-offs, so they'd had to start meeting later. Last time, they had decided to meet twenty minutes later each time until mid-July. But that would mean many after-midnight meetings. Matthew thought that maybe they should revise their plans, but more and more redcoats were patrolling as the days wore on.

Faith snuck in the side door of the meetinghouse. "Hi," she whispered, and they slipped over to the corner they liked the best. "Sorry it took me a bit longer to get here tonight. The patrols are out in full force, and I had to travel in several circles before I could get here.

The moonlight streamed through the window and gave her an angelic glow. "I am

231

glad you are safe. But it does make me worry." The tension behind his eyes wouldn't ease. Probably from all the looking out and lack of sleep. "They have basic control of Boston, but not as much here on the outskirts. I am concerned they have brought more troops in through the harbor and will be pushing at the barricade lines soon."

She nodded. "I had the very same thoughts." Another packet tied with a ribbon was in her hand. "Here. There is some very important news in these. I do not understand it all, but please, promise me you will be careful?"

"I promise." He took the missives. The worry etched lines on her face. "Let's talk about something happier."

She looked puzzled for a moment, and then her face broke into a smile. "Oh, I have quite the story to tell you today."

He didn't miss the rolling of her eyes. It must be a good story. "Please, go on."

As she recounted her adventure with Anthony Jameson, he laughed along with her. "He really fell onto the floor?"

"With a great resounding *splat* on the marble." She shook her head. "His girth made him bounce quite a bit, and I must admit that replaying the image in my mind is quite humorous."

As they laughed together, the words replayed in his mind. "And you said that he *insisted* you would marry him?" His smile faded as a knot of tension formed in his stomach.

The smile fell from her face as well. "Yes. I must admit the man has been very persistent, and I have had to plant my foot on the ground to convince him otherwise. Although I think he was too preoccupied with my shoes." Her laugh was a bit too forced.

Probably for his benefit. "But it doesn't sound like you convinced him. He seems dead set on the idea that he will not take no for an answer and that you will be his bride." The more he thought about it, the more he didn't like it. At all. This man was a threat to Faith, and jealousy raged through his system. "We need to do something about this." He stood up, flexing his hands at his side. He'd been pent up too long as a battle raged around him. If he could just punch this Jameson fellow, he'd probably feel better.

"I have not given him one ounce of encouragement." Her voice raised in pitch. "Not one. And neither has Clayton. So you just need to calm down."

Matthew held his hands up. "Whoa. Hold

on, Faith. I was not accusing you of anything untoward. I am just feeling warning bells go off about this man's insidious behavior. You should be concerned."

"I am not your horse, so please do not tell me to 'whoa' as if I were under your command." She made a face at him and crossed her arms over her chest. "There is nothing to be concerned about. I told him to leave and that I did not wish to see him again. Clayton physically removed the man from my home."

"I still do not like it. It is unsafe for you in Boston anymore. Especially with that man on the loose. He is unpredictable and a threat." He paced in front of her. His long legs ate up the floor.

"Quit your stomping, Matthew. Someone will hear you." Faith scolded him. Yes, scolded him.

What was going on between them? His temper flared. "Like someone will hear your raised voice? I do believe that is what we refer to as the pot calling the kettle black." Raising his eyebrows at her, he sat on the bench beside her.

She huffed.

Which made him snicker. She was entirely too adorable when she was worked up.

"You stop that laughing this instant, Matthew Weber or I will —"

The side door whooshed open and Matthew grabbed Faith and pulled her to the floor in an instant. Thankfully, his reflexes were lightning fast and her voluminous skirt muffled their landing. He put a finger to his lips. Faith's eyes were wide, but she remained silent.

Footsteps sounded for about ten paces. " 'Twas coming from in here, I tell ya."

"What did ya hear?"

"Noises. Possibly voices."

"But it is empty. There ain't nothing there, Jones."

"Don'tcha want to check it out?"

"I am checking it out. Look around ya. There is no one here."

Footsteps again.

The door closed.

Faith released her breath

Matthew put his finger over her lips this time. He then inched his way around the corner on his hands and knees. From the open aisle, he couldn't see any boots. Which was a good thing. He crawled back to her and whispered, "I think they are gone." Whoever they were, they weren't the brightest of recruits. Of lower rank. Which gave him a small sense of relief.

She sat up from her sprawled position on

the floor. Her skirt billowed around her. "Let's wait a moment just to be safe."

He nodded again, and they sat on the floor in silence.

As the minutes passed, he remembered how her lips felt against his touch. He suddenly wished he'd shushed her with his own lips rather than with his hand. A slow, small smile started to work its way onto his face — he couldn't help it.

Faith eyed him and whispered, "What is so amusing, Matthew?"

He looked at her and tilted his head. "Now wouldn't you like to know?"

She gave him a scolding look again. "I am sorry for my outburst earlier."

"I am sorry too."

"Good. You are forgiven." She got to her knees and peeked over the top of the bench. She must have been satisfied with what she saw, because she stood to her feet and brushed off her skirt.

"I am still quite concerned about this Mr. Jameson."

"That is fine. But do not forget you have your own job to do. Let me handle mine."

He looked heavenward. *Lord, she is spirited. But You know, I'm pretty sure I love her. Give me patience and wisdom. Please. I beg You.*

"What pray tell are you doing?" Hands on her hips again, she was quite the vision.

His only option was honesty. "Praying for patience."

She adjusted her lace gloves with a completely expressionless face. "Good luck with that, Matthew. My mother did it a lot. I wish you could have known her." Walking to the door, she threw over her shoulder, "She had lots of practice on me, she always said. And one more thing . . . her name was Patience. See you in two days." With a wink, she went out the other door.

Thursday, June 15, 1775
Philadelphia

The day had been exceedingly long for George. As he walked into his home away from home, the butler took his hat and handed him a letter.

George recognized the seal immediately.

Faith.

"It came from Mount Vernon, sir."

George nodded and headed into the parlor, opening the letter as he went. As he scanned Faith's missive, he jumped back to the top of the page. Almost two months ago, she'd penned this letter. A lot had happened in two months. A lot more was about to happen.

Moving directly to the desk, he pulled out paper and the inkwell. Even in his exhaustion, he knew that if he didn't write her back tonight, he might not get to it for too long a time.

He leaned back in the chair and stretched out his long legs. Being tall had its advantages, but it also had many disadvantages. Especially when a lot of sitting was involved. And there'd been a lot of that during the Congress.

Taking the time to read her letter thoroughly, George smiled at the pages. Faith could almost read his mind sometimes, even from many miles away. Their bond was like that of dearly loved siblings and George wouldn't want it any other way. He adored her.

After he read the letter through twice, the words for his response came to mind so fast, he couldn't put the quill to the paper quick enough.

June 15, 1775

Dear Little Faith,

It had been his greeting to her for so long, he couldn't imagine beginning a letter to her without it.

238

I apologize for such a long delay in writing to you, but your letter went to Mount Vernon, and I left early May to come to the Congress. It was sent on to me here, but supplies take precedence over letters, sadly.

As you may know, things have moved forward with great speed. And with that knowledge, I must insist that you leave your home. I do not believe it will be safe for you much longer. Take care of who you can, but please leave.

To address one of your other points, I believe it would be a wonderful idea to visit your family. The region is fairly stable. Reestablish those familial connections, and I feel it will bring you great joy. I know it will bring joy to them. I wrote on your behalf to a few of your relatives there when you were much younger, but it was just to let them know of your well-being. They would love to hear how you are faring, I am sure.

Family is a wonderful thing, Faith. Savor it.

To address another of your topics, I must answer: yes. I believe we are beyond the years of seeking a compromise via words and letters. War is upon us and will be for some time, I am most certain.

Which reminds me, today I was voted in unanimously as the commander-in-chief of the army. It will be a humbling and rigorous job, but I take it on for my fellow man. I would greatly appreciate your prayers during this time.

Your last topic is not at all surprising. I fancy myself a pretty good match-maker. It worked the first time, did it not? While I approve of this mutual friend, it is too dangerous of a time right now. Do not put yourself at risk. He has taken on a task that is far beyond what you and I understand. No one can know his true allegiance, and so you must stay away. Do not put yourself in harm's way or in any jeopardy of any kind. Did you read that? More than once?

Good.

Now please, let me know when you are safely out of your home. My prayers go with you, and I know yours go with me.

Martha sends her love as well. I miss you both.

George

He'd given her the facts.

Leaning back in the chair again, he contemplated all that he *hadn't* said.

Would she understand that for him to ac-

240

cept the position of commander-in-chief, he was guilty of high treason against England? In fact, everyone that had gathered for the Congress would be guilty of that charge.

If he should fail? He'd be dragged behind a horse and hung by the neck — but not until dead, just enough to weaken him. After that, they'd slice him open and burn his entrails while he was still alive. Then they'd quarter him. Not a fun way to die.

So this decision was no easy one. The cause before them had to be determined to be worth their very lives because that would be what they would give up should they fail.

Going up against the world's most formidable forces didn't seem like the smartest or most logical thing to do. But passion and purpose drove the Patriot cause. People with heart. Who longed for freedom and to be out from under the rule of Britain.

People were tired of being taxed to death so that England could repay her debts. And there was very little respect for a king that sat on a throne across the ocean and dictated rules to them.

Yes. The choice he had made was the correct one. Faith could read between the lines better than anyone he knew.

He just wished he could keep her safe

But that would have to stay in the Lord's hands.

Because George had to find a way to somehow win an impossible war.

CHAPTER 15

Sunday, June 18, 1775
Plymouth, Massachusetts

The early morning light on the dewy ground that Sunday morning made Faith feel as if all the troubles of the world could wait for just a little while longer. As she walked to the carriage, the beauty around her called her to join in glorious worship of the Creator. The morning dove's call, the fresh scent of wildflowers, and the sweet taste of honey left on her lips as she ate from the basket her family had packed for her.

Her family.

What a joyous reunion it had been. She assured them that it would not be the last and as soon as this conflict was over, she would make regular visits. She also wanted them to come visit her. But she'd invited them all to the farm in Virginia. Her parents' farm. Her legacy.

Did that mean that she thought she

wouldn't be in Boston much longer? Probably. She took another bite of the soft, homemade bread dripping with honey.

There was so much that needed to be done to help people in her town.

The women that remained had been called upon to help soldiers, feed people, mend wounds, and help provide shelter and clothing. Now there were only a few of them left. And much more work to do.

She climbed into her carriage and told the driver it was time to go back home to Boston. She was supposed to meet Matthew tonight, and she had much to tell him. If there were letters waiting at home to be coded, she'd have to hurry to get them done in time.

How she missed going to church. Things hadn't been the same since the British had occupied Boston. And while her church was still there, the atmosphere was decidedly different. Maybe one day soon, all would be right again.

The carriage lulled her as it traveled the miles back to Boston. It was a lengthy trip, a good forty miles, but her driver would make it before midnight. Sleep had been difficult once again last night as she'd thought about Matthew and the dangers surrounding him. Maybe she could just take a little nap.

A cacophony of sound woke Faith up. She rubbed her eyes and looked out the window of the carriage. People carried belongings, dragged carts and animals, and pushed children along on the side of the road. What was going on? As they slowly passed more and more people, the carriage eventually came to a halt.

The conveyance rocked, and she knew her driver had gotten down. Several minutes passed, and then there was a tap on the door.

Her driver opened it and peered in. "Ma'am, there has been a battle."

"In Boston?" Again? The thought upset her more than she wanted to admit.

"Yes, ma'am. On Bunker and Breed's Hills. The Brits have gained ground."

Oh no. A great sigh left her lips. The Colonists had held those two high points for some time. This was a severe blow.

"But the Colonists injured more than half the redcoats from what I hear, ma'am."

The news wasn't warming at all, even though she knew he meant it as an encouragement. What would happen now? Was it safe to stay in Boston?

She must. People needed her.

"Would you like to continue, ma'am."

245

"Yes, please."

"As soon as the road clears a bit, I will continue on." He closed the door and left her to watch out the window. The exodus of people made her heart sad.

It took several more hours to make it to the outskirts of her town. It only made her more anxious to see Matthew. Perhaps they could pray together over what should be done. Surely there was still hope for the many people who remained.

The carriage halted once again, and Faith leaned back. Whatever the issue was, she hoped that they would make it in time for her meeting. She'd hate for Matthew to worry over her.

Shouting came from outside.

A voice she recognized. And loathed.

Closing her eyes, she prayed he would leave.

But a banging on the carriage door interrupted her petition to God.

She composed herself and went to the door and opened it a crack. "How may I help you, Mr. Jameson?"

"It is imperative that you come with me now, Mrs. Jackson."

"I tried to tell him, ma'am." Her driver looked spent.

Jameson puffed out his chest and stepped

in front of the driver. "I will neither be interrupted nor ignored."

Faith huffed. "I do not believe you were ignored, nor were you interrupted, Mr. Jameson. Now I believe it is in your best interest to calm down."

"I am not a child, Mrs. Jackson." He held a hand up to her. "Now I insist. You must accompany me to a safer place. My coach is more comfortable than yours." His condescending smile looked pasted on — did the man not realize his odiferous behavior?

"Mr. Jameson, I will do no such thing. Now if you will excuse me."

"It is not safe — especially for a woman of your status — to be alone in the town, Faith."

"Please, I do not believe I have granted you the permission to be so familiar, *sir*."

"Come now." He looked at her as if she was a half-wit. "We both know that you and I will be married soon —"

"I know of *no* such thing, I assure you!" That was it.

"But —"

"Excuse me, Mr. Jameson. I am not finished." She slammed the carriage door open against the side. It probably did a bit of damage, but she was tired of this horrible man thinking he could tell her what to do.

247

Everything boiled within her. "We most certainly will *not* be marrying." She'd had more than enough of him and would not restrain her temper a moment longer. Her voice turned to a shriek when she was mad — which she hated — but the man had gone too far. "I *refuse* to marry you. Ever. Do you understand me? Or do I need to spell it out for you *again*! No. No means *no.*"

His face turned deep red and then darkened to a truly ugly shade of purple. "You are simply upset, Mrs. Jackson. That is all there is to this rant. When you have calmed yourself and come back to your right mind, I will call upon you again."

"You will do *no* such thing!" She stomped her foot. Who cared about propriety or manners at this point? The man was insane. Or a complete fool. "I do not wish to ever see you again, Mr. Jameson. I will never marry you. And if you dare to come to my home again against my wishes, you will see how good my aim is with a musket." She yanked the door back toward her and slammed it again — this time closed — and practically screeched through the roof, "Drive on!"

Faith was late. But with so many skirmishes

happening all over town, Matthew was giving her a little extra time to maneuver her way to him. It'd been too many days since he'd been able to see her beautiful face and lovely smile. He'd had important meetings to attend, and she'd finally gone to see her family. Which was good. A refreshment for her in this horrible time of drought and dreary.

But he feared that the news he must share tonight would be devastating for them both.

Boston was no longer safe. With the militias fighting the red-coats in several locations, and after the battle at Breed's Hill, he really had no choice. They'd have to meet for only a minute or two at most. There was too much at risk for anything else. Especially since they'd both been followed at one time or another. It had been easy to confuse the follower when circumstances were simpler. But now? The dangers were too great.

The thought just about did him in. He'd gotten so used to being able to see her. Touch her hand. Hear her laugh.

At least they'd had a little bit of time.

Soon the war would be over. At least, he prayed it would be soon.

He heard a noise behind him and turned.

It was Faith. Looking far beyond weary.

There was a bit of agitation and fear lurking in her eyes.

"What happened?" He kept his voice as low as he could.

"Anthony Jameson." She shook her head. "I do not wish to explain. 'Twas horrible."

"Did he hurt you?"

"No." She reached into her skirt and pulled out a small note and handed it to him.

He tucked it into his waistcoat. "I am sorry."

" 'Tis not your fault, but I believe I am done in from the debacle. Are you all right?"

"Yes, I am quite well."

She nodded and looked down. "My apologies, Matthew, I probably should just go home. I do not feel alert enough to do my job well, and I need to check on my staff and make sure everyone is sound."

Matthew took her hand. " 'Tis becoming too dangerous as it is, I am afraid. We should probably keep our handoffs to brief visits."

Her face fell.

"I know. And I am deeply sorry, but I fear for your safety. It is for the best." He held out a note for her. "It is nothing official. Just from me. Maybe we could correspond that way — through coded letters." In the chance he could wipe the sadness from her face, he smiled and hoped she'd say yes.

Footsteps! "Hey! Who's there?"

Matthew pulled Faith into his arms and kissed her. He wrapped his arms tight and lowered his head to keep her whole face covered. Not the way he wanted to share their first kiss.

"Nothin' but a couple of lovers sneaking around late . . ." The voices went past them and turned to mumbling.

Matthew got lost in the feel of Faith in his arms. She'd stiffened at first, but then melted against him — whether in exhaustion or passion he wasn't sure — and kissed him back. He pulled away gently and then kissed her softly one last time. Keeping her in his arms, he lifted his head an inch to look around. "They are gone."

She pulled back. Cheeks flushed, lips curved into a smile. "Thank you for your quick thinking." The mischievous sparkle in her eyes gave away more than her words.

"Thank you for your participation." He took her hand again and squeezed.

"I look forward to next time." With a swish of her skirts, she turned and slipped around the corner.

Whether she spoke of seeing him again or

of their first kiss, Matthew didn't mind.
Either way he was the winner.

CHAPTER 16

Tuesday, June 20, 1775
Boston

Looking into the long mirror in his bedroom, Anthony let out a sigh. His clothes were pristine. His hair was immaculate. He was a dashing man if he said so himself.

He lifted his chin — yes, the lines of his jaw were quite striking. His eyes? Commanding and compassionate.

If truth were to be told, he was everything that a woman would desire in a man.

What was wrong with Mrs. Jackson? Why was she ignoring him? And worse, why had she rejected him?

Turning to take in the view from the other side, he couldn't understand why she wasn't falling at his feet. He might be a tad bit thicker around the middle than he had been when he was younger, but his servants told him it was distinguished and very becoming for an older gentleman.

He looked one last time and shook his head. There was absolutely nothing wrong with him. So Mrs. Jackson must be over-wrought with stress and not thinking clearly. He'd have to fix that.

Maybe if he watched her for a few days and followed her, he could find out what it was in her life that was affecting her in such a way.

He wanted to be angry at her for speaking to him in such a manner, but the more he thought about it, the more he realized that she just needed his guidance. Once they were wed and she was under his care, she'd go back to the lovely and amiable woman that he knew.

Yes, once they were married.

But first, he needed to find out what was bothering the woman. Once he eliminated that, he could move on with his plan.

Saturday, June 24, 1775
Hingham

Night had fallen, and every muscle in Faith's body ached. From making bandages, to dressing wounds, to helping women and children escape the town without the harass-ment of the redcoats, she had done it all. But she hadn't had enough rest.

As she smoothed her hair to go meet Matthew, she sighed. Would he notice her weariness? How was he doing in all this?

Her driver brought the carriage around and she climbed inside. The smells of gunpowder hung in the air. Pretty soon, she'd have to leave Boston. She knew that. But she wanted to help as many as she could before that moment. And she wanted as much time as possible with Matthew.

That was probably selfish, but it was honest.

The kiss they'd shared last time had taken her by surprise. But it was also exciting. Passionate. And she longed to do it again.

What a scandalous thought! Hands to her cheeks, she felt the warmth that flooded her face. This was why the scripture spoke of taking a spouse rather than burning with passion, wasn't it? Did he enjoy it as much as she did? Forever grateful for his quick thinking, he'd completely covered her identity with what started out as a facade. But she knew that it had been real.

Gracious. She needed to clear her mind of these thoughts before things got out of hand. Focus is what she needed. Clarity of thought and mindfulness of her surroundings.

The carriage came to a halt. From here, she always had to walk. Her driver would leave and then pick her up in a different location. The air was thick with humidity and the stench of decay. Would their world ever be normal again?

Tonight's meeting would be back at the meetinghouse. Things had once again gotten trickier, and it might be too dangerous to slip inside, but they would at least try.

The nights of long conversations were over. But at least now, she was sure of Matthew's care for her. Anything could be endured for a little while when there was so much to look forward to.

Silence permeated the air around her. Even the wind was still.

But it was too quiet. Not a cricket. An owl. Nothing. Was it a trap of some sort? *Oh, Lord, help me to be alert. Please keep Matthew safe.*

Circling around the building, Faith looked in every direction. There was nothing to be seen. Anywhere.

And for some reason, that made her very nervous.

She headed for the side door and made her way inside the building. Waiting for her eyes to adjust to the dim interior, she paused at the entry. Then scanned the large room. The wooden benches, railings, and rafters were the only occupants. No one human was there.

The same silence that had pressed on her a few moments before was here. Why did her stomach feel uneasy? What was she missing?

With every nerve on edge, she slipped into the bench far in the corner. Was she that early? Hopefully Matthew would get here soon. The eerie feeling around her grew. Her heart picked up its pace.

The door opened and she started to smile, but then she caught a glint of red and slid to the floor as silently as she could. Footsteps echoed on the wood floor.

Her senses weren't as keen as Matthew's. She couldn't tell which direction they were headed. So she slid all the way under the bench and tried not to breathe.

The steps slowed as the floor creaked, then stopped all together.

If only she knew where the soldier was now. She took tiny huffs of air in through her nose and out through her mouth hoping that there wasn't any sound.

A chill raced up her spine in the quiet. What was he doing?

Creak!

Then another step, then two more. They sounded closer. A lot closer.

Her heart pounded in her ears Surely, the

redcoat would be able to hear it and come drag her out from under her hiding place.

A tiny squeak from behind her made her jump in the confined space. *Thump!*

The steps stopped.

No. Not now.

Skittering movement made her fear what she knew was back there. The unmistakable sounds of a mouse. She hated mice. More than spiders and snakes. She took in a slow, deep breath and closed her eyes. If she didn't see it, maybe she wouldn't do anything foolish. Like scream and make a mad dash for the door. She could do this. It was just a mouse.

Little feet tickled her backside as they ran up the outside of her skirt. Lying on her side underneath the bench, she tried to shrink away from the animal. This couldn't be happening. There was not a mouse crawling over her. There wasn't. She squeezed her eyes closed even tighter. And didn't breathe.

The larger vermin's footsteps hadn't begun again. He must have heard the noise. What could she do? She couldn't give away her location. And she definitely didn't want to wait until he found her. Maybe she could play dead.

She might die of fright right here and now

anyway if this mouse didn't hurry up and go away. Then she wouldn't have to play dead.

The prickly feeling of the critter climbing all over her almost did her in, and she couldn't hold her breath any longer.

The steps started again and she inhaled as quietly as she could.

Finally, the mouse crossed over her and she heard the tiny feet skitter in front of her. Faith opened one of her eyes just a smidge to see if it was gone.

The foul thing had to stop not more than a foot in front of her and look back.

As much as she wanted to tell it to shoo, Faith couldn't give away her hiding place. Instead she pleaded with her eyes. If it would just keep running away. Away from her at least.

Of course, the poor mouse was probably wondering why she had invaded its space.

Poor mouse, indeed. She'd lost her mind.

Ears twitching, the mouse studied her and then ran the other direction.

Faith closed her eyes and listened.

"Ahh!" The soldier's voice raised a whole octave during the shout.

Then the large vermin footsteps ran away from her. The door slammed.

Could it be? The mouse had scared the

big, bad soldier away?

She made herself count to one hundred before she moved. When she was certain the coast was clear, she began to crawl out from under the bench.

Click. Thud. If she wasn't mistaken, that was the door. Was it the same soldier or another one? At this rate, she'd have to spend the night on the floor of the meeting-house. *If* they didn't find her. What would her driver think? And where was Matthew?

She slid back into her hiding spot as quietly as she could.

Steps. Quick and light. They came toward her.

She held her breath again.

"Faith?" Matthew's voice was hushed and strained.

Relief flooded her brain, and she let out a long sigh. Finally, she could breathe normally. She crawled out from under the bench one more time. "I am over here."

"Thank God." His steps came toward her until she saw his black shoes. "Are you all right?"

"I do not know. I think so."

He reached down with his hands and lifted her up off the ground.

Wiping off her skirt, she gave him a smile. "Although I was most certain I would die

260

of fright."

"Because of the soldier?"

"No, because of the mouse that climbed over me." She sighed. "I am going to have to scour this dress when I get home. I can still feel its feet." Her body shook with a shiver. "Ew."

Matthew laughed. "So that is why I heard the soldier scream. I was afraid you had clobbered him."

"Well, I would have. Had I not been stuck under the bench having a stare down with a very fierce mouse."

"I am sure." Mirth filled his eyes. He put a hand to his chest. "But I am much relieved that you are all right. When I saw that soldier enter, I thought for sure you would be caught."

"You have so little confidence in me, Mr. Weber?" It was nice to tease him after the events of the evening. She needed her heart to regain a normal rhythm.

"I have the utmost confidence in you, milady." He bowed dramatically. Then his face turned serious. "But it is too dangerous for us to linger." He reached into his waistcoat. "This is for you."

Sad that the moment was over, Faith knew that this was how things would be. They were at war, and lives were at stake. With a nod, she took the missive and pulled one of her own along with a packet of other messages out of her pocket underneath her skirt.

"I will see you in two days." He leaned forward and kissed her on the lips. It was all too brief, but she still felt his warmth when he pulled away a few inches. "I will think of you every moment."

"And I you." Faith soaked in the features of his face. Tried to memorize every line.

"Faith?"

"Yes?"

He moved an inch closer. "I think . . . well, that is —"

A noise by the door made them both jolt and duck.

Matthew looked, waited, and then shook his head and turned back to her. "My apologies. What I was trying to say is that . . . I love you."

Her heart soared. "Oh, Matthew. I love you too."

He kissed her one more time and then rushed for the door. "I will check and then you leave first, agreed?"

After he exited, Faith reveled in the words. He loved her. *Thank You, Lord!*

Thump!

The muffled sound came from beside her. And it was definitely too big to be a mouse.

CHAPTER 17

He thought she'd never leave.

Anthony took a deep breath and released it. He'd have to hurry if he were to catch up with whomever that fellow was she'd met with. He'd seen enough to know that the man needed to be eliminated so there would be no more obstacles in his way. Faith would be his soon.

He'd paid his driver to find two men to help him follow today. Hopefully, one of them followed the tall man out. If not, Anthony would find him. He knew what he looked like now.

After exiting the meetinghouse, he found his carriage. His driver opened the door and leaned in to whisper. "One of the men is following that fellow. Do you want to follow him or Mrs. Jackson?"

"Follow him. I will deal with Mrs. Jackson in due time."

The driver closed the door, and soon the

263

carriage was in motion.

A plan began to form in his mind. He could play both sides. Either way, Faith would have to see his power and realize he wasn't playing games. He was a winner. He always won. This would be no exception.

The rocking of the carriage soon lulled him into leaning back onto the seat. No. He couldn't sleep. He needed to remain alert. Tonight, he would finish this business and get on with his life.

What seemed like hours passed. Finally, the carriage slowed. It shifted as his driver climbed down. Soon the door opened. "Sir, the man has gone into that large house over there. We almost lost him at one point, he made several circles, but the man I hired stayed with him on horseback and we doubled back with the carriage."

"Good thinking." Anthony climbed down and snuck his way up to the house. One of the windows was open — probably because of the oppressive heat. But who would be up at this hour of the night? He crept to the edge of the window and knelt underneath.

"You sent for me?" One voice spoke.

"Yes, I did. Thank you for coming so quickly." The other voice answered.

"My apologies it took so long. I was in Boston delivering your message." Ah. So that was the man who'd met with Faith.

"Quite all right, I appreciate your duty to the Crown." The man was a Loyalist? What was Faith doing fraternizing with Loyalists? He thought she was a Patriot. Or had he assumed wrong? This changed everything. As much as he disliked King George right now, the Brits *did* have the upper hand when it came to war.

"I will do whatever I can to help what I believe in."

Anthony didn't like the guy. Whoever he was.

Their voices moved away and became muffled Drat. He needed to listen. Anthony lifted his head just a bit so he could peer into the window. Instant recognition hit him. The man talking was none other than the Governor of New Jersey. William Franklin.

That confirmed it. They *were* Loyalists. He didn't need anything more than that.

It was time to confront Faith.

Sunday, June 25, 1775
Boston
The incessant banging on the door about drove her mad. Faith had sent Clayton on an errand and really didn't want to answer the door without him there. But the person

265

was persistent. Maybe it was someone who needed help. If so, she couldn't leave them outside.

Laying aside her letters and the coding, she covered it all with a blanket and went to the door. She stopped for a moment and went back to ring the bell in the parlor.

Marie and Sylvia both appeared in a matter of seconds.

"Ladies, Clayton is not here, so I just wanted to have you present as I answer the door. I'm not sure who is banging, but they don't want to give up. There may be someone we need to help, but I wanted you to be ready, just in case it is someone with foul intentions."

"Yes, ma'am." Sylvia blocked the hallway.

"Yes, ma'am." Marie went to the fireplace and grabbed the poker. "Just in case."

Faith nodded and tried to hide her smile. Her maid was smart.

The banging continued. Wasn't the person getting tired? Wouldn't their hand hurt?

She took a deep breath and unlocked the door. She opened it a few inches.

"Finally. That is the worst —" Anthony Jameson bellowed.

"Good afternoon." Faith raised her eyebrows. "The worst what?"

"Never mind." He narrowed his eyes and

pointed a finger in her face. "Mrs. Jackson, you and I must speak immediately."

She closed the door to less than a three-inch gap and put her foot behind it. "No, we do not. I think I was very clear after our last meeting."

He leaned close to her. "And I think after your meeting last night, you will want to hear what I have to say." Rancid breath washed over her.

She felt the color drain from her face. Last night? Had he followed her?

Marie and Sylvia were right behind her. She could feel their presence. What could she do? Other than allowing the foul man entrance, she couldn't think of any other choice. She'd have to find out what he knew.

Putting a mask of indifference in place, she turned to her staff. "Mr. Jameson and I will be meeting briefly in the parlor." She opened the door to give him entrance.

Jameson threw his gloves and hat at Marie. "I will require some tea and refreshment. I am famished." He waltzed past them all like he owned the place.

Faith took a deep breath and whispered to the girls, "Please get some tea and sandwiches as quickly as possible, Sylvia. Marie, I need you to stay by the door. If I call for you, come in. With the poker handy."

Sylvia nodded and ran to the kitchen. Marie narrowed her eyes and held the poker. "I will be right here if you need me."

"Thank you." Faith collected herself and went into the parlor, closing the door behind her. "Now, how can I help you, Mr. Jameson?"

"I saw you last night, Faith."

She cringed at his use of her Christian name. "I do not know what you are talking about."

"In Hingham. I followed you."

"I think you are mistaken. I was asleep in bed by eight thirty last eve. I had a dreadful headache."

"Play the part all you would like, Faith, but I know the truth. I know you went and met a Loyalist. A *Loyalist*! I have been doing some investigating today. Now what would your friend George Washington say about that? Especially since he is the new commander of the Colonists' army? Hmmm?" He smirked. "What do you have to say for yourself?"

Thankfully, she'd been working on how to mask her expressions. Something Matthew's sister had passed on from Benjamin Franklin. "I do not have anything to say. You must have followed someone else, because I was here."

"That is untrue, and you know it!" His face mottled red.

"I know nothing of the sort, Mr. Jameson." She kept her voice calm. "Perhaps you had too much to drink?"

"I say! You will not speak to me in such a manner!" He stomped toward her.

At that moment, Marie entered with the poker in her hand and quite visible. Sylvia held a tray with tea and sandwiches.

Faith nodded to the offering. "Would you like something to eat? Perhaps that will cool your foul temper."

"How dare you speak to me in such a way! I am not a child."

"As you wish." Faith turned to Sylvia. "Please take the tray to the kitchen. Marie, please stay." She kept her voice calm and smooth.

Anthony stomped toward her again. "I know what you are up to, and it is going to stop. You will marry me! Or I will report your behavior to the authorities." His spit spewed forward.

"There is nothing to report, Mr. Jameson. I am afraid you are gravely mistaken. I am but a lowly widow." She turned around and took a few steps toward Marie and raised an eyebrow. What could they do? She turned back around. "And if you will remember, I

269

told you quite emphatically at our last meeting, that I will not be marrying you."

"Oh, yes, you will."

"No, I will not." How could she get rid of this man? Panic began to creep up her throat, but she couldn't allow it to win. She couldn't. Where was Clayton? "Besides, I am leaving Boston."

"Good, it is quite unsafe here anyway. When you return, maybe you will have some sense, and we can resume plans for the wedding."

The man must have been hit in the head with a bag full of bricks. There was no other reason for him to be this crazy. Why, the man was obsessed! "There will be no wedding. I am not returning." She wasn't sure where the words came from, but as soon as they were out, she felt they would be true.

He narrowed his eyes and moved toward her. "Where are you going? I will go with you."

"You will not. And I will never tell you." Her calm voice obviously had done nothing to dissuade him. She felt her temper rising again. "You are the most bull-headed man I have ever met. You do not listen. You do not care what anyone thinks or feels except for yourself. There is no way I would ever marry you." It was her turn to stomp. And she did so without remorse. All the way to the door. "It is time for you to leave."

"No one tells me what to do!" He bellowed and lifted his chin. "We are not done."

"We are most certainly done! Get out of my house!" As unladylike as it was, she found herself feeling empowered by her screaming match with the irritating man.

At that moment, Clayton appeared and took the poker from Marie. He jabbed it in Jameson's chest. "I believe the lady requested you leave."

Anthony narrowed his eyes again and slowly made his way to the door, the poker in his chest the whole way.

Clayton shook his head. "You should have listened the first time, Mr. Jameson."

"We are not done here." Anthony looked at her. "Wait until I give your Patriot friends the news of you sneaking around and meeting Loyalists. You will have no choice but to do as I say." He sneered and turned on his heel.

Clayton slammed the door behind the odious man and locked it. "Ma'am. I am so sorry I wasn't here for this."

Faith shook her head. "It's not your fault. I was the one who sent you on an errand."

"Are you really leaving Boston, ma'am?" Sylvia stepped forward.

"No. Yes." Faith had her hands on her hips as she paced the room. "Not yet. But I believe it will be time very soon."

"What are you going to do?" Marie came and put a hand on her shoulder.

"I do not know." Who knows what Anthony would say to George or others — if he indeed went, which she wouldn't put past him — to get his way. The man was . . . well . . . *insane* was the only word she could think of. "But I know that we cannot put the cause in jeopardy. I fear I have made a grave mistake."

CHAPTER 18

Wednesday, June 28, 1775
Hingham

Faith paced inside the smelly barn. It didn't look like anyone had been in here to clean up for several days. It smelled much worse than normal too. She'd taken to having Marie pin her nose-gay much closer to her face on days they met in the barn.

But the smell was the least of her problems.

Anthony had disappeared the day after his verbal assault in her home. Clayton had checked and it seemed very likely that yes, Mr. Jameson was off to tattle on her to someone.

She was unsure of who he would go to first, but the horrible man could cause serious damage to the Patriots. If he actually knew anything. But she didn't know how to even find out because she had to deny everything. Had he actually followed her?

On top of all of that, the man seemed bound and determined to see them married. What was wrong with his mind? Had no one ever told him no?

A horse's whinny brought her attention back to the reason for why she was here. Too much time had passed. Again.

Matthew hadn't shown up on Monday, and now he didn't appear to be coming today. Did he get word that she'd been followed? Was their mission compromised now? Or had something happened to him? She had coded three messages of extreme importance for him. What should she do now?

Removing her lace gloves, Faith lifted her right hand to her mouth and chewed on her thumbnail. A nasty habit from childhood, she hadn't done it in years. George had seen to it that she shook the dreaded fidget, but tonight, her nerves were too frayed.

She took a deep breath. Logic and reasoning needed to take over. This had happened before, and Matthew had been fine. He had to be all right this time too. She would just keep coming to meet him and soon he would return and explain. If there wasn't already some kind of message awaiting her at home.

Hopefully.

But just in case he was simply — well, extremely — late, she'd wait another ten minutes or so. There wasn't anyone around. It would be fine.

It would.

But Matthew did not appear. The carriage ride home did nothing to calm her nerves. As much as she wanted to believe that Matthew was detained in some way, deep down, something didn't feel right. What could it be?

Weariness bore down on her whole body, and she felt her shoulders droop as she entered her home. A bath sounded lovely, but it was too late, and she was too tired.

She came to an abrupt halt. Three red-coated men stood in the parlor.

Her heart sank. " 'Tis awfully late to be asking for beds for your soldiers, is it not, sir?" She gave a small smile.

"You, Mrs. Jackson, are under arrest."

"Excuse me?" She narrowed her gaze at the man who'd spoken. "And you are?"

"Who I am is of no importance to you. We know that you are conspiring against the British and so you are under house arrest until the charges can be substantiated." The man lifted his chin. The two on either side of him looked a bit young, but their faces were stone.

"Exactly what have I done to conspire against the British?"

"We have testimony from a valuable source that you have been working with the Patriots. That is all I have to tell you." The man raised his eyebrows and gave her a scathing look.

"Who is this valuable source?" She was exhausted, but she didn't want to back down. Not now. Not ever. It didn't matter what they knew, she needed to distract them as long as possible so that Clayton could get the staff out of the house. He'd seen and heard it all, she was sure. The man saw everything in her house.

"He said that he knew you would ask that question. And he actually wants you to know. Mr. Jameson was very helpful. Informing us of your meeting location and names of other women he'd seen here . . . helping." He sneered at her. "Now if you cooperate, we might allow the other women to avoid the humiliation —"

"You would believe Anthony Jameson as a source?" She laughed out loud and put a hand to her mouth. Hoping the dramatics would convince the soldiers. "You must be really desperate for information." She gave the man a look that she hoped showed her confidence and lack of worry about the threat.

A flash of doubt flickered across the soldier's face, then disappeared. "It doesn't matter what I think, Mrs. Jackson. It's what the man knows and his connections with the King." He stepped closer to her, his hat under his arm. "You will remain under house arrest until further notice."

He walked to the door, and the two soldiers beside him followed. Making a quarter turn, he looked over his shoulder at her. "Get used to the redcoats, ma'am. We are everywhere. It's best you learn that now and realize there is no chance for a rebellion to gain any ground here. King George and the British *will* rise victorious."

The soldier who had spoken to her the whole time nodded and walked out the door. The other two stood guard inside her home.

"Would you not rather stand outside?" Faith quirked an eyebrow at them.

"No, ma'am." The shorter one looked at her. "We have been ordered here. There are two more at the rear. And a number of soldiers around the house, so please don't try anything stupid." He looked away and stared straight ahead. The steel in his eyes told her that he was trained. Being a soldier was his career. Even if he did look to be far too young.

What could she do now? "Very well." She walked back to the kitchen as if she didn't have a care in the world.

Clayton stood by the table. "I tried to get everyone out, ma'am. But they have soldiers everywhere." His words were a hushed whisper.

"Did you succeed in getting anyone out?" Her throat choked on the query.

He shook his head. "But I do believe we have come up with a plan."

All she could manage was a nod. " 'Twas Anthony Jameson who told them to come here and arrest me." Her hand flew to her mouth, and she started chewing on her nails again. "That man. He is the most detestable man I have ever met."

"Which makes me wonder what he is up to."

"What do you mean?"

"He told you he wondered what George Washington would think of you meeting with a Loyalist, and then he went to the British." Clayton shook his head. "The man is more dangerous than we gave him credit for. I worry for your safety."

He had a point. "But with these soldiers guarding the house so I cannot go anywhere, certainly, they wouldn't let anyone in, either?"

"We can but hope." Clayton winked. "Now, let me tell you about the plan."

Saturday, July 1, 1775
Unknown detention camp

Matthew's stomach rumbled for the millionth time. It was so raw that it felt like it rubbed up against his backbone.

He'd lost track of the days somewhere. Or even the last time he'd been given anything to eat. He remembered a small cup of water sometime yesterday. But his cracked lips begged for more.

The straw on the floor did nothing to give him comfort or ease the odor of his surroundings. The chamber pot was overflowing. The floor full of droppings from an uncountable amount of vermin. The stench of death surrounded this place.

Having no idea where he'd been brought, he attempted to sit up. He needed to take note of his surroundings, be observant, look for some way to escape.

So far, all they'd done was beat him. Ask for information. Then beat him when he refused to speak.

At this point, he was so weak he wanted to give in and beg for food. If they only knew who he really was, they wouldn't treat him this way.

But that was the problem. He couldn't tell them. Here he was: a Patriot. Captured by other Patriots while he was playing the Loyalist. But he'd been taken captive with a number of other Loyalists. Men that he'd been meeting with. Men that knew him. Recognized him. If any of them were released, Matthew's cover had to remain intact. They'd never be able to get another Patriot entrenched into the upper ranks like him.

If Matthew gave away who he really was, all would be lost.

During the last beating, he'd asked to see the senior officer. But there didn't appear to be anyone of any rank among this ragamuffin troop. He asked to get a message to General Washington. They all just laughed in his face.

Matthew was left to suffer — and possibly die — known as a Loyalist.

Not a Patriot sacrificing his life for the cause as a spy. No.

He'd chosen this course. He'd made his promise. He'd have to live with the consequences.

What would Faith think? She already probably thought him dead. If she was even still in Boston. Things had gotten bad so fast that he couldn't predict what would happen next. Would she wait for him?

Unlikely.

Especially if he was dead.

The thought made him think about the afterlife. Heaven was a better choice than the suffering going on here. If it was his time to go, he was ready. He'd given his life over to the Lord years ago. He had no regrets.

Other than Faith.

He hated hurting her.

But she wouldn't be alone.

She'd have George — her friend and guardian. And she had all her family in Plymouth now that she'd reconnected.

Plymouth. His sister would be distraught with the news of his death. But hopefully she would know his sacrifice. If he died at the hands of the Patriots because they thought him a Loyalist, someone would have to let her know the truth, wouldn't they?

Everything within his body ached. Maybe it *was* his time.

An incredible weariness overwhelmed him. It would be gracious of God to take him in his sleep. Maybe he should beg for that.

If only he could see Faith one last time . . .

CHAPTER 19

Wednesday, July 5, 1775
Outside Boston

George rode his horse down the line as he inspected his troops. They'd be attempting to take Boston back soon. These men had seen a lot of battle already. They weren't the same trained, career soldiers that the British had. But they had heart, and that is what mattered.

In the two weeks since he'd been unanimously voted in as the Commander-in-Chief of the Continental Army, he'd surveyed troops, read military stratagems, and made plans. This wasn't a war they could lose. Every single one of them had put everything on the line.

He'd been in command two whole days, and the weight on his shoulders grew heavier by the minute.

There wasn't time to prepare each militia for what George knew was coming. He'd fought for the British, after all. And had worked side by side with General Gage of the British back when they were both aides for General Braddock.

But now they were on opposite sides. And Gage had the upper hand when it came to troop readiness. It was a daunting challenge.

As George made his way back to his tent, a scuffle took place off to the side. Some overweight, fancy fellow was causing quite a ruckus. George shook his head and continued on.

"General Washington! General Washington, I *must* have a word with you." The portly man's voice squeaked on the end. "Unhand me, man! Washington, I demand to speak to you! It's about Faith."

George halted his horse. Not that anyone should demand his attention, but the man obviously had something devious up his sleeve because he knew to mention Faith. Very few knew his relationship to his ward or her Christian name. He turned his horse and rode over to the man.

Taking his time, he dismounted and stepped up to the frivolously dressed, pompous-faced man. He allowed himself a moment to size up the visitor.

Everyone around them quieted.

The stout man raised his chin.

George stood straight and tall. His frame soared more than half a foot over the man who'd made the demand. "Exactly what is it that is so urgent that you demand my attention, Mr. . . . ?"

"Jameson. The name is Jameson." He bowed. "And I am at your service."

George raised his brows. Really?

"I have come to you to speak about Faith. Mrs. Faith Jackson. I am sure you know of whom I speak?" The man looked entirely too confident.

What was his game? "I do. What of Mrs. Jackson?"

"Not so fast." The man shook a finger at him. "This discussion is delicate and should be in private. Offering some refreshment to your guest would also show some manners."

"Mr. Jameson. Might I remind you that we are at war. Do you understand what that means? Do not come in here commanding attention and then expecting high tea. I have more pressing matters at hand." He turned on his heel. "You may follow me to my quarters for a word, but I will only give you a few minutes of time. I'm sure you understand that is all I can offer."

"Well. I say!" Jameson sputtered and spewed.

George didn't look behind him to see if

the man followed. Either he did or he didn't. It was his choice. George didn't play games.

He reached his tent and walked inside. Shockingly, the portly little man kept up and huffed beside him.

"Washington, I will not insult your intelligence, nor will I waste your time."

"Good."

The man straightened his waistcoat and then clasped his hands behind his back. "I have disturbing news about Mrs. Jackson, and I am here to gain your approval for our marriage."

George shook his head. "Your what?"

"Our marriage." The man looked a bit too confident.

"Faith has told me nothing about you, nor your intentions. I find it a bit odd that you are coming to speak to me about marriage."

" 'Tis my purpose, whether you think it is odd or not, and I believe you will agree that I am most suited for her."

"I will, will I?" Who was this man? And was he crazy?

"Yes, of course. Now back to the disturbing news. I caught her meeting a Loyalist the week or so past. I knew this news would be disturbing to you, and so I confronted her. She denied it because I fear she didn't want to disappoint me, but rest assured, I knew I needed to handle this with you. I let her believe that I would take care of everything. Thus, my visit to you."

George shook his head again. What on earth was this man up to? He crossed his arms. "Exactly how are you going to 'handle this with me'?"

"Why, by securing Faith's hand in marriage." The man looked at him as if he was daft.

Were they even speaking the same language? George couldn't figure out how this man thought this all made sense. "To whom?"

Jameson rolled his eyes. "To me! Were you not listening?"

"Why would she want to marry you?"

"Because I am the best match for her and because it is what is best for her. Surely you can see that."

At this point, George wasn't sure he saw anything clearly. He lifted his hand up to his face and pinched the bridge of his nose. "I'm not sure I see that at all, Mr. Jameson."

The portly fellow stepped closer. "She was meeting a Loyalist. She has been up to all kinds of no-good in that house of hers with a bunch of gossiping women. I am telling you, the woman needs straightening out."

"I beg your pardon, sir. But Mrs. Jackson is one of the smartest women I have ever known. I doubt she needs straightening out." George crossed his arms over his chest. This man needed to leave. And fast.

"I do not think you understand what I am saying. I will be marrying Faith Jackson. You will give your permission. Or . . ."

Ah, so there was the threat. But of what? "Or you will do what, Mr. Jameson?"

"I will go to the general of the British troops and hand over the evidence I have against Mrs. Jackson. She is already under house arrest for her conspiracy against the Crown."

"House arrest? And what evidence? I thought you said you caught her meeting with a Loyalist? How is that damaging to the Crown?" George tried to follow the twisted mind in front of him. Obviously, this man thought he held some kind of power, but over what or whom, there wasn't any clear idea.

"Yes, house arrest. I went and told the general myself." Jameson seemed awfully proud of that fact.

"And you did this on purpose? To the woman you wish to marry?"

"Of course." Jameson huffed. "She needed to know who was in charge."

"Of course." George couldn't hide his sarcasm. But the man appeared oblivious.

"She was meeting with a Loyalist. I saw her with my own eyes. And I saw them exchange messages. Then I followed the man she met with." He clasped his hands behind him again. "I know you care for Faith. And you want the best for her. Well, if you do not agree to my terms, then I will have no other choice than to tell them that she is spying for both sides."

"You wouldn't dare!" George could not believe the man in front of him. "You dare to come in here and tell me that you are the best thing for Faith and then if you do not get your way, you are going to turn her in as a spy . . . to both sides? Do you want to get her killed?"

The man crept closer. "I believe the question is, do you want to get her killed." He sneered and showed his white teeth.

But the nasty breath of the man made George want to vomit all over his guest. Not taking an eye from Jameson, he shouted, "Thomas, Edwards!"

Two of his best soldiers ran into his tent. "Yes, sir?"

"Arrest this man for duplicity!"

The soldiers yanked Jameson by the arms and started to drag him away.

288

"Wha— what?" Anthony Jameson looked around him. "You cannot arrest me! I know the King! I will have your head for this, Washington! What do you think you are doing?"

George walked up to him, and the soldiers stopped dragging the poor man, but he hung from their arms. "You, my good sir, have no honor. How dare you threaten a poor woman and have her arrested for doing good? You say you care for the woman, yet if she doesn't do what you wish, then you punish her?

"You are not a man. You are a monster. You do not care who you side with as long as you get your way. Well, in my book, guess what that is? Treason. And you, sir, are guilty. You know what the King does to those who commit treason. Well, here in the Colonies, it is much worse." He straightened to his full height. "But now that I think about it, maybe King George would like to know what his 'friend' is up to."

He nodded to Thomas and Edwards. "Take him away and make sure he has two men guarding him at all times. No food or water. Let's give him a couple of days to think about this, and then I will deal with him personally." He didn't care if he sounded harsh. He couldn't believe the brashness of the man!

"Washington! You cannot do this! How dare you!" The man blustered as the soldiers dragged him away.

George turned back to his quarters. In the distance, he heard the man cry out in a very pathetic-sounding wail.

Good. Let him suffer. What on earth had the man put Faith through?

He rubbed his forehead. Now he had to find Faith and make sure she was all right. But how? He was in the middle of a war. How did he even know that Jameson told the truth? Was it all a ruse to use blackmail against him?

Knowing Faith, if she had indeed been put under house arrest, she'd already escaped anyway. But if Jameson had told the Brits she was a spy, then she could be in grave danger.

Thursday, July 6, 1775
Boston

With her knitting in her lap, Faith listened closely to the guards at the door. Not more than a half hour had passed since she'd given them the wonderful cookies Sylvia had made.

Cookies laced with some herb root that caused abdominal distress.

The woman was a genius. Ever so thankful that she had such people in her employ, Faith smiled to herself. Their plan had been brilliant.

All this time, Faith had been the gracious hostess and fed all the guards from her sumptuous kitchen. Sylvia prepared the very best of everything they had to impress the guards. It worked so well that the soldiers began to fight over who would run to the market to get her supplies, and if they didn't have it all, they'd go to the British to get what they could out of their supplies.

They'd earned the trust — at least the hunger-trust — of the guards. Faith hadn't tried anything sneaky. She had done nothing but mundane, lady-of-the-house things. Knitting. Sewing. Mending. Overseeing the staff. Reading books. And reading her Bible aloud. Just in case the soldiers needed reminders from the Good Book. Oh, she always chose scripture that would apply to them. Verses about oppression, widows and orphans, taking care of the needy. She'd found all kinds of passages to read to them. That had been the fun part.

Hopefully it all looked normal to the guards. But to her it was far from it. She'd developed the mundane skills expected of women in carrying out their duties, but she'd always used them for a bigger purpose. Like the Patriot cause. Not that sewing and knitting weren't useful employ and honoring to the good Lord above in their normal capacity. But Faith wasn't normal. Hadn't followed normal patterns for most of her life.

Now that the guards had been lulled into a false sense of security, she and the staff put their plan into action. Sylvia made her cookies. They fed them to all the guards before bedtime. Soon — prayerfully very soon — those same guards would have some sort of symptoms.

A groan from the foyer reached her ears. Then another.

Laying her knitting back in her sewing basket, she went to play the gracious hostess. "Is there anything wrong?"

Both guards groaned.

One was crouched near the floor.

"What did you give us?" The one still able to stand narrowed his eyes. He looked quite green.

Clayton snuck up behind them, a candlestick in each hand.

"I didn't give you anything. Why would you think such a thing?" She reached out and patted the soldier's hand. "Is there anything I can do?"

Now both soldiers were close to the floor.

Clayton stepped closer and clobbered each of them over the head with his make-shift weapons.

The guards crumpled the rest of the way to the floor.

Faith didn't waste any time. She ran up to her room and grabbed her two carpetbags.

Racing back down to the foyer, she saw her staff gathered at the bottom of the stairs. "Is this everyone?"

"Yes, ma'am." Clayton held a bag as well. "The guards have been tied up. Two in front, two in the rear, and four outside. The wagons are full."

Faith nodded. "Good job, everyone. Thank you so much. Now somehow we have to make our way out of town without being seen. Most of you will have to hide in the back of one of the wagons, and we will lay blankets over you. We have several women and children we're trying to get to safety, so I need everyone to work together and protect each other."

Nods made a wave around the room.

"It will take us many days to get to where we are going. But we can't stay here. The battles are happening all around us now, and it won't be safe for us any longer."

She pulled out her Bible. "I'd like to read

a short passage before we begin our journey. It's from the book of Second Samuel, chapter twenty-two." She flipped to the page she'd marked earlier that morning and began to read:

"The Lord liveth; and blessed be my rock; and exalted be the God of the rock of my salvation. It is God that avengeth me, and that bringeth down the people under me. And that bringeth me forth from mine enemies: thou also hast lifted me up on high above them that rose up against me: thou hast delivered me from the violent man. Therefore I will give thanks unto thee, O Lord, among the heathen, and I will sing praises unto thy name."

Clayton nodded. "Amen."

Several others breathed soft *amen*s as well.

"Let's load up the wagons." Faith picked up her bags again and led everyone out the back door.

Marie touched her elbow. "Ma'am. Once we're in the wagons, do you think we could pray?"

"Of course. That's a wonderful idea. I'm sorry I didn't offer it myself." As her gaze went to all the people piled into the wagons, she noted the fear and hesitancy on their faces. Many of them had never been outside Boston. With the war and everything else, this was quite a challenging experience.

"Could we recite the Lord's Prayer, ma'am?" Marie bit her lip.

"Yes, Marie. Thank you for the suggestion."

Faith climbed up in to the front wagon with Clayton. She was responsible for all these people, and she wouldn't hide. If they came upon danger, she would meet it head-on. "Let us pray."

With heads bowed, their little group began the whispered prayer.

"Our Father which art in heaven, hallowed be thy name. Thy kingdom come, thy will be done in earth, as it is in heaven."

Faith looked around and her eyes swelled with tears. *Lord, protect us, please.*

"Give us this day our daily bread. And forgive us our debts, as we forgive our debtors. And lead us not into temptation, but deliver us from evil: For thine is the kingdom, and the power, and the glory, for ever. Amen." A hush fell over the group.

Faith nodded. "We are in God's hands." She faced forward, and Clayton lifted the reins. The horses moved ahead.

Would they make it out of Boston? She wasn't sure. And Virginia was such a long way off. The thought of the journey worried her, but they'd brought plenty of provisions. And she had lots of gold and silver coin sewn into the hem of her dress. So did Sylvia, Marie, and several of the others.

God would go before them.

Of this she was certain.

As Clayton steered them to the outskirts of town, they stayed hushed in the wagons. Faith had time to let her thoughts go to Matthew. There had been no word from him, but how could there be when she and her household had been under the watchful eyes of guards every hour of the day.

Her heart ached for him. Prayerfully he knew that she was all right.

As soon as they reached Virginia, she would find out how to get word to him. George would have to know.

But for now, she had to get all these people to safety.

Her butler broke the silence. "You are concerned about Mr. Weber, are you not?"

Faith turned to Clayton. "Yes. How did you know?"

"I know everything, ma'am. 'Tis my job, remember?" His voice sounded weary.

She gave him a little smile. "Well, do you know anything of him?"

"No." he shook his head. "Sadly, all

anyone knows is that he disappeared. But as soon as we get to our destination, rest assured, I will help you find him."

"Thank you." Her heart plummeted. Disappeared? No one knew where he was? She wanted to cry but couldn't allow the emotions to take over.

Oh, Matthew. Where are you?

CHAPTER 20

July 8, 1775
Unknown detention camp
The walls closed in on him again. No matter how hard he tried, he couldn't keep them from moving. Matthew prayed for relief, but none had come so far.

Oh, Father . . . how long do I have to wait?

As his mind played the horrible tricks on him again, he closed his eyes. Sleep came a lot lately. Weak, beaten, and half-starved to death, it was no wonder. And it was the only relief he had. At least in sleep, he could dream of Faith. Could hear her voice. Feel her touch. Sleep was welcome.

But today it wouldn't come.

Footsteps sounded outside his cell. "Hey you. Weber." The man flung a tin plate toward him. "Eat." He set a tin cup on the ground, and in his haste, the liquid sloshed over the edge.

Matthew crawled to it as fast as he could.

His hands shook as he reached for the food. The bread was hard as a rock, but the water at least quenched his thirst.

He only managed a few bites of bread before a lump formed in his throat, so he stuffed the rest of the bread into his coat pocket.

The Lord above saw fit to keep him alive. As far as Matthew could tell, this little group of soldiers was keeping prisoners for the Patriots to trade or negotiate or kill. He wasn't sure. But they weren't anywhere near any other encampments. There were no officers that Matthew could plead his case to in secret. And he was in too deep. The other prisoners had already told all they knew. Which meant Matthew was implicated as a Loyalist.

The only thing for him to do was pray. And try to stay alive as long as he could.

Wednesday, July 12, 1775
Somewhere between Boston and Virginia
Faith felt the wagon roll to a stop and she took a deep breath. She wiped the sleep from her eyes and sat up. Far above, the stars winked at her — peeking through the thin clouds as they skimmed past. Was Matthew looking at those same stars?

She hoped so. With every fiber of her being.

Clayton climbed down from the wagon and she followed suit. Most everyone else was still asleep. But she and Clayton took turns driving the lead wagon. They'd each sleep for a while, drive for a while, let the horses rest and eat, and then they'd start again. She'd paid for new horses three times already. And soon would probably need to again. The price was steep since horses were in high demand for the war, but she had the money. And she needed to get these people to a safe place.

Virginia was a lot farther away than she remembered. But she'd always come via hired carriages.

When they had to travel so slow and with so many people, the trip lengthened.

She followed Clayton to a stream and washed her face.

"I have been thinking, ma'am."

"That is always a good thing."

Her butler chuckled. "Yes, I suppose it is." He shook his head. "But what I was thinking is that you have enough men to help you. I could purchase a horse and ride back to see what I could find out about your Mr. Weber."

"Oh, Clayton." Her heart thrilled at the

thought of being able to do something for the man she'd come to love. "Would you? That is a lot for me to ask of you. It's such a long journey, and you are worn out. But let me pay for the horse."

"I will gladly do what I can, ma'am." Clayton stood and looked back to their little entourage. "I am hesitant to leave you, but I know you will be in good hands. Besides, we seem to be past most of the danger."

"I appreciate all you have done for me these many years, my friend. Thank you."

"You will see me soon. I promise." He put his hat back on his head. "Well, if you do not mind, I will go find a horse and start my journey. I might even make it back to your farm before you do."

"Let me pack provisions for you."

The hours trudged by as Faith drove her wagon. Clayton had left in a rush of horse's hooves, and she prayed that he would succeed in finding Matthew.

But what if he found that Matthew was no longer alive? What would she do?

The Lord was her rock. He was her salvation. She wouldn't be afraid. Just like the scripture said.

A sob choked her. Her mind and her heart were at battle. She knew the Lord would sustain her, but her heart . . .

She didn't know if her heart could take the blow of losing Matthew. Hadn't she lost enough? The more she thought about him, the more she realized how much she loved him.

All the months of meeting in secret. Passing messages back and forth. They'd shared their hearts in little moments of quiet.

He'd cared for her. She knew that. Even said he loved her.

Straightening her shoulders, she lifted her chin. Exhaustion had worn her down. She wouldn't allow doubt and worry to overcome her. She wouldn't.

Clayton would search until he discovered Matthew.

No matter the news, she had to know.

Thursday, July 13, 1775
Unknown detention camp

Matthew rolled over onto his side. His mind wasn't clear anymore. Sometimes he heard someone in the cell with him, talking to him. Then other times his delusions took him to a faraway place.

Dysentery had set in to all the prisoners. They were weak, and they stunk.

The smell alone in the little makeshift prison building was enough to make the guards gag. They didn't come often, and when they did, they exited in haste.

At least he was being fed. That was something to be thankful for. It wasn't much, but at least it sustained him. The others had stopped talking a few days ago. It became very lonely, but the sounds of sickness at least alerted Matthew that the other men were alive. For now.

Each day, he tried to quote a verse from the Bible, but his mind had become so muddled that he couldn't string words together in a coherent manner anymore.

The dreams that came to him in the night were another form of torture. Everything just out of his reach. No hope of escape.

How long were they going to be held here? Until one side or the other won the war? That didn't give him much hope.

The soldier who had attacked him when the Patriots ambushed them had taken the missives Matthew had carried. Had they been trying to decode them all this time? Would they realize that he wasn't a Loyalist?

He gripped the sides of his head with his hands. The thoughts plagued him day and night and became a new form of torture. If only he'd told them the truth when they'd first captured him.

If only George or Ben knew where he was.

If only he could see Faith . . . just one more time.

Tuesday, July 18, 1775
Fredericksburg, Virginia

The sun crept over the eastern horizon as Faith urged her horses on. She was on her land. The farm would come into view soon, and they all would have some relief. A bath sounded beyond lovely. And a soft bed. Where she could sleep for hours — possibly even days.

The weariness that overwhelmed her was more intense than anything else she'd ever experienced.

They'd suffered tragedy along the way. One of the Miller children had taken ill and died. Then an axle had broken on one of the wagons.

It truly was a miracle that they were even here.

They'd all woken before three in the morning since Faith had told them last night that they were almost there.

As light streaked across the sky above them, she heard some of the children singing in the wagon behind her. What a joyful sound. It lifted her spirit.

The horses pulled and crested the hill

they'd been climbing. Before her, Faith could see the whole farm. The pond that she'd victoriously crossed with her own band of "soldiers" sparkled in the morning light. It looked like diamonds.

Her heart lifted with the thought of being home. Home where her parents had created an atmosphere of love and caring. Home where she always thought she'd want to raise her own family.

Tears pricked her eyes. Prayerfully, that would still be possible.

Prayerfully, Matthew was still alive.

Prayerfully, they would all survive this war.

Little Betsy climbed over the back of the bench from the wagon. "Mrs. Jackson, is that your farm?" Her chubby finger pointed.

Faith couldn't help but smile at the sweet child. "It sure is."

"That means we really are almost there. Not 'almost there' but it's days away like Mama has been saying."

Laughter bubbled up. "Yes, Betsy."

"Good. 'Cause my feet hurt from when we walk. And my back side hurts from when we sit." Her little face scrunched up in the cutest expression.

"You will love it here. Lots of room to run around."

"Good. I'm fast at runnin' around."

"I bet you are."

"You didn't do the Bible readin' today yet, did ya?" Betsy pointed to the book on the bench. "I was asleep."

"Nope, not today." She nodded toward the book. "Do you want to read?"

"Can I?" The child's eyes grew wide.

"Of course. We were on Psalm twenty-four." Faith looked down at the young girl. "Do you know how to find it?"

"I do! Papa taught me a *long* time ago."

"That's wonderful. Let me know if you need any help."

"Uh-huh." The little girl's tongue hung out a bit as she turned the pages. She looked so serious. "Found it!"

"Oh good. So what does it say?"

" 'The' " — Betsy's pudgy index finger slid underneath the next word — " 'earth — is — the . . .' "

The pause stretched. "That's very good, Betsy."

" 'The earth is the Lord's.' " The little girl clapped her hands, and the heavy book slid off her lap and onto the floor beneath her feet. "Oh, Mrs. Jackson, I'm so sorry!"

"It's all right. Just pick it up, and we will keep going."

Mary — Betsy's older sister — leaned over

the seat. "Would you like me to help you, Betsy?"

Tears perched on the little girl's lashes as she nodded. "I'm so, so sorry I dropped your Bible. Papa said we should never drop God's Word 'cause it's the most important book ever."

Faith adored the sweet child. "Your papa is right. But I'm not upset with you, Betsy, and it looks like my Bible is fine." She looked to Mary. "Would you like to continue reading? Betsy can learn by pointing to the words as you read them."

The sweet smile that came from the quiet, older sister warmed Faith's heart. The far-too-thin young lady read over Betsy's shoulder as her younger sister pointed to the words:

"The earth is the Lord's, and the fulness thereof; the world, and they that dwell therein. For he hath founded it upon the seas, and established it upon the floods. Who shall ascend into the hill of the Lord? or who shall stand in his holy place? He that hath clean hands, and a pure heart; who hath not lifted up his soul unto vanity, nor sworn deceitfully. He shall receive the blessing from the Lord, and righteousness from the God of his salvation. This is the generation of them that seek him, that seek thy face, O Jacob. Selah.

"Lift up your heads, O ye gates; and be ye lift up, ye everlasting doors; and the King of glory shall come in. Who is this King of glory? The Lord strong and mighty, the Lord mighty in battle. Lift up your heads, O ye gates; even lift them up, ye everlasting doors; and the King of glory shall come in. Who is this King of glory? The Lord of hosts, he is the King of glory. Selah."

Betsy looked up at Faith with her finger still on the page. "Mrs. Jackson? I don't think I understood what that meant."

"You know, Betsy, I've been reading that book my whole life, and I still don't understand everything, but I keep reading it and keep learning." Faith smiled.

Mary patted Betsy's shoulder. "It sounds like a song. See?" The older girl put a melody to a couple lines of the text and sang it. Then she shrugged her shoulders. "Seems pretty simple to me. The earth is God's, and He is the King of glory."

Out of the mouths of children. Simple and yet true.

The wagon rolled into the side yard of the estate. Faith pulled the team to a stop and set the brake. "Well, girls, I believe we are here."

They cheered and woke up the rest of wagon. People stretched and climbed down. Their journey had come to an end.

Thank You, Lord.

Faith picked up her Bible and two bags and headed for the house.

Mr. Harrison — her trusted steward for her parents' estate — walked out to greet her. "Welcome home, ma'am." He bowed. "Mr. Clayton arrived in the middle of the night and has urgent news for you. I told him I would wake him as soon as you rode in."

Her heart thudded inside her chest. The news had to be of Matthew.

CHAPTER 21

Faith paced the large study in her parents'
home waiting for Clayton to come down.
The staff was seeing to the needs of the rest
of the people, making sure everyone had a
place to sleep, and putting away the remaining provisions they'd brought with them on
the journey. Normally, she'd want to oversee
it all, but at this moment, the only thing she
wanted to do was hear Clayton's news.

Her beloved butler came into the room,
and she went to his side.

"Please tell me he is alive?" She bit her
lip.

Clayton nodded. "Yes, ma'am. He is
indeed alive. As far as I know. But he is a
prisoner."

She gasped and put her hand to her
mouth. "The British found out he's a spy?
Where is he being held?"

This time, he shook his head. "I am afraid
it's complicated, ma'am. He's being held by

the Patriots. As a *Loyalist* spy."

"What?" He wasn't spying for the Loyalists.

"While meeting with Loyalists, he was captured by a small band of soldiers. They have been holding them, beating them, and trying to get any information they can out of them. But the men are all weak, sick, and I am afraid it is quite grim."

The news took her aback. "But we just need to get word to them that he is a Patriot. Right?"

"I do not think it is as simple as that, ma'am. The soldiers who captured these men have been trying to get those in charge to come deal with it and tell them what to do. But there has been a bit too much confusion and they have been told to just hold them as prisoners. Since their captors haven't gained any significant information to share, the others have been too busy fighting the war to know what is going on in that tiny camp."

"That is ridiculous! I must get a message to George." She stomped over to the desk.

Clayton followed her. "Ma'am. General Washington is in the middle of a war."

"Well, someone has to do something. They cannot just leave Matthew there."

"I agree, but I could not find any senior

officer who could help me. That is why I came home to bring you the news." He sighed, lines etching his face. "War is ugly business, Mrs. Jackson. The Continental Army needs every man they can get, and they are doing all right holding their own for the moment. I just don't think they are completely organized. Whoever commanded this small band of soldiers obviously forgot about them. They have been in the same place for over a month, and it is pretty foul."

"What about Benjamin Franklin! He knows Matthew well. Maybe I can get in touch with him?"

"Hmmm . . . Franklin is in Philadelphia, so that might be helpful. Matthew is being held in a remote location in New Jersey."

"New Jersey? I don't think I've ever been there."

"It's not too far from Philadelphia. Much closer to us than Boston."

"What do you think he was doing in New Jersey?" The puzzle didn't make sense to her.

"Apparently, the man the Patriots wanted to nab was with the Royal Governor of New Jersey. Who just happens to be Benjamin Franklin's son. They'd heard that he had been gathering secrets from the Patriots and wanted to know how. They just missed the governor and his aides, but they took all the others."

A horrible thought crashed into her brain. Matthew knew a lot of secrets of the Patriots. And she brought him message after message . . .

He couldn't be the man they were looking for, could he?

Matthew couldn't be giving secrets to the Loyalists. No. It couldn't be. The governor had to be getting his information from somewhere else. It was all just a coincidence. She simply needed sleep. How could she ever suspect the man she loved?

"What is troubling you, ma'am?"

Clayton's words made her look up. She tried to wipe her face of expression. "Oh, nothing. Just trying to figure out how to get there."

"You are not thinking of going, are you?"

"Of course." She went to the stairs. "Do you think you can get me a uniform?"

Marie assisted Faith with the alterations to her new outfit up in her room. The lovely bedchamber had been part of the section that George rebuilt after her parents' death. She didn't have any memories up here from before her mother and father died. But she'd love to have memories here with a

313

family. *Her* family. Prayerfully, one day.

That's why she was doing what she was doing. Exhausted as she was, she had new determination to spur her on.

She had to save Matthew.

"I think it's ready, ma'am." Marie held up the garment.

"It's perfect. Thank you, Marie."

"Are you certain this is safe?"

"Of course not." Faith shook her head. "But who else can do it?"

"I will finish packing your things, then." Her maid gave Faith the look that showed she clearly disapproved but would do her duties nonetheless.

Marie would just have to get in line with Clayton. He certainly didn't approve. But neither of them could stop her.

Before she could make the journey, she needed to write George a letter. Let him know what she was about. Just in case. He wouldn't be pleased, but he was the least of her worries right now.

First, she needed a plan. How could she rescue Matthew? She couldn't just traipse in there and demand his release. Second, she needed some rest before she rode all the way to Philadelphia. By herself. Something she'd never done before. Third, she needed to figure out how she would change her clothes without a maid. That might prove difficult. Maybe she'd just wear the same thing every day until she saved him. That would be the easiest. She might not smell the greatest by the time she got there, but she didn't care about that.

She sat down at her desk. "Marie?"

Her maid came to her side. "Ma'am?"

"How long will it take you to finish packing?"

"Not long, ma'am. Maybe fifteen more minutes."

"Good. That will give me time to write a letter, and then I am going to lie down and rest before I start the journey. Please make sure I am not disturbed unless it is urgent."

"Of course, ma'am."

Faith put her elbow on the desk and leaned her forehead on it. How on earth would she tell George?

Wednesday, July 19, 1775
Continental Army Camp

The troops in front of him were getting better. George was pleased with their progress but had them in training numerous times a day when they weren't marching toward the next battle. He'd worked with many different battle groups now as he'd traveled New England, surveying what made up his Con-

315

tinental Army.

Still amazed at all they'd accomplished, he thanked the good Lord each day for His provision.

He'd gotten word from one of his aides that Faith had indeed escaped the house arrest in Boston. Assuming she went to Virginia, he thought she should be there by now. Unless she went to Mount Vernon. It was closer. He'd have to send a letter to Martha and check. If Faith hadn't gone to Mount Vernon, then maybe she could check on her at the farm in Virginia.

He shook his head and smiled. Of course Faith had escaped the British soldiers. He'd expected nothing less. But his heart still worried after her. For years, he'd thought of her like a little sister, but as he got older, he was beginning to feel much more parental.

Matthew better take good care of her. The man was a good choice for her, of that he had no doubt, but everything was so unstable right now. There wasn't much of a chance for romance when he was a spy within the Loyalists.

Clark — his aide — rode up next to him. "Sir, I have an urgent message for you." He held out a folded paper.

Washington nodded and took the note. He opened it and read the contents.

His heart dropped. Poor Faith.

But maybe she didn't know?

Matthew had been captured by the Patriots as a Loyalist spy. George would have to get word to the encampment immediately so that Matthew could be released.

If he was still alive.

George quirked an eyebrow as he thought it all through. If she didn't know, then perhaps George could save the day without her ever having to know.

Another scan of the note urged him to his quarters.

Prayerfully, Matthew was still alive.

CHAPTER 22

The sun wasn't up yet, but Faith had been
awake for over an hour. She was ready to
go. Marie had helped her to dress and send
word to the groomer to ready her horse.
She'd carry only what she needed in her
bedroll on the animal's back.

It was up to her to save Matthew, and she
would do it. Even if she died trying.

As she walked down the stairs, she knew
Clayton would try to talk her out of it, but
rather than sneak away to avoid him, she'd
remind him that she was the mistress of this
house and that she could handle herself.

She'd been in tough scrapes before.

When she reached the foyer, she heard a
gasp and knew it was her devoted butler.
"Ma'am. I see you are ready to go."

Faith cringed and closed her eyes to turn
and face him. But when she opened them,

318

she had to blink several times. Clayton was a mirror image of herself.

His blue breeches, gold waistcoat, and blue coat all matched hers perfectly.

She put her hands on her hips. "Clayton! What are you about?"

He bowed and smirked at her. "Well, since I was getting one uniform, I figured I could get two. . . ."

"Or perhaps three." Marie's voice echoed from the top of the stairs. And down strode her maid. Dressed in the same livery as Faith and Clayton. The velvet coats were trimmed in gold embroidery at the wrists.

They really were quite stunning liveries, but why did all three of them need them? Faith pinched the bridge of her nose. "Marie, why are you dressed like that?"

Her maid walked up to her with confidence.

Faith understood the walk. There was something quite freeing about wearing men's breeches. Not that she would ever say that aloud. But she definitely felt like she could conquer the world without the skirts and petticoats in her way.

Marie lifted her chin a bit. "There's a very good explanation why I'm dressed this way. You need someone to help you with your clothes on the trip. As you know — excuse

me Clayton for the delicate conversation —
it isn't easy to hide your feminine virtues in
men's clothes. Simple as that. I refuse to allow you to go alone."

Faith couldn't argue with her on that
point. The wrapping they'd had to do of her
chest before Marie put on Faith's stays was
quite the chore and Faith was quite sure
she wouldn't survive wearing them around
the clock. Honesty had always been her
policy, and poor Clayton had seen and
heard much in his years of service to her.
She found she didn't even mind the turn of
conversation in front of him. Raising her
eyebrows, she turned to her butler. "You
knew my reasoning. I couldn't go traipsing
around soldier encampments dressed as a
woman asking about prisoners. They
wouldn't have told me a thing. But what
exactly is your excuse?"

"I promised General Washington I would
do something, and I plan to keep my promise."

George. She should have known. And a
very vague answer. "You promised him . . .
something?"

"Yes, ma'am. And I will not tell you what
that something is."

Of course he wouldn't. The man knew
every secret there was to know it seemed.

Faith didn't have time to argue. "I didn't pack provisions for you."

"We did."

The two answered in unison.

"All right then, let us be on our way. Matthew needs our help."

Friday, July 21, 1775
New Jersey

Matthew could taste the fear of the other prisoners. They'd been sick so long that they were weak and confused. Just like he had been.

Collins had died. Just this morning. And the other two men were much younger. They didn't have as much experience and had worn down over time. They cried at night and whimpered during the day. The nighttime was so much worse.

The only thing that had saved Matthew thus far was when he stopped drinking the water they brought him in the cup. One day he'd been so delirious, he thought he saw something in the cup and it tasted horrid. So he threw it up against the wall.

What he saw in the next morning's light made him lose what little contents he had in his stomach.

From that moment on, he emptied the cup and wiped it out with his shirt. Then he prayed for rain. He rigged up his jacket under the hole in the ceiling. When the Lord sent rain, he drank his fill and more. But only from the sky. If there wasn't rain, Matthew didn't drink.

Thankfully, it had rained a lot this summer.

And the past few days, he'd begun to regain his strength. Not a lot, but he wasn't sick all the time. Which helped.

As darkness closed in around him once again, he prayed. Something he'd done a lot more of while he was a prisoner. He found such peace in doing it, and it also kept his mind off the horrific cries of the other prisoners.

If only he could figure out a way to escape. But the lock on the bars was solid. He'd tried it more times than he could count.

Closing his eyes, he thought of Faith. What he wouldn't give to see her again.

As sleep began to claim him, he thought he heard someone humming. It was actually quite a lovely tune. This would be a nice change to fall asleep peacefully.

Faith. He tried to focus on the last time he'd seen her. Her beautiful smile.

Thunk! "Ow!" Something had hit him in the head. He sat up in the straw. Just as something else pelted him from above. Matthew looked up.

"Yoo-hoo." The ugliest woman he'd ever seen waved at him from the hole in the ceiling. Then something was lowered on a string.

When it reached Matthew, he realized it was the key. Scrambling to the door, he whispered a quiet "thank you" to the old hag and unlocked the bars. Within seconds, he was outside running for all he was worth. Which wasn't much more than a fast walk, he was so weak. He reached the edge of the woods and kept going into the thick forest. After a minute, he was too winded to go on, and he stopped to breathe in the fresh air. His first fresh air in weeks.

"You ungrateful boy." Someone came toward him.

Wait a minute. He recognized that voice. Matthew turned. "Ben!"

Franklin reached him and nodded, limping along.

Matthew rubbed his eyes. "Are you wearing . . . a dress?"

The old man chuckled. "I certainly am. And it worked too." Then he grabbed at his skirts, lifted them, and took off at a fast pace past him. "Come on. Let us get you out of here."

Matthew had no choice but to follow. "I

thought you were the ugliest old hag I had ever seen." He chuckled and half walked, half stumbled through the undergrowth.

"I shall take that as a compliment." For an old man in a dress, he was surprisingly agile.

They reached a river. A really wide river. "What is your plan, Ben? I am weak and haven't had a decent meal in more than a month."

"This is where we swim." Ben's voice was a bit muffled as he tugged the dress over his head, leaving him in his underclothes.

"I do not think I have the energy to swim, my friend. Go on without me." Matthew collapsed in the grass at the bank of the river. The escape had taken its toll on him, and he didn't feel like he could move.

"Oh no, you are not giving up on me now. I did not come all this way to rescue you to have you give up on me. You do not have to swim. I am an excellent swimmer and will help you across." Ben rubbed his hands together and then stretched his arms above his head. "It's not that far, and the river is slow moving."

"But —" He wanted to say, *"You're old,"* but he didn't think that would go over too well. The man had gotten him out of a locked cell. Dressed as a woman no less.

"Trust me."

Matthew nodded.

"Lie on your back and float. You need only to kick your feet a bit to help move you along."

It made absolutely no sense to him, but Matthew obeyed. The water was cold, but it soothed his weary, bruised body. Ben gripped his arm and literally dragged him across the river. While Matthew had always thought of him as a stout — even paunchy — little man, Benjamin Franklin was quite athletic and strong.

Within minutes, Matthew crawled up on the other side of the river, feeling cleaner than he had in weeks. "Thank you, Ben."

His mentor and friend looked down at him. "You are most welcome, my boy. I couldn't very well allow you to shrivel up and die in prison, now could I?"

A small laugh escaped his lips. The fresh air smelled sweet. "I *am* quite shriveled up, but thankfully not dead. It will probably take a good deal of time to build up my strength."

"General Washington was quite concerned for you, as I am sure Faith is as well."

Faith. He'd despaired of never seeing her again and putting her through such sorrow. The war was just beginning, and the horror it already brought was devastating.

"Have you told her yet?"

Matthew turned to Ben. "Told her what?"

"That you love her?"

The thought brought a smile to his face as he watched the clouds float in the sky above. "Yes, I have. I asked her to wait for me."

Ben jumped to his feet, his long shirt dripping from their swim. "Wait for you? Are you daft?"

Matthew pulled enough energy together to sit up. "I did not think it would be very kind to ask her to marry me in the middle of a war."

His friend smacked his palm against his forehead. "You are quite addled, I fear. When you see her again, my suggestion is that you do not wait one more moment. Marry the girl." Ben's features softened. "Time is short, my dear boy. Shorter than you can imagine. Why, look at what you just went through. I am most certain that you feared you would not survive, and in fact probably prayed for Almighty God to take you from this life."

The words were truth. Matthew nodded.

"If you love her, marry her. Do not let the circumstances of war stand in the way." He pointed a finger in Matthew's face and nodded. Placing his hands on his hips, he scanned the horizon. "Now if I can just remember where I hid my breeches, we can journey on and find some food for you, then get you back to Faith where you belong."

CHAPTER 23

Wednesday, July 26, 1775
New Jersey

"This is the place where Matthew is being held," Clayton whispered.

Faith nodded. It had been grueling to get here. She was tired and dirty and hungry. Their ruse had worked so far, and no one thought a thing about three gentleman riding off to aid the Continental Army. They'd asked lots of questions about soldier camps, where to find the officers in charge, etc. But today was the day. It was time to rescue Matthew.

"I still think we should have gone to see Mr. Franklin and get his help." Marie crossed her arms over her chest. "I am just a maid. I have no knowledge or experience for this sort of thing." For the first time on the trip, the girl sounded a bit frightened.

"We ran out of time. It would have taken us more time to get there and back." Faith

328

put a hand on her maid's shoulder. "Why don't you stay here — hidden in the trees — and wait for Clayton and me to return?"

Marie nodded. Then shook her head. "No, I said I would go with you, and that is what I am going to do." She drew in a shaky breath.

Clayton looked around. "Something isn't right. There doesn't appear to be any movement."

"Well, I am not just going to sit here." Faith took off at a run across the open field until she got to the edge of a ramshackle building. Running was so much easier when there wasn't a dress involved. Clayton and Marie were right behind her.

Clayton spoke in a low tone. "I will go see if I can distract the soldiers in their quarters. You see if you can find where they are holding Matthew."

Faith nodded and watched her butler sneak across the yard without making a sound. Once he entered into the other building, she grabbed Marie and took her toward the other building. The one that looked like a place they'd hold prisoners. It was disgusting.

Opening the door, the stench that filled her nose was worse than anything she'd ever encountered. She lifted the hem of her coat and covered her nose.

Marie did likewise.

It took a few seconds for her eyes to adjust to the dim room around her, but soon she saw cell doors at the end of the hallway in front of her. Matthew!

She ran toward them and the smell got worse.

When she looked into the first cell, she choked back a cry. The man on the ground was obviously dead. Marie started shaking beside her.

Faith moved to the next cell. Nothing.

Then the last one.

Nothing.

Matthew wasn't here.

Dragging Marie out of the building, Faith couldn't wait to breathe in some fresh air. Never in her life had she seen anything so horrid. Was that where they'd kept her beloved? No. It couldn't be.

Clayton met them outside. "There is no one here. Looks like they packed up and moved on."

Faith nodded. "The cells were empty. Except for a dead man." Her knees felt weak. "He cannot be dead, Clayton. My heart cannot abide it."

"We will keep looking. Come on." Her stoic butler led them back to the horses.

Marie was awfully quiet as she climbed onto her horse.

Faith didn't know what to think. What had she missed? Was there a clue here somewhere? She turned to mount her horse when a smelly hand clamped over her face.

"Do not make a move!" Whoever had her pointed a knife at Clayton.

Clayton raised his hands. "Let him go. He's just a boy." Just a boy? Who was he talking about?

Faith looked at Marie. For a moment she wanted to smack herself. Of course, he was talking about her. She was dressed as a man.

Marie's eyes went wide.

Her captor waved the knife toward her too. "Stay back. I need your horse and your supplies."

A wave of nausea hit Faith. The man smelled. Just like the cells. He had been there. He knew something!

With every ounce of strength she had, she stomped on his foot and jabbed her elbow into his midsection. As a child, she'd used the move many times on the boys when they captured her during their battle games.

The man with the knife bent over and moaned, letting her go. But when Clayton approached him, he stuck the knife out again.

Faith couldn't wait any longer. "You were there, were you not?" She pointed back to where the encampment was. "Where is Matthew?"

The man's eyes went wild, and he waved the knife around. "I am not going back. I escaped. They are all dead. All of them."

Faith screamed. "No!" She flung herself at the man, and he collapsed to the ground.

Clayton grabbed the knife as Faith slapped the man's face. "You are lying. He cannot be dead. Where is Matthew?"

"He's dead. Just like we were all supposed to be. Those stinking Patriots captured us. Gave us rotten food and diseased water. I am the only one who survived." The man curled up in a ball and cried.

Faith didn't know what to do. A deep sob started in her gut. She shook her head. Matthew couldn't be dead. He couldn't.

Clayton tied the hands of the half-starved man. The man was a Loyalist but had obviously suffered a great deal. Her butler picked up the pouch the man had dropped. He opened it and peered inside. "Look, Faith."

"I do not care what is in there. It doesn't matter now." She sniffed and wrapped her arms around her middle.

Clayton nodded, picked up the man as if

he weighed nothing at all, and then threw him over his horse. "We need to take this man in. There are messages in this bag."

All she could manage was a nod. Faith climbed on her own mount and rode back into the woods, letting the tears stream down her face.

Hours later, Faith didn't have any tears left to cry. She'd spent them all. Marie came up beside her. "I am so sorry, ma'am."

" 'Twas all for naught. I thought I could get here before anything bad happened. I thought I could save him." She shook her head. "My plan did not work."

"God's plans are always a mystery to us, ma'am. What you did was very brave."

"I do not care if it was brave or not. I just wish Matthew were still alive."

Clayton rode up next to her. "Mrs. Jackson, why don't you let me ride on ahead and get this man turned in. We will meet up in the little town we ate dinner in last night."

"That is fine, Clayton." She didn't have the heart to make any more plans.

Everything she'd done for the cause, every message she'd coded, every person she'd helped . . . It all felt worthless without Matthew. Why?

"You loved him a lot, didn't you, ma'am?" Marie interrupted her thoughts.

"Yes, I did."

Friday, July 28, 1775

Matthew rode toward Fredericksburg, Virginia. That's where Faith's family farm was. He couldn't wait to see her. And after a lengthy talk with Ben, he'd decided he wasn't going to wait to marry her. Not after all he'd been through. He was much thinner than he had been a couple of months ago, but each day he gained a little strength. He was almost to the point where his stomach could handle a full meal again.

After Ben had dragged him across the river, the old man had taken him to a doctor friend of his and had him patched up. Some of the wounds would take time to heal, but there was nothing more beautiful than freedom. Ben wrote a letter to the leaders so they would know what had happened to Matthew. He also gave a scathing report about how the soldiers had treated their prisoners and how the commanding officers had a total lack of knowledge in the situation. Over time, they'd have to get more organized if they were going to win this war.

When Matthew had rested, eaten enough to give him some strength, and cleaned himself up — *several* times — he told Ben he had to go find Faith.

334

His mentor had nodded and given his blessing. "I'll get word to Washington."

Matthew had been riding ever since.

Virginia was beautiful country, but he hoped he didn't have too much farther to go. His backside was sore, and he was hungry. Again.

He crossed a field and saw two men dressed in liveries. They must be servants on one of the local plantations. Maybe he could ask directions.

As he galloped closer, he realized the men must be young boys because they were awfully small. Then he saw a shock of golden hair.

He gained ground and almost caught up with the riders. "Hello there!"

The blond turned and looked at him then back to the road. Then back at him.

Shock filled his — no *her* face. It wasn't a man at all. It was Faith. "Matthew?" She yanked back on the reins.

The other horse stopped as well, and Matthew tried not to stare. Faith and her maid were both dressed as men. Servant men at that. He dismounted.

Faith practically fell off her horse and ran to him. "Matthew! You're alive!" She hit him with such force that he had to brace himself against his mount as she wrapped her arms around him.

"Yes, I am very much alive. Why did you think I was not?"

She pulled back. "Because I went to rescue you, and no one was there. The crazy man we met said he escaped and that everyone else was dead."

"Huh? What crazy man?"

"A young Loyalist. He said you were dead."

"One of the others survived?" He sighed. He'd carried around guilt for abandoning the other men. Even though they were Loyalists. No one deserved to be treated the way they had been.

She stepped back and looked at him. "Oh, Matthew, what did they do to you?"

Now that the shock had worn off, he took the time to drink her in. "Do not worry about me. I am quite well now." He took her hands and looked her up and down. Oops. Big mistake. "Umm, exactly why are you wearing breeches?"

"I couldn't go off to rescue you in prison wearing a dress." She laughed.

"Why not? Benjamin Franklin did."

"What?!" Her face was puzzled.

Marie joined them, eating an apple. "See? I told you we could have worn our dresses."

Faith rolled her eyes and put her hands

on her hips. "So you are telling me that Benjamin Franklin rescued you?"

Matthew nodded. And looked at her fine figure again. It was quite distracting.

"And he was wearing a dress?"

"Um-hm." He took one last glance at her legs and then forced his eyes up. "I promise I will tell you the story later, but I need to say something." He stepped closer to her. Then pulled her into his arms.

A sly smile split her lips. "Why, Mr. Weber. This is awfully forward."

"It's all right, we have a chaperone."

Marie giggled.

Matthew lowered his head until it was only a few inches from Faith's. "You look far too good in men's clothing, Faith Lytton Jackson. And I find that it is a distraction from my mission at hand."

"And what mission would that be?" She licked her lips.

"Asking you to be my wife."

She tilted her head.

"Please do not leave me in agony, Faith. I love you more than I could have ever imagined. Please, will you do me the honor of becoming Mrs. Matthew Weber?"

That mischievous smile returned. "Yes. The answer is most definitely, yes!"

CHAPTER 24

Faith placed her hands on either side of Matthew's face and pulled him closer to her. She kissed him with every ounce of love she had in her heart. Tears squeezed out of her eyes and spilled down her cheeks. This man. This wonderful man. God had saved him for her.

Matthew pulled back, a fiery passion in his eyes. "Oh, milady, if you are going to do that again, warn me." He kissed her again soft and sweet. "I do not wish to wait to get married."

She shook her head and tasted his lips again. "No. Let's not wait. Please."

Marie tapped Faith on the shoulder. "Didn't you say the church your parents were married in is over in the next town?" Her maid grinned.

Faith laughed. "Marie, you are brilliant." She grabbed Matthew's hand. "Let's get married today."

"I like this plan."

"We can just go to the church right now and track down the preacher."

"Let's do it. As long as you wear those breeches for the wedding."

Faith strode to her horse with a giggle and practically jumped in the saddle. "You got it. I will race you there."

The next morning, Faith awoke with the most wonderful sensation. She was held in her husband's arms.

Lord, thank You.

Fresh wildflowers sat on the windowsill and gave the room a cheery feel and filled the air with the scent of life. Oh, how thankful she was that Matthew was alive!

"Good morning." Matthew whispered in her ear. His arms felt warm and safe.

She turned to face him. "Good morning." For the first time as Mrs. Matthew Weber, she had the privilege of waking up and seeing his face first thing. It was wonderful. "I bet you are hungry."

"Famished. I know it may be hard to believe, but I didn't get fed a lot the past few weeks."

Faith laughed and kissed his cheek. "Well, let me get Marie, and she can help me dress. Then we can see what this establishment has for food."

She'd been so excited to marry him yesterday that she hadn't even paid attention to where they went after the wedding. Prayerfully, the inn would have food for them. Otherwise, she'd have to hunt down her horse and sad little pouch of provisions. Her husband needed food.

He dressed quickly and leaned over and kissed her on the neck. "I will leave you to get ready and meet you downstairs."

A shiver raced up and down her spine. Oh, how she loved her new husband.

As he left the room, Marie curtsied and entered. "Good morning, Mr. Weber. Mrs. Weber."

Faith couldn't help smiling like she was on top of the world. "Good morning, Marie."

"Clayton is here. And he has news to share."

"Oh, wonderful." A tinge of guilt hit her. Would he be upset that she'd married without him present?

"I am afraid the only gown we have with us is quite wrinkled." Marie cringed.

"It does not matter one bit. I am not worried about it, besides we should be home later today." *Home.* Such a wonderful word. And it meant so much more to her now, because it truly was home to her family. With Matthew.

Marie did her best to smooth out wrinkles. "We need to dress you as the lady you are."

"I think as long as I do not show up downstairs in breeches again, Mr. Weber will be happy."

Marie giggled. "Oh, he was quite happy to see you in men's clothes, ma'am. But he definitely would not wish anyone else to see you in them."

Through much laughter, Faith was finally fit to be seen. She and Marie made their way downstairs, and Clayton came forward to hug her.

"I hear congratulations are in order, Mrs. Weber." Her butler bowed.

"Thank you, Clayton. I am so sorry you were not there. We missed you."

"I am just so thankful you found him, ma'am." He smiled. A deep, genuine smile that made Faith's heart soar. This man had become so dear to her. He nodded toward her husband, who sat at the table with a heaping plate of breakfast.

"I hear you have news to tell us." Faith quirked an eyebrow and sat down at the long table.

"Indeed. Well, the fellow that you helped capture?"

Matthew swallowed. "You helped capture someone?"

Marie chimed in. "Yes, she even slapped the man in the face. Of course that was after he had said you were dead. She was quite distraught."

Her husband's brows raised, and he lifted a napkin to his lips and wiped them. "Do tell, Clayton."

"Well" — the butler turned to Matthew — "after your wife tackled him and hit him, the man didn't have any fight left in him, so we tied him up."

Faith shook her head and laughed. "Goodness, you make it sound like I won the war single-handedly. Just tell us your news."

Clayton laughed and looked back at Matthew. "Come to find out, the pouch he'd been carrying had some of your coded messages, as well as some other missives. Secrets that someone was going to pass on to the Loyalists."

"So he was the one?" Matthew shook his head.

Faith lowered her brows. And to think that she had thought Matthew had been guilty — even if for only a moment. Her heart ached with the thought. "What do you know of him?"

"Only that Ben's son — William — was

342

getting secrets from someone. Part of my job was to try to find out whom." He shook his head. "I would have never guessed."

Clayton nodded. "Apparently the young man confessed everything once I took him in. He was starved and half out of his mind."

Looking at the plate of tasty treats in front of her, Faith felt horrible for how she'd treated the young man. It was sad that he had been a traitor, but she still felt bad. "Matthew?"

"Yes, dear?"

"I would really like to go home."

He looked concerned. "Of course. Anything you like."

"There are a lot of people at our home."

"That's fine."

"And I would like to see if there are others we could help."

"I would not want it any other way." He stood and walked over to her and held out his hand.

"The cause still needs our help."

Matthew nodded. "Yes, and I need to report to General Washington soon. We have a war on our hands."

"We will win it together. Side by side." She smiled. It would be hard to let him go. But freedom never came without sacrifice.

"I love you, Mr. Weber."

"And I love you, Mrs. Weber."

EPILOGUE

Thursday, July 4, 1776
Fredericksburg, Virginia

In the wee hours of the morning, Matthew heard a cry. He ran up the stairs and met Marie at the door to the bedroom he shared with his beautiful wife. Dr. Livingston stood by the bed, holding a squirming baby.

His baby.

His stomach felt like it jumped to his throat as he took slow steps forward.

Faith lay in the bed, a sweet glow on her flushed cheeks. "He is beautiful, is he not?"

Matthew reached the bed and leaned down to kiss his wife's forehead. "Not as beautiful as you, my love. Are you all right?"

She nodded. "You need to meet your son."

At that moment, the doctor handed him the tiniest little human he'd ever seen. "Well, hello there." His heart swelled with feelings he couldn't put into words. This little life — this little human being was flesh of his flesh and bone of his bone. With gentle hands, he pulled the infant — his son — close to his chest. He looked to his wife. "Thank you."

Her smile was soft. "I love you, Matthew Weber."

"What should we name him?" He looked back down at the baby in his arms. The soft tuft of blond hair on his head was softer than velvet. He stroked his son's cheek with his finger. Awe. That was this feeling. Pure awe.

"I was thinking George is a fine name. . . ."

"A very fine name indeed." Matthew nodded and put his finger in front of the tiny fist waving in the air. His son opened his hand and grabbed onto Matthew's finger. Was there anything finer in the whole world? "And I was thinking Benjamin. After your father and another fine gentleman we know."

Faith's soft laughter filled the room. "I love it. Then I believe we have chosen a name. George Benjamin Weber."

"I like it too," Doc said from the washstand. "Not that you asked for my opinion. But I am old and have been around a long time." He chuckled and walked back over to Faith. "Take it easy for a while. 'Twas

346

not an easy delivery. Your maid knows what to do."

"Thank you, Doctor." Faith smiled up at the man who had delivered her as an infant in this same house.

Matthew couldn't feel prouder.

Faith sighed, and he looked back at his beautiful wife. Is this how every man felt when their firstborn entered the world? This complete joy? Absolute, unconditional love that overwhelmed his whole being? He hoped he would feel this way about every child the Lord blessed them with because he never wanted it to end.

"I love you so very much, my dear."

"I love you too." She gave him a little smirk. "But one of us has just done a lot of work and needs a nap."

Little George yawned. Matthew pointed to their son in his arms. "You mean, him? You are right, he does look tuckered out."

Thursday, July 18, 1776

Faith leaned over little George. He was so sweet as he slept. To think of all that God had done in her life to get her to this moment. It overwhelmed her with gratefulness and thanksgiving.

Matthew would have to leave her soon and go back with the Continental Army. Faith knew that Matthew and George would look out for each other, but it still made her heart ache to see her husband go off to battle.

Martha had been a gift from the good Lord above. She'd come as soon as she'd heard and ran the household for Faith so she could focus on her newborn. They had many people to take care of, and Mrs. Washington never tired of helping.

"Oh, Faith!" Martha appeared at the doorway. "I have received a letter from George. Is Matthew around? George wants me to share it with all of you."

"I believe he's down in the study." Faith kissed the forehead of their sleeping son and covered his legs with a blanket. "I'll come down with you."

Martha chattered about exciting news all the way down the stairs. She obviously couldn't wait to share whatever it was that George wrote about.

As they entered the study, Matthew stood from his seat behind the desk. "Well, you look beautiful this morning, my dear." He came and kissed Faith on the cheek. She'd never tire of the butterflies she felt inside whenever he was near. He belonged to her. And she to him. It was a wonderful thing.

"Thank you. Martha has a letter from George that is of some import." Faith sat in one of the tall wingback chairs by the fire.

Matthew offered a chair to Martha and then sat on the arm of the chair next to Faith. She adored that he loved being close to her.

On the edge of her seat, Martha beamed a smile at both of them. " 'Tis exciting news. Let me share it with you." She pulled her glasses up from the chain that hung around her neck, perched them on the end of her nose, and began to read:

"Dearest Martha,

This letter is for you to read to Matthew and Faith. Please give them my sincerest congratulations on the birth of their son. I am honored that they chose to name him George.

Personally, I feel rather grandfatherly. Is that all right? I long to hold the child and run with him around the pond, just like I did with you, dear Faith.

Matthew, raise him up in the Lord, and you will not go wrong.

I have wonderful news to share with you all. On the day of George's birth, July the fourth, the Declaration of Independence was signed by fifty-six men representing their Colonies. Benjamin Franklin was there and sent word to me.

The excitement that is here is almost so thick you can taste it.

So our little George will share his special day with this auspicious occasion. For I believe it to be the birth of our new nation. July the fourth of 1776 will go down in history as the day we declared our independence.

Matthew, I know it will be difficult to leave your little family, but your presence is greatly missed here.

Faith, I long to see you again. Take great care of yourself and precious little George. Prayerfully soon we will meet again.

Martha, my love, I will write to you again very soon.

In honor of our family's newest addition and the birth of our nation, I give you a written copy of the Declaration.

All my love,
George"

IN CONGRESS, JULY 4, 1776

THE UNANIMOUS DECLARATION OF THE THIRTEEN UNITED STATES OF AMERICA

When in the Course of human events it becomes necessary for one people to dissolve the political bands which have connected them with another and to assume among the powers of the earth, the separate and equal station to which the Laws of Nature and of Nature's God entitle them, a decent respect to the opinions of mankind requires that they should declare the causes which impel them to the separation.

We hold these truths to be self-evident, that all men are created equal, that they are endowed by their Creator with certain unalienable Rights, that among these are Life, Liberty and the pursuit of Happiness. —That to secure these rights, Governments are instituted among Men, deriving their just powers from the consent of the governed, — That whenever any Form of Government becomes destructive of these ends, it is the Right of the People to alter or to abolish it, and to institute new Government, laying its foundation on such principles and organizing its powers in such form, as to them shall seem most likely to effect their Safety and Happiness. Prudence, indeed, will dictate that Governments long established should not be changed for light and transient causes; and accordingly all experience hath shewn that mankind are more disposed to suffer, while evils are sufferable than to right themselves by abolishing the forms to which they are accustomed. But when a long train of abuses and usurpations, pursuing invariably the same Object evinces a design to reduce them under absolute Despotism, it is their right, it is their duty, to throw off such Government, and to provide new Guards for their future security. — Such has been the patient sufferance of these Colonies; and such is now the necessity which constrains them to alter their former Systems of Government. The history of the present King of Great Britain is a history of repeated injuries and usurpations, all having in direct object the establishment of an absolute Tyranny over these

States. To prove this, let Facts be submitted to a candid world.

He has refused his Assent to Laws, the most wholesome and necessary for the public good.

He has forbidden his Governors to pass Laws of immediate and pressing importance, unless suspended in their operation till his Assent should be obtained; and when so suspended, he has utterly neglected to attend to them.

He has refused to pass other Laws for the accommodation of large districts of people, unless those people would relinquish the right of Representation in the Legislature, a right inestimable to them and formidable to tyrants only.

He has called together legislative bodies at places unusual, uncomfortable, and distant from the depository of their Public Records, for the sole purpose of fatiguing them into compliance with his measures.

He has dissolved Representative Houses repeatedly, for opposing with manly firmness his invasions on the rights of the people.

He has refused for a long time, after such dissolutions, to cause others to be elected, whereby the Legislative Powers, incapable of Annihilation, have returned to the People at large for their exercise; the State remaining in the mean time exposed to all the dangers of invasion from without, and convulsions within.

He has endeavoured to prevent the population of these States; for that purpose obstructing the Laws for Naturalization of Foreigners; refusing to pass others to encourage their migrations hither, and raising the conditions of new Appropriations of Lands.

He has obstructed the Administration of Justice by refusing his Assent to Laws for establishing Judiciary Powers.

He has made Judges dependent on his Will alone for the tenure of their offices, and the amount and payment of their salaries.

He has erected a multitude of New Offices, and sent hither swarms of Officers to harass our people and eat out their substance.

He has kept among us, in times of peace, Standing Armies without the Consent of our legislatures.

He has affected to render the Military independent of and superior to the Civil Power.

He has combined with others to subject us to a jurisdiction foreign to our constitution, and unacknowledged by our laws; giving his Assent to their Acts of pretended Legislation:

For quartering large bodies of armed troops among us:

For protecting them, by a mock Trial from punishment for any Murders which they should commit on the Inhabitants of these States:

For cutting off our Trade with all parts of the world:

For imposing Taxes on us without our Consent:

For depriving us in many cases, of the benefit of Trial by Jury:

For transporting us beyond Seas to be tried for pretended offences:

For abolishing the free System of English Laws in a neighbouring Province, establishing therein an Arbitrary government, and enlarging its Boundaries so as to render it at once an example and fit instrument for introducing the same absolute rule into these Colonies

For taking away our Charters, abolishing our most valuable Laws and altering fundamentally the Forms of our Governments:

For suspending our own Legislatures, and declaring themselves invested with power to legislate for us in all cases whatsoever.

He has abdicated Government here, by

declaring us out of his Protection and waging War against us.

He has plundered our seas, ravaged our coasts, burnt our towns, and destroyed the lives of our people.

He is at this time transporting large Armies of foreign Mercenaries to compleat the works of death, desolation, and tyranny, already begun with circumstances of Cruelty & Perfidy scarcely paralleled in the most barbarous ages, and totally unworthy the Head of a civilized nation.

He has constrained our fellow Citizens taken Captive on the high Seas to bear Arms against their Country, to become the executioners of their friends and Brethren, or to fall themselves by their Hands.

He has excited domestic insurrections amongst us, and has endeavoured to bring on the inhabitants of our frontiers, the merciless Indian Savages whose known rule of warfare, is an undistinguished destruction of all ages, sexes and conditions.

In every stage of these Oppressions We have Petitioned for Redress in the most humble terms: Our repeated Petitions have been answered only by repeated injury. A Prince, whose character is thus marked by every act which may define a Tyrant, is unfit to be the ruler of a free people.

Nor have We been wanting in attentions to our British brethren. We have warned them from time to time of attempts by their legislature to extend an unwarrantable jurisdiction over us. We have reminded them of the circumstances of our emigration and settlement here. We have appealed to their native justice and magnanimity, and we have conjured them by the ties of our common kindred to disavow these usurpations, which would inevitably interrupt our connections and correspondence. They too have been deaf to the voice of justice and of consanguinity. We must, therefore, acquiesce in the necessity, which denounces our Separation, and hold them, as we hold the rest of mankind, Enemies in War, in Peace Friends.

We, therefore, the Representatives of the united States of America, in General Congress, Assembled, appealing to the Supreme Judge of the world for the rectitude of our intentions, do, in the Name, and by Authority of the good People of these Colonies, solemnly publish and declare, That these united Colonies are, and of Right ought to be Free and Independent States, that they are Absolved from all Allegiance to the British Crown, and that all political connection between them and the State of Great Britain, is and ought to be totally dissolved; and that as Free and Independent States, they have full Power to levy War, conclude Peace, contract Alliances, establish Commerce, and to do all other Acts and Things which Independent States may of right do. — And for the support of this Declaration, with a firm reliance on the protection of Divine Providence, we mutually pledge to each other our Lives, our Fortunes, and our sacred Honor.

Signed:

Connecticut: Samuel Huntington, Roger Sherman, William Williams, Oliver Wolcott

Delaware: George Read, Caesar Rodney, Thomas McKean

Georgia: Button Gwinnett, Lyman Hall, George Walton

Maryland: Charles Carroll, Samuel Chase, Thomas Stone, William Paca

Massachusetts: John Adams, Samuel Adams, John Hancock, Robert Treat Paine, Elbridge Gerry

New Hampshire: Josiah Bartlett, William Whipple, Matthew Thornton

New Jersey: Abraham Clark, John Hart, Francis Hopkinson, Richard Stockton, John Witherspoon

New York: Lewis Morris, Philip Livingston, Francis Lewis, William Floyd

North Carolina: William Hooper, John Penn, Joseph Hewes

Pennsylvania: George Clymer, Benjamin Franklin, Robert Morris, John Morton, Benjamin Rush, George Ross, James Smith, James Wilson, George Taylor

Rhode Island: Stephen Hopkins, William Ellery

South Carolina: Edward Rutledge, Arthur Middleton, Thomas Lynch, Jr., Thomas Heyward, Jr.

Virginia: Richard Henry Lee, Francis Lightfoot Lee, Carter Braxton, Benjamin Harrison, Thomas Jefferson, George Wythe, Thomas Nelson, Jr.

NOTE FROM THE AUTHOR

I hope you enjoyed *The Patriot Bride* as much as I did writing and researching it. I always discover fascinating pieces of history when I'm researching a book. One of the things that struck me the most is the instantaneous world that we live in now and how hard it is to imagine a world where it took months to find things out. For instance, in January 1775, orders were given for General Gage to march on Concord and destroy the arms that were there. That news didn't reach the British troops in America until much later, and of course, we know that on April 18, those orders were carried out and thus the famous ride of Paul Revere. In the same manner, Parliament declared that Massachusetts was in a state of rebellion on February 9, 1775. We don't know how long that news took to reach the colonies, but by the time it did, those in America would have said something like the modern equivalent of, "Duh, ya think?"

This length of communication created quite a mess during the war. Parliament and the King were unaware of things as they happened in America, while the British troops in America were carrying out two-month-old orders (at least). If they'd had the technology and communication of today, would there have been an actual war? We can't know, but it does give us a chance to learn from the past once again.

Back to Paul Revere — many of us have heard what has become his legendary phrase, "The British are coming! The British are coming!" In fact, that is not what happened or what he said. The way I portrayed it in the story is much closer to the actual truth. For more fascinating tidbits, see https://www.paulreverehouse.org/the-real-story/, http://www.history.com/news/history-lists/ 11things-you-may-not-know-about-paul-revere, http://www.masshist.org/database/99, and http://www.masshist.org/database/viewer.php?item_id=98.

I was taught as a child that George Washington had wooden teeth. Also not true. But he did have false teeth. His face was pock-marked from his horrible bout with smallpox, and he chose not to wear a wig but to powder his own hair.

One thing I never learned in school was his actual height. I think I might have heard that he was "tall," but to a kid, *tall* could mean five feet. His executive secretary — Colonel Tobias Lear — wrote after Washington's death that the general was six feet, three and one-half inches *exactly.* Lear was an exact man and had to measure the general for his burial. All of this simply reinforces the fact that Washington was an impressive figure.

Our first president was such a remarkable man. I want to write numerous stories with him in it because he was just that amazing. Some interesting facts about him that I used in the story were that he wore his military uniform to the Second Continental Congress. Did he know what was about to take place? He was the only one there in uniform. And when he left Mount Vernon for that Congress on May 4, 1775, he was then gone from his beautiful home for eight long years. (He did have one short documented trip home in 1781.) All those years, he spent his time with the Continental Army in the field. Martha often visited in the winter, and it was uplifting to the troops and obviously to

George.

The lady's fire screen mentioned in chapter five was inspired by an actual fire screen stitched by our first First Lady that resides at the Rosedown Plantation in Louisiana. I've been to every plantation in Louisiana and Mississippi, and the artifacts are truly amazing. But since the first time I laid eyes on that fire screen when I was a teen, I was fascinated with our first president and his wife. For a picture of it, go to www.daughtersofthemayflower.com under *The Patriot Bride*.

I had the incredible opportunity to speak to some preservationists at Mount Vernon on my visit there. Thanks to a rainy, dreary day, I was almost by myself at the historic home, and it gave me lots of time to ask questions. As an author, I do a ton of research — ninety percent of which the reader never gets to see — and it's a privilege to include tidbits here and there. Mount Vernon's last expansion was technically done by 1775, but that only meant that the exterior was done. So while I mention the study in this book, and it is fashioned after what we know of to be George Washington's study after the Revolutionary War, the experts who spend day in and day out studying Mount Vernon don't know for certain which rooms were used for what prior to this expansion. To make things easier, I used the study from the existing Mount Vernon as inspiration so that if you have the chance to visit the incredible location, it will be the same.

Benjamin Franklin along with Washington played major roles in this story. But it is important to note that Franklin was actually in England from late 1774 through May 1775 (so he was not even home when his wife died). Rather than give a lot of tedious backstory to you about the relationship between him and Matthew, I chose to show Benjamin Franklin as present in the beginning of the book. Again, it is a fictional story, but I didn't want anyone to think I didn't have my facts straight or to mislead about actual historical events.

Benjamin has become another of my favorite characters of all time. The man was simply fascinating. Eccentric. Amiable. Brilliant. If you read comments from any of his peers, you'll find he's more than just fascinating to us. He was to them as well. Something new I learned about him this year was his love of "air baths." Apparently, it was one of his oddities, and we have no record of what his neighbors thought of this practice as he sat disrobed in front of the open windows, but he proved that he was well ahead of his time with the reasoning behind those baths. He believed that fresh air would aid in airing out the rooms and thus the body because he suspected that people closed up together in houses (especially in winter) tended to spread sickness and disease faster. Hm. Interesting thought.

The women who were involved in the Patriot movement truly did accomplish the tasks listed in the book (producing over 40,000 skeins of yarn and weaving 20,522 yards of cloth). They also took care of soldiers, helped the wounded, sent messages, and much more. It's fascinating to me to see how many were involved.

Fascinating books, articles, and other resources show how spies were used to aid in the war efforts. While Matthew and Faith are purely fictitious characters, their activities are based on true accounts. The tunnel in the secretary's home, however, was purely from my imagination.

If you'd like to dig for some history yourself, the following websites are good places to start: www.legendsofamerica.com, www.mountvernon.org, and of course, keep

up to date on this series at www.daughters
ofthemayflower.com.

As always, it is a privilege to have readers
like you. Thank you for once again traveling
with me.

Enjoy the journey,
Kimberley Woodhouse

ACKNOWLEDGMENTS

I could never write enough thank-you notes to the people in my life who make this all possible.

First and foremost, I want to thank my Lord and Savior. Writing is a ministry for me, and as much as I would love to impact millions, if my books touch just *one* life, I am content with that and know that was His plan. It's all written for Him. To God alone be the glory.

My husband — Jeremy — is the best man I've ever known. He puts up with a lot from me and my crazy-creative-writer brain. He's superman. Who's been known to run the vacuum, do laundry, and cook fabulous meals when he knows I'm hunkered down on deadline.

Our two amazing kids are two of the best cheerleaders I have. Josh and Kayla — I adore you. And I thank God for giving me the opportunity to be your mom. Love you both!

While I was researching this book, our family expanded with the addition of my new daughter-in-law. Ruth, you are precious, and I'm so excited to have you as part of the Woodhouse clan. Hopefully having an author as a crazy mother-in-law won't be too taxing on you!

Barbour Publishing — our journey together has been so interesting. Fiction and nonfiction, I always look forward to what God is going to do next through our working relationship. You all have been a joy to work with. Thank you for all you do. The cover is absolutely gorgeous! Thank you for capturing Faith's personality and for matching the dress I found so perfectly. I am in awe.

Becky Germany, thank you for believing in me. It has been a joy to get to know you over the years.

Becky Fish, thank you again for your hard work on this manuscript. Your input and encouragement were wonderful.

Jackie Hale, friend and cheerleader. Thanks for being there.

My critters: Darcie Gudger, Becca Whitham, and Kayla Woodhouse — where would I be without you? Becca — thanks

370

for traipsing to Mount Vernon with me. Your insight and questions were wonderful. (I'm amazed neither one of us got sick in the chilly rain.) We need to do more research together. It's entirely too much fun.

My friend and mentor — Tracie Peterson — you've blessed me in more ways than I can count. Thanks for cheering me on and whacking me upside the head when I need it.

And to you — my readers, I couldn't do this without you. Thank you, thank you, thank you.

Grabbing onto God's joy,
Kimberley

ABOUT THE AUTHOR

Kimberley Woodhouse is an award-winning and bestselling author of more than fifteen fiction and nonfiction books. A popular speaker and teacher, she's shared her theme of "Joy Through Trials" with more than half a million people across the country at more than two thousand events. Kim and her incredible husband of twenty-five-plus years have two adult children. She's passionate about music and Bible study and loves the gift of story.

You can connect with Kimberley at www.kimberleywoodhouse.com and www.facebook.com/KimberleyWoodhouseAuthor.

The employees of Thorndike Press hope you have enjoyed this Large Print book. All our Thorndike, Wheeler, and Kennebec Large Print titles are designed for easy reading, and all our books are made to last. Other Thorndike Press Large Print books are available at your library, through selected bookstores, or directly from us.

For information about titles, please call:
  (800) 223-1244

or visit our website at:
  gale.com/thorndike

To share your comments, please write:
  Publisher
  Thorndike Press
  10 Water St., Suite 310
  Waterville, ME 04901